Be Bold and Coura
In all you do! G

Joshua 1:9

bush
PUBLISHING
& associates

FIVE
MINUTES
to LIVE

The Matt Davenport Chronicles Book 1

DAVID PORTER

bush
PUBLISHING
& associates

FIVE MINUTES TO LIVE

ISBN 978-1-944566-22-7 (Paperback)
ISBN 978-1-63732-871-2 (ebook)

Printed in the United States of America.

First publication in 2020 by Bush Publishing and Associates, LLC.
www.bushpublishing.com
Tulsa, Oklahoma

Cover Art, Layout and Design by Bush Publishing and Associates, LLC.

Editing by Writing By Michele, LLC.

Dedication

To my wife, Lauren, who inspires and motivates every day; and to my parents, Dave and Virginia, who laid a godly foundation and are beautiful examples of His unconditional love.

Author's Note

I'm so thrilled that you've decided to read this book! *Five Minutes to Live* is a work of fiction; however, various elements of it are steeped in truth. Outside of our main players, many of the people mentioned in the book are currently living; they are real people. Much of the science in this book, while diverging from the mainstream school of thought, is real nonetheless. Most of the locations mentioned in the book are places you may actually visit. I encourage you to take the time to follow the links included in the footnotes, learn about these places, these peoples, these *truths*. Look at the pictures, read the biographies, and watch the videos. It will only add to the excitement and adventure of the book. And possibly, it will open your eyes to things you've never considered or even imagined…

David

Israel was not created in order to disappear—Israel will endure and flourish. It is the child of hope and the home of the brave. It can neither be broken by adversity nor demoralized by success. It carries the shield of democracy, and it honors the sword of freedom.

— John F. Kennedy

Contents

Prologue

My eyes explode open.

It's an unusual feeling, like being torn from a lifelong coma. My ears are ringing, and my head is pounding, and I have no idea why. Desperate to figure out where I am and what's going on, I try to look at my surroundings, but the pain is unbearable. I gasp as each shift of my weight, each movement, is torture to my body. All I know is that I have to keep going. I must save her.

My face is pressed into sun-bleached pavement. It's a colorless grey and warm to the touch. I can smell dirt and exhaust fumes. Shifting my weight again, trying to roll over, every muscle groans and spasms. I'm stiff from physical exertion, bruises cover my body, and for some reason, there is blood all over me.

I must save... her.

I'm finally able to turn to see the sun, hanging low and still in the sky. It's either early morning or very late afternoon, I can't tell which. The air is dry and crisp with no hint of moisture. There is something familiar yet unusual in the air. Sirens are wailing in the distance, an alarm clock call to my stiff, tired body.

Slowly, I press up onto my hands and knees. The pain takes my breath away. I'm forced to stay in that position to regain my strength, my composure. Each breath in and out feels like it takes hours to inhale and expel. There is no traffic on the street, but I know I need to get out of the road, so I press up to one knee and see more of my surroundings.

On either side of the street, cars line the curb, parked close to one another, bumper to bumper. City parking. Past the cars, there are two-story buildings as far as I can see, framing the street. The bottom levels are littered with shops, not yet open or closed for the evening. The glass windows are barred shut, and there are colorful signs in an unknown language.

The signs hang perpendicular to the buildings, over the sidewalks. The sidewalks act as a boundary to the cars, keeping them several feet from the buildings. The language on the signs isn't English. I can't read it. It's Hebrew or Arabic, unfamiliar. I must be in the Middle East, Egypt, Israel, Sudan, or Iran. This doesn't surprise me and, incredibly, it doesn't scare me.

I'm different now.

I flex my fingers, roll my wrists, and extend my elbows. Nothing seems to be broken or dislocated, so I stand. The pain is excruciating. Immediately, I am supporting my weight, my hands on my knees.

Something in the air reminds me of camping as a kid. S'mores... Stories around the campfire... Smoke... Smoke is in the air! A heavy smell of smoke. Something is burning. The sirens are louder now, closer.

The city is waking up.

Like me.

I step a few feet toward one of the cars parked along the street, a heavily dented machine, and place my hand on its roof for balance. There is a metallic clunk as my hand touches down. Gripped in my palm is a gun, a Smith & Wesson 1911, .45-caliber automatic.

A feeling washes over me, a knowing, a comfort. A still, small voice. *I am alive. I am ready. No matter what comes at me, there is no weapon, no enemy, formed against me that can prosper against me.[1] Nothing can stand in my way. I am undefeated. I am more than a conqueror.[2] I choose to win. I choose to... fight.*

---

1 Isaiah 54:17
2 Romans 8:37

I say a quick prayer under my breath, thanking God for His protection and asking for His help. I can't explain it but, in some way, I know I am still alive because of Him.

A knowing. Somehow, I know to check my pockets. There, I find a couple of cell phones with no power and broken screens, a visitor's pass to somewhere, two wallets—a woman's small wallet and mine—and incredibly, I see that I am also holding a tube of lipstick. I notice my shoulders feel heavy, weighed down and I realize I am wearing a bulky backpack on my shoulders. It's clipped securely across the front of my chest.

The black smoke billows. It's incredibly close. Something is burning. The sirens scream, incessantly and loud. They are close.

People start spilling from the buildings and into the streets, families, men, women, children. Not American. Not Caucasian. Not happy. I begin to realize I am the cause of all of this.

Panicked screams fill the air. English screams. A woman's screams. I see her now, running toward me from the opposite direction of the smoke.

"Matt! Matt! Maaaaaaaaaaaaaaatt!"

Chapter One

Two Days Earlier

"**M**att. Matt! Are you listening to me?"

I had to admit that at that very moment, I hadn't heard a word that Jessica had been saying. My mind was elsewhere, thinking about how I looked like a secret agent in my new tuxedo.

Jessica and I had met a few years earlier and, remarkably, because of the circumstances of our first contact, a friendship had grown. Some people might call it dumb luck, but I choose to think of it as Divine Providence. I was at the Charlotte International Airport, standing in what I figured had to be "the world's slowest-moving line" at the Starbucks on Concourse B. At the time, there were only two people working in the tiny coffee shop and they were working as fast as they could, but the line just continued to grow. Now, you would think standing in line for that long would give people a chance to figure out what they want to order by the time they arrived at the cashier. That did not seem to be the case on this day.

Growing more and more frustrated, I kept checking my watch, becoming more upset with each passing second because of how long it was taking in line. I honestly don't know why I was in such a hurry—it was probably the circumstances of the days leading up to my time at

Starbucks—but my connecting flight didn't leave for several hours, so I had the time to spare. It was during one of those moments, lost in my own world, checking my watch for the hundredth time in just a matter of minutes, that I heard a woman's voice behind me say, "You're not alone," and my life changed forever.

That woman was Jessica, and she was just trying to make some small talk. She said, "You're not alone" with the implied meaning, "You're not the only one who thinks this is taking forever" or "You're not alone in checking your watch a hundred times." What she wasn't expecting to happen next, did.

At that moment, when I heard those three words, *"You're not alone,"* the tears began to flow. I couldn't stop them. Rivers and rivers of tears streamed down my face. The floodgates were opened. Looking around for something to use, I grabbed one of the world's least comfortable tear-wipers, the only thing I had at my disposal right then. I grabbed one of those brown-colored, eco-friendly, made-from-recycled-material Starbucks napkins and tried to stymie the tears streaming down my face. Clear tears ran down my cheeks. Clear snot poured out of my nose. All of this because a complete stranger said, "You're not alone."

To anyone else, that would have been a clear sign that I was mentally unstable. It would have been the easiest thing for Jessica to politely apologize, step out of the shop, and leave the weirdo sobbing in the Starbucks line, alone. Incredibly, that's not what she did. Jessica reached into her purse, pulled out one of those travel Kleenex packs, and handed me something soft to wipe the tears from my face. I saw the genuine concern in her eyes and a tenderness in her touch as she placed her hand on my shoulder.

What Jessica didn't know, what she couldn't know, was that I had just spent the weekend at my father's funeral. My mother was too emotionally spent to give me much comfort or to help with what I was going through emotionally. Additionally, she just wasn't up to doing all the necessary things, so it fell on me to plan the funeral, purchase the casket, organize everything from ordering flowers to ordering the food for the family. On top of it all, I wanted to be strong for my mother. Speaking at my dad's funeral was hard and brought tears to my eyes, but it wasn't until I was standing in line at Starbucks, feeling completely spent, tired, empty and alone, that the emotions finally really surfaced. Jessica said, "You're not alone" meaning, "You're not alone in this line," but to me, it sounded like a message delivered directly from God… "You're not alone, and you never will be."

Finally, I was able to regain my composure as Jessica and I quietly made our way out of line. One of the great things about Starbucks is that they are everywhere, *everywhere*, and that includes the airport in Charlotte. As we left Concourse B, we found another Starbucks, on Concourse C, two doors down from a frozen yogurt shop. This particular Starbucks only had one person in line and three people working behind the counter. Jessica ordered some fancy drink with several Italian-sounding words in it, and I ordered my coffee black. I paid, and we made our way to the frozen yogurt shop and each had a small cup of the frozen goodness.

Over a cup of mountain blackberry yogurt, I learned that Jessica was returning from a business trip to Israel, that her father had died toward the end of her senior year in college and that she had been recruited to her job shortly after. The elderly gentleman who recruited her had been a guiding presence, taking her under his wing and helping her through the pain of loss. She could relate to what I was going through, but I simply couldn't believe that she would help a complete stranger like she did. Tenderness radiated from her. By the time I needed to make my way to my connecting flight, my attitude had changed, my emotions were restored, I felt alive and I knew in my bones, I wasn't alone. God, somehow, was *with* me.

Jessica stayed with me, right up until the moment I boarded the airplane. We exchanged telephone numbers and hugs, and I thanked her profusely. If that had been my last contact with Jess, my life would have been forever changed. She made that type of an impact. But incredibly, it wasn't the last time I had contact with her. She actually called a few days later to check on me! We picked up right where we had left off at the airport, spending most of that afternoon on the phone.

Over the following months, we found we had many things in common, and it was effortless to have lengthy conversations; it was easy to spend hours on the phone together. In particular, we connected through our mutual Christian faith. This was, I think, something new for both of us. Some people click over a shared hobby, a sport, a particular hangout or bar. Connecting over a shared belief in God and the way He worked was something new to both of us. As we got to know each other more and more, we realized our Christian faith was more than just a Sunday morning religion to either of us; it was a way of life.

Jessica and I both grew up in church, living what we called a 'life of faith.' This form of Christianity, this doctrine, places a high value on the Bible and Jesus' words. If Jesus said it, we consider it true. We choose to believe it. So, when Jesus said things like, "Whatsoever things ye desire, when ye pray, believe that ye receive them and ye shall have them,"[3] we believe that if we want or need things, like Godly direction or wisdom, we can pray and believe, and He said we will receive those things! We believe it is true! I don't know why, but sometimes this gets a negative connotation with people, even with fellow Christians. I guess they think in terms of getting 'things' from God, like money or fame. To us, to me and Jessica, if it's in the Bible, that settled it, and that shared faith in what God's written Word said, even through the pushback of other Christians, brought the two of us even closer.

But there was something different about Jessica's relationship with God, something I had never really experienced. She spoke of a personal, intimate relationship with Him, of speaking with Him on a *daily* basis … and that God would respond to her and help her, give her direction, lead her and guide her! That sounded completely crazy to me

---

3 Mark 11:24

because I had never experienced anything like that. I didn't know how that could even be possible, but the more I got to know her, the more I believed Jessica when she said it. I wanted to find out if God would speak to me on a daily basis too.

Hours were spent on the phone, FaceTime, Skype, even on Xbox Live. We talked, laughed, played games; we even had a regularly scheduled Bible study together where we explored many different topics. We studied things such as the authority that resides in the follower of Christ, God's grace on us, Old Testament heroes like Abraham, Ruth, and Noah, and the different teachings of the apostles. Jessica had even begun sharing with me how to communicate with God and how to hear His voice.[4] She said it was an easy thing and that I would be able to do it … and I believed her, even if I didn't know what I was doing. She lived halfway across the country and worked halfway around the world, but that didn't hinder our growing friendship.

The company Jessica worked for was based in Israel, and because her lab was there, she traveled extensively all over the world. We tried to meet occasionally, as our schedules would permit, times when she would be in my part of the country or a part of the country where I happened to be.

We met one time for a weekend in San Diego where we toured the USS *Midway* and walked along the boardwalk. Once it was a springtime trip to Nashville to see the city; we even watched a professional hockey game there. We still hadn't visited her lab in Tel Aviv; in fact, I'd never been out of the country. But tonight she wanted me to witness her work or at least witness the *results* of the work she had done. This trip, tonight, was for a lecture she was giving at Penn State University. That's where Jessica had completed her graduate studies in geology a few years before we met and where she changed from Ms. Adams to Dr. Adams. Jessica was what she termed a 'histo-geologist,' and even though I didn't know exactly what that was, it sounded impressive.

---

4 John 10:27

Tonight's invitation gave me the opportunity to finally reconnect, in person, with my friend. Jessica didn't want to show up to her formal presentation, a $500 per plate dinner fundraiser, alone, so she invited me as her plus-one. The evening had been presented to potential donors as a "once in a lifetime event." It gave me a chance to see Jess, finally be able to learn about the work she has been doing, and almost equally as important, it gave Jessica a chance to see me in the new tuxedo I had recently purchased.

"Every time I get to put this thing on, I feel like James Bond," I said as I looked at my reflection in the mirror. "What kind of car are we riding in? Please tell me they are picking us up in a Bentley limousine! Little flags on the corners. Something like that?"

"Matt! Are you listening to me? I'm trying to practice this part of my speech. It's really important." She continued rehearsing. "The presence of water trapped within the ringwoodite indicates vast amounts of water beneath the Earth's surface layer."

"I'm sorry. No. I'm lost," I interrupted again. "What were you saying? I was trying to find the James Bond theme song on my phone. Jess, I need a gun. Don't you think? Yeah, I need a gun. '*Davenport. Matthew Davenport.*'"

"Matt, you look great, but I really need to practice this speech. Will you listen, at least until the car gets here to pick us up? It's important I get this out, that it's clear, so that the scientific community can't refute it. And, no. You absolutely *don't* need a gun."

She tried to continue her speech. "The presence of water trapped within the ringwoodite indicates vast amounts of water beneath the Earth's surface layer. Along with the findings of Dr. Pearson[5] from the

---

5 Jason Koebler, "There's an Ocean Deep Inside the Earth," *Motherboard Tech by Vice*, June 12, 2014,
https://motherboard.vice.com/en_us/article/ypwvmy/theres-an-ocean-deep-inside-the-earth?utm_campaign=engagersLAL1&utm_source=mbfbads

University of Alberta and Dr. Jacobsen[6] of Northwestern University, my research shows a sizeable amount of water trapped between the upper mantle and lower mantle regions in what is known as the 'Transition Zone.'" She paused and then said to me as an aside, "I'll have a couple of slides right here that will give a diagram of the different water levels and…"

"Time-out, Jess. Where is the water? Underground? How deep did you say? And what is the Transition Zone? I thought that had to do with when dinosaurs went extinct. Wasn't that millions of years ago?"

"No, Matt. You're thinking of the K-T boundary layer, not the Transition Zone. Similar names, but so vastly different in every other respect, and scientists have them both wrong. Did you even take basic science classes in college?"

"You know that I've got a chemistry minor, thank you very little!" I responded with a chuckle.

Jessica continued, "The K-T boundary is the layer separating the so-called Cretaceous and Tertiary periods. We're talking shallow, surface of the Earth stuff here, Matt. The K-T layer is exposed in most places and where it's not exposed, it's only a few hundred feet below the surface at its *deepest* point. The K-T layer is where they dig for fossils. The Transition Zone, on the other hand, is *miles* below the surface of the Earth. And by the way, the dinosaurs didn't go extinct millions of years ago." She paused before adding, "And I can prove it."

She let that last sentence hang in the air for a beat longer than normal.

"Listen. I know this isn't the most riveting stuff to you, Matt, but I invited you here to be with me tonight for a couple of reasons. Not just because you're my best friend and I didn't want to be dateless, but also

---

6 Andy Coghlan, "Massive 'ocean' discovered toward Earth's core," *New Scientist*, June 12, 2014,
https://www.newscientist.com/article/dn25723-massive-ocean-discovered-toward-earths-core/

because tonight will be one of those course-altering points in history, and I didn't want you to miss it. I haven't been able to tell you what I have been working on all this time, but tonight, some of God's handiwork will be revealed. I *think* tonight will be one of those times you'll be able to tell your kids, 'I was there when it happened.' I *know* that tonight will be life-changing for me, for science, for the truth about the creation of our planet. The impact will be felt in several scientific areas of study including the theory of evolution, the dinosaur extinction, history, geology, anthropology and even the Big Bang. I know the answers. God has shown me the answers. And I want you to be a part of it, Matt…with me."

I was a little speechless as she dropped this news on me. What could she have discovered, and kept hidden from me, that would revolutionize science?

I think she saw the look on my face, that stunned, opened mouth, searching for the words expression and bailed me out.

"I don't know how these distinguished and accomplished scientists will take this news. They have spent their whole lives working toward an established paradigm that I will essentially prove is incorrect, revealing it this evening. It's revolutionary in thought. It's a radical new approach. I will be kicking over a lot of sacred scientific beliefs, those things that seem to form the foundation, the bedrock of science today. My conclusions are backed by years of research, but I think I'm going to anger a lot of people tonight. There *will* be a significant amount of backlash. I *need* you there with me."

I stood there, proud to be her friend, proud to be here with her, proud that she called me, proud that she wanted me there, that she *needed* me there.

"Do you remember the first three words you ever said to me?" I asked.

A smile flashed across Jessica's face. "Of course, I do," she replied. "You're not alone."

"Well, tonight *you're* not alone," I said, then added, "I'm here for you and always will be." I personally thought she was probably overre-acting, and I was just about to try and settle her down when her phone chimed. A text message.

She picked up her phone, unlocked it, read the message and said, "The car is here to pick us up. Come on, James Bond. It's time to go."

I grabbed my things and slipped them in my pocket—cell phone, Chapstick and a pack of gum—and started walking toward the door. Jessica, a few steps behind me, had her hands full.

"Matt," she said, "Do you know the *real* reason I invited you here tonight? Pockets."

"What?"

Laughing, she said, "Yep. I don't have any pockets in this evening gown, and I don't have a purse that matches it, either. You get to carry my stuff. You have pockets!"

"Got it! I'm the pockets!" I said, joining in her laughter.

Stepping through the hotel door and closing it, we heard the elec-tric lock click into place. Jessica handed me her cell phone, a tube of lipstick and a small wallet that was only large enough to carry a couple credit cards and maybe a couple dollar bills. When I saw hers, I realized that I had forgotten my wallet in the suite. I said, "Wait, Jess. I need to work a Bible verse."

"Huh? What are you talking about? *Work* a Bible verse?" she said with a puzzled look on her face.

"Matthew 7:7," I replied. "*Ask*, and it shall be given you; *seek*, and you shall *find*."

"Knock, and it shall be opened unto you,"[7] she finished the verse, obviously familiar with it. "What are you talking about?'

I said, "I need to *ask* you for the key to the suite, so that I can *seek and find* my wallet!"

---

7 Matthew 7:7

She laughed and handed me the key card for the suite, the last thing she had in her hand. I quickly went in and, after looking in the usual obvious places, found my wallet trapped between the two cushions of the navy-blue loveseat. I grabbed my wallet and was back with Jess in the hallway in a matter of seconds.

We made our way through the hall to the elevator, and as I stepped back from pressing the *down* button, Jessica slipped her arm into mine. I could tell she was excited and maybe a little nervous about the evening. She squeezed into me and bounced on the balls of her feet. She was a paradox. If you hadn't seen her and only spoke with her on the phone, hearing the intellect ooze from her lips, you could easily forget she was an incredibly gifted athlete, a tennis star in college. If all you did was see her, and that natural beauty, you could easily forget she was one of the most brilliant minds in science, or at least that's what I thought about her. Obviously, others did as well, which is why we were all gathering to listen to her tonight.

The sound of Jessica's voice brought me back to the moment as she said, "I really wish Dr. Kaplan had felt well enough to make the trip. Please don't get me wrong. I'm so pleased you're my date, but I hate that Dr. Kaplan had to cancel. I feel like I owe all of this to him. He started me on this path, helped with the research and development, and encouraged me all along the way. Not to mention the funding he has always provided. Anything I ever needed or wanted, Dr. Kaplan was able to secure it for me, sometimes even before I knew I would need it."

Although I had never met Dr. Eli Kaplan, I felt like I knew him. Jessica had talked about him throughout the years. He was a mentor. A helper. A guide. A benefactor. He was a facilitator and an introduction maker. He and his company had recruited her right out of college, and Jessica quickly became one of the lead scientists in the firm. But their relationship was more than just work. Dr. Kaplan was the man responsible for helping Jess through the devastating loss of her father, and she felt a sense of devotion to him. From what I could tell, they had a wonderful father-daughter type relationship. She was Dr. Kaplan's friend and 'go-to girl' whenever a new project or lead came along. I'm not exactly sure what was considered a 'new' lead to a histo-geologist, but she was always on the move and his firm was never short of funds.

"Aw. I know, Jess. How about we call him when we get finished this evening. He should be awake by then. What's the time difference? Seven, eight hours?"

"Seven! Yes! That's what we'll do! Don't let me forget to call when we get back to the hotel. That's your other job tonight. To be my re-minder." That beautiful smile flashed across her face, and her brown eyes lit up.

"You got it. I'm the pockets and I'm the reminder. Let me set the mental alarm, and we'll be good to go!"

The elevator arrived and I held the door for Jessica. She stepped on and I followed her in. I pushed the button for the ground floor and began humming along to the Muzak version of *Eye of the Tiger*.

"How do you know every song that comes on a radio?" Jessica play-fully asked me.

"Oh, that? That's my superpower. That, and spouting random bits of useless trivia," I said.

"Pretty specific superpowers you've got there, Double-O Daven-port. Hmm. What should I call you? *Agent Davenport* doesn't begin to express your true abilities! You'll need a better superhero name than that. Let's think. Mega-Music Man? Captain Trivia?" she laughingly asked. "Do you normally wear a cape?"

I put my hands on my hips, standing in my best superhero pose, and blurted, "Nope. I've got bright yellow spandex!" We were both laughing as the elevator reached the ground floor. It was nice to get her mind off of the seriousness of the evening for a few minutes.

It was an inexpensive hotel, but we felt like a million dollars as we stepped into the lobby, all smiles. Well, I felt like a million dollars in my *Double-O Davenport* costume. Jessica *looked* like a million dollars, especially in the emerald-green evening gown she was wearing. She stepped out of the elevator a beat before I did, and a handsome man in a dark, well-tailored suit smiled and made his way toward her. I followed from the elevator a second later and noticed that the man's face flashed a moment of surprise. It passed in an instant. I felt a moment of jealousy that I hoped he didn't notice, but that also passed in an instant.

"Dr. Adams, I'm Omar, your driver this evening." Even his British accent was cool. "If you and your guest will come with me, we'll be on our way."

Jessica nodded and then turned to me. I can only describe the smile on her face as giddy. This really was the culmination of all those years of devotion to her work and the sacrifices she had made. She was *bubbly*.

I wasn't a gambling man, but if I were, I would say that Omar was one of the most handsome men I had ever seen in my life. Like, celebrity good-looking. He was athletic and tall, easily a couple of inches taller than six feet. His shoulders were broad, his hair was jet black and his skin was the color of cinnamon. It glistened. His face was square, his cheeks were high, and his jaw was strong. I genuinely had a hard time believing this Omar guy wasn't a model who had been hired to be a driver for the night. The suit he was wearing looked like it was made just for him, like he should never think of wearing anything else, though he would probably look equally as good in a soccer jersey and shorts. He was much more Cristiano Ronaldo without the earrings than David Beckham without the tattoos, though. I really had to fight a negative gut feeling every time I looked at him. Was it just jealousy or something more?

We crossed through the lobby and as we passed the reception desk, the woman who had checked us in earlier in the afternoon said, "Have a great evening." Jessica just smiled.

"Thank you. You too!" I said over my shoulder as we stepped into the cool evening air.

Omar walked toward his black Cadillac Escalade, the brand's luxury SUV, and opened the rear driver's side door for Jessica. The SUV was new, and that *new car* smell hit us as the door opened.

"It's not a Bentley, but this is still pretty cool," she said as she slid across the leather to the passenger side.

Omar held the door for me, his left hand resting on the top of the door, above the window. The slightly awkward position made his buttoned jacket flair. My weight had already shifted, and I was falling into the seat, but that's when I noticed it. He was wearing a gun in a shoulder holster under his suit coat. *That's weird for a model,* I thought, but before I had time to say anything or even acknowledge what I had seen, Omar had shut the door and was getting in behind the wheel.

I grew up around guns. My family was in law enforcement, so guns never bothered me. But tonight, I had an eerie feeling. Just another slight, contrary feeling, like sandpaper on the inside, about what I had seen. I didn't want to take anything away from Jessica's moment, so I let it pass.

"Make sure my cell phone is set to silent, please. Will you?"

Jessica's question snapped me back to the moment, and it took me an instant to understand why she was saying that to me. I am fairly sure her reason was twofold: she didn't want her phone to ring while I was holding it, and she was trying to distract me from the fact that she wasn't fastening her seat belt. She loathed seat belts. It was one of the very few things that we argued about.

"Oh. Yeah. Of course. That'd be awful if *your* cell phone rang in *my* pocket during *your* speech! And buckle up!" I found her phone and flipped the switch on the side, turning the ringer to silent.

"Thank you." She chuckled as she said it, but still didn't buckle her seat belt.

A couple of minutes later, a cell phone rang in the car. Jessica shot me a look, asking without saying a word, "Is that yours? Put it on silent!" But it wasn't mine.

"Apologies, madam, sir," Omar said. "This is my wife. May I take the call? I'll only be a moment."

"Of course!" I said, before I realized it really wasn't my place to give him permission. I looked to Jessica, who was smiling and thinking of something else. She was all smiles tonight. Excited smiles. Nervous smiles. Tonight was going to be big for her, and she knew it.

Omar answered the phone, but when he spoke it wasn't English. Jessica and I made eye contact, but she just shrugged her shoulders. Because of her travels, she heard different languages all the time, so it wasn't a big deal to her and in a moment, she was lost in her thoughts again.

I have noticed that different languages have familiar patterns depending on what part of the world you live in. It's pretty easy to recognize Latin-based languages, Spanish or Italian. It's easy to recognize Germanic languages. It wasn't easy to recognize what Omar was speaking. It was something that I'd never heard before. He spoke in low, even tones, but there was a constant 'hacking' to the language, like he was constantly clearing his throat or something.

Omar continued his conversation for a few moments longer.

"I do apologize. My wife is pregnant, and she was asleep when I left. She just wanted to know when I would be back. She's due any day now," Omar said as he continued driving, never looking back at us.

"That's so sweet!" Jessica exclaimed, snapping back to the present. "Is it a boy or a girl?"

"A boy, madam. Omar Jr. But please, excuse me now. Unlike those Uber drivers, *professional* drivers are meant to be seen, not heard." He said *Uber* with so much disdain you could taste it.

Okay, he really is a driver. I wonder if he's ever even considered modeling.

Jessica was smiling, I'm sure, thinking about Omar Jr., the night ahead, and what it would mean. Sitting there lost in her thoughts, she looked incredible. She really had it all: brains, beauty, success, and a great sense of humor. I could feel the argument coming.

She really is perfect. Why haven't we ever dated? Idiot! Just get the guts and tell her how you feel!

It was an argument I had with myself often. It kept me up at night. I didn't want to jeopardize or even sacrifice our friendship by making an unwanted advance. Not knowing how she felt made it all the worse. I was in the "friend zone," but was there a way out? Did Jessica feel trapped in the 'friend zone' too? Did she even want out?

Just as a way to move myself away from that never-ending self-argument, I started thinking about Omar's gun. I still had an uneasy feeling for some reason. Seeing that gun had given me a moment of pause, and I couldn't put my finger on why. For whatever reason and out of nowhere, that feeling, that 'negative nudge' was back. With Jessica's help, I was learning to listen to that 'still, small voice'[8] inside. Was this God trying to tell me something, or was I still just feeling jealous of Omar? Was this what it was like to hear God speaking directly to you? Was He telling me to—

Tires screeched across the pavement and headlights were right beside me, coming at me, full speed. *Impact.* The Escalade rocked on two side wheels, shuddering from the impact. I heard Omar grunt and glass breaking. I heard the deafening roar of airbags being deployed. Our forward momentum spun the back end of the heavy truck around so that we were facing the wrong direction in traffic, but somehow, we were still upright. I was stunned, in shock and unable to breathe, but I instinctively knew that I had buckled my seat belt and I was still in my seat. I knew I was alive. It was the tension from the belt that had knocked the wind out of me and was making it difficult for me to breathe. My ears rang with a high-pitched squeal. Jessica's passenger

---

8 I Kings 19:12

window was splintered into a thousand shards, like a glass spider's web woven from the impact with the side of her head. She never made a sound. *Why didn't she ever buckle her seat belt?* Jess laid there, slumped, unconscious and bleeding. Omar was draped over the steering wheel— woozy? Concussed? Alive? Leaning on the horn. Lights blinked all around us. A car alarm was screaming incessantly. It was a tangled mess of utter chaos.

I began to regain my senses, a little, and started to regain my hearing. All around us tires screeched and horns honked as traffic struggled to avoid impact. In the distance, I heard crushing metal and the sound of headlight glass being broken. We weren't the only ones who had been in an accident tonight. Suddenly, Jessica's door violently swung open and two men in black balaclavas reached in. Like a choreographed dance, each man had his routine. One pointed a gun at me while the other reached under Jessica's arms and dragged her out. I saw the panic in her eyes when she realized what was happening. I struggled to move. I could feel my arms and legs and they were responding to my instructions, but I couldn't determine why I was still in my seat. The seat belt. Fumbling with the latch, I unbuckled it and tried to follow after them, falling out of Jessica's passenger door. I looked up just in time to see her being shoved in the side of a black Humvee. I heard one final scream, "*Eli!*" before the doors were closed on her. The engine rumbled and in an instant, the truck was out of sight.

What do I do now? Call the police. I should call the police. "Help! Somebody, help!"

Suddenly, Omar was standing in front of me, blood dripping from his nose. "Dr. Adams is in grave danger. Come with me now if you want to save your friend."

Before I could protest or ask questions, Omar was running full speed toward the stopped traffic. In a flash, he pulled out his gun and was removing a driver, a scared teenage boy, from his car. Omar and I made eye contact, and he shouted, "*Get in!*"

I stumbled to my feet, my head still not clear. The owner of the car was shouting but moving away as he did it. Car horns blared from every side. Headlight glass crunched beneath my feet.

"Get in! Now!" a bloodied Omar again shouted through the windshield.

I was trying, but my body wasn't responding as quickly as I wanted.

"I'm sorry!" I shouted to the car owner, passing him as I moved toward the sleek Camaro.

What is going on?

Finally, able to get in the passenger side of the car Omar had commandeered, I frantically shouted at him, "Is she okay? Omar, what's going on? Who were those guys? Why do they want Jessica? Where are they taking her, Omar?"

"My name is not Omar. It's Aaron. I'm with Mossad. Shut up and let me drive."

Chapter Two

"I will say of the Lord, He is my refuge and fortress, my God, in Him I trust. Surely, He will deliver me from every trap, and protect me from deadly disease. He shall cover me with his feathers, and under His wings I will trust: His faithful promises are my armor. I will not be afraid of the terror by night; nor for the arrow that flieth by day; I do not dread the disease that stalks in darkness, nor the disaster that strikes at midday. A thousand shall fall at my side, and ten thousand at my right hand; but it shall not come near me."[9]

I honestly didn't realize I was praying the 91st Psalm under my breath, in a whisper. It was a habit that formed in childhood. From an early age, I *knew* that the Lord loved me and always wanted the best for me. I *knew* it. Even though I had never heard Him say it directly to me, it was as real to me as the shirt on my back. Grabbing hold of His promises found in the Bible always brought me comfort. If there was something I needed now, in a high-speed car chase, comfort was it. Praying a 3,000-year-old text[10] gave me peace, but it was the look on Omar's, scratch that, *Aaron's* face that brought me back to the reality of the moment.

Until now, nothing had phased Aaron. He was calm and cool from the moment Jessica and I first saw him. Even when he was shouting at

---

9 Psalm 91:1-7 (combination King James & New Living Translation)
10 "Probable Occasion When Each Psalm Was Composed," *Blue Letter Bible*, Study Resources, Charts and Outlines, https://www.blueletterbible.org/study/parallel/paral18.cfm

me to get into the car he was stealing, Aaron was not panicked. He was not scared. He was not surprised. He was… determined. But as I was rehearsing the 91st Psalm, Aaron gave me a look unlike anything I had seen from him tonight. What was it? Was it rage? Hatred? Shock? Surprise? I reasoned it away, thinking anyone hearing a scared and confused man in a tuxedo rehearsing Bible verses would have that type of look on their face. Screeching tires and a revving engine brought me back to the moment.

I quickly realized that a high-speed car chase isn't like what the movies make it out to be. When you're watching a movie, you can see the different angles; you know where the cars are at all times. You know if the lead car has turned. You know if the chase car is about to catch up. There is exciting music playing and while your adrenaline might get pumping, it's just a movie, and you realize there's no real danger. In real life, with the adrenaline pumping, headlights blinding you, taillights distracting you and streetlights flashing all around as you pass them at speed, chasing a Humvee is not easy to do. Especially when they have a considerable head start, it's dark and they have a black vehicle. It's a lot like watching an ice hockey game, in person, for the first time. Most of your evening is spent trying to find the puck, and the closer you are to the ice, the harder it is to follow the game.

"Where'd they go? Where'd they go?!" I shouted at Aaron.

He ignored me and turned a hard left in front of oncoming traffic. For the second time in a matter of minutes, headlights were heading directly for me. I screamed and covered my head. Aaron downshifted and the white Camaro we were in rocketed forward as we narrowly avoided the collision. Maybe Aaron had chosen this vehicle with purpose. I was almost laughing with relief because we had safely made the turn when I heard a quick, chipping, *pwink, pwink* sound.

Aaron ducked behind the steering wheel, getting as low as he could. He screamed, "Get down!" and I heard another *pwink*.

"Get! Down!"

It took me a moment to realize those *pwink* sounds were bullets slicing through the front windshield. I racked the seat all the way back and slammed my body into the mud-covered floorboard, getting real small, real quick. Another *pwink*, and the headrest where my head had just been sitting puffed as a bullet tore through the black leather. White stuffing fabric exploded into the front and back seats. *He truly delivered me from the terror by night and that "arrow" that was flying straight at my face!*

This whole time, I hadn't noticed that the Camaro we were in was a stick shift, but now that I was eye level with it, I sat in awe as Aaron drove. He was smooth as he weaved through traffic. A hard right turn slammed my face into the gear shifter and knocked the car into neutral. I heard the engine rev. Aaron shouted something in that other language, tires squealing in the distance. We were slowing down. Aaron grabbed the shifter and thrust it into fourth gear. The car shot forward.

Pwink. Pwink. Pwink.

This is nothing like the movies. I can't hear the gunshots. The windshield and back glass haven't exploded, blown out in little pieces everywhere. Aaron is way too calm. Don't freak out! Don't freak out!

That's when I heard it, a thunderous *Boom!* The car lurched and then went dead. We limped to a stop. It was then that things dawned on me. Whoever was in the Humvee wasn't necessarily trying to shoot *us.* The shots through the windshield were actually misses, as they were trying to disable the engine. A large caliber bullet to our aluminum engine block had done the trick. The Camaro was dead in the water. Maybe Aaron hadn't chosen so wisely after all.

"Come on! We've got to go!" Aaron was already moving out of the car and beginning to chase the Humvee on foot.

I spilled out of the floorboard and onto the street. Traffic was heavy all around me.

He ran twenty yards and stopped. Turning back to see if I was coming, Aaron shouted, "Hurry up! Your friend is in danger! We can still stop them!"

An instant of paralysis. Thoughts ran through my head in a fraction of a second.

Decision time. Fight or flight. Stay here and be safe, or save Jessica and be the man? The Lord is by my side. He'll never leave me nor forsake me.[11] I told her, "You're not alone…and you never will be." I gave her my word.

Instantly, I was at a full sprint, top speed. I could tell my speed and determination surprised Aaron. Within a half-second, I had caught up to him, but I didn't know where we were going. I had been on the floorboard and didn't know which direction the Humvee had gone, so I had to slow down to allow Aaron to lead.

"Through here," he shouted, turning down an empty alley. We ran a city block and turned left onto a crowded street. The running was much more difficult here than it had been prior. People were milling around, sitting outside at sidewalk coffee shops, window shopping. The place was alive with people. Moms pushing babies in strollers. Couples walking hand-in-hand. A living organism determined to prevent our rapid progress. Half a block later, Aaron screamed, "This way," as he found another deserted alley for us to use.

I was beginning to understand the direction we were going, but still didn't know why.

"If we don't find another car, there's no way we'll catch them," I shouted ahead to Aaron. He slowed down a beat as if considering what I had said. Then off he went again, full sprint, toward something I couldn't see around the corner. By the time I reached the place where he had been, I saw the chain link fence with Aaron dropping over it. He had used his suit jacket to protect him from the razor wire that ran along the top of the 10-foot fence. I was standing across the small street, outside of the fence, looking in at an airport runway. Aaron was already sprinting toward the hangars.

How did he get up and over that fence so quickly? Who is this guy?

---

11 Hebrews 13:5

I sprinted as hard as I could, and with the energy I had left, jumped onto the fence. I climbed as quickly as I possibly could, something I hadn't done since I was a kid, and did my best not to slice myself open as I used Aaron's jacket for protection against the razor wire.

How did he do this so quickly? Athletic isn't a strong enough word for the ease with which this guy moves.

My feet hit the ground, but my energy was spent. My shaky legs wobbled unsteadily. It had been too long since I had run like this, and the adrenaline rush was wearing off. I ran as hard as I could, which was little more than a jog until I saw the black Humvee in the far distance. Seeing the truck gave me one final energy boost. It slewed to a stop, big knobby wheels on loose gravel, and came to rest at the rear of a large cargo plane. The airplane's engines were already running, and the propellers were turning. I was so far away, but I could plainly see Jessica being hustled up the rear ramp of the airplane by two men dressed in black. She looked tiny against the mass of the hulking propeller plane, but she was unmistakable in her emerald-green evening gown. A group of men followed them into the belly of the plane and even before the ramp was up, the plane lurched forward. The wheels began their slow rotation. Time was running out.

My eyes searched the darkness, and there in the distance I saw Aaron, running full speed toward the airplane. Even though it was barely moving, and he was moving quickly through the freshly cut grass, I knew there was no way Aaron was going to cover the distance before the plane's wheels were off the ground. I think Aaron sensed it too. I watched as he pulled his gun again, took up a steady shooting position, feet shoulder-width apart, left foot slightly in front of his right, and began firing in the direction of the airplane. It almost seemed like the whole action happened in slow motion.

"No! Stop! Quit! Stop it!" I breathlessly shouted at him. I couldn't take the risk that he would injure Jessica. I was still a distance behind him, and he had emptied his clip before I made it to his position. I heard the gun *click, click, click,* as he continued to pull the trigger.

I summoned all of the strength I had left and pushed him in the back with both hands. "You could have killed her!" I screamed at the top of my lungs. Stumbling and then wheeling on the ball of his right foot, Aaron backhand slapped me with the hand that was holding the gun. He turned back again toward the airplane, seeing the wheels all off the ground. The blow dropped me to my backside. Landing with a thud in the damp evening grass, it knocked what little breath I had left out of me.

Stunned and with blood pouring down my cheek, Aaron looked me directly in the eyes and said, "Never touch me again. I would never do anything to harm her. I was aiming at the tires. I was trying to stop the plane from taking off. Never touch me again. Are we clear?"

It was a sharp rebuke, but I nodded in agreement. I wasn't about to do anything to get even further on his bad side. Aaron pulled a white handkerchief from his back pocket and tossed it at me. It hit me in the chest. "Clean yourself up. It's going to be a long night, and you need to focus if you're going to be a part of it. I need you to be a part of it. Jessica needs you to be a part of it." He turned to move away from me, then stopped. "By the way, what is your name?"

"Matt. Matt Davenport."

"Come on, Matt-Matt Davenport. We've got a lot to do and a short time to get it done." Aaron, who was already walking toward the hangars from where the airplane had taken off, pulled a cell phone from his pocket, dialed a number and began speaking in that other language to someone, barking what I guess were new orders, within just a few seconds.

I stood up and dusted some freshly cut grass off of my hands and my rear-end. I didn't know if taking it to the cleaners could help my new tuxedo after this night. I was dirty from the floorboard of the car, and now I was covered in grass stains and blood from the unexpected slap. I didn't know if Aaron thought my name was actually Matt-Matt, but at that moment I wasn't about to correct him. I was catching my breath, following his slow pace.

I'm dressed like James Bond, Double-O Davenport, playing pretend. This guy actually is James Bond.

I waited until he clicked off the call and then stepped up beside him and asked, "What do we do now, and what's going on? Please tell me."

"Your friend, Dr. Adams, is in possession of some unbelievably valuable information. She doesn't realize what she has or how valuable it is. There are people, organizations, that will pay millions of dollars for the information. There are organizations that want to keep the information hidden, no matter the cost, even if that means taking your friend's life. What we do in the next few seconds, minutes and hours will determine the course of human history and whether your friend lives or dies. I'll tell you more when we get airborne. Please, hurry up." With that, he picked up his pace.

I stopped and under my breath, looking at the distant blinking lights of Jessica's now airborne cargo plane, I said, "You're not alone," and I meant it.

Chapter Three

That contrary, negative nudge was back.

Aaron had said truly little to me since we left the grass of the airfield. Sitting in the sleek jet now, it amazed me how quickly things had been arranged. From seemingly nowhere and in no time, people arrived at the airport and the small jet was fueled and readied on the runway. I could tell by the activity level that we would be taking off very soon.

Flying commercial was one thing. Security checks. Long wait times. Delayed flights. People being herded on and off the airplane like cattle. Not that I had ever had the opportunity to do it, but I imagine that flying in a private jet would be a different experience altogether. However, being in a privately owned, government operated, passenger jet airplane was something spectacular and completely next level to any flight I had ever experienced.

At one point, Aaron's activity, phone and physical, slowed and I took the opportunity to try and find out some information. When I asked where we were going, hurriedly Aaron told me we were flying to Israel; then he started to walk off.

"I don't have a passport," I blurted. It just came out. It was almost an excuse, almost a protest, almost a complaint, and I knew it sounded stupid the moment I said it. The truth was, flying to Israel wasn't exactly in my weekend plans. None of this was. I had a normal life, a job to get back to, a flight home to catch, plans for the summer to make. On the other hand, Jessica had been kidnapped and I had given her my word that I would always be there for her. Besides, Aaron wasn't exactly giving me an option.

Aaron's shoulders slumped as he turned back toward me and exasperatedly said, "Man up and grow a pair." He turned away and went on with his business.

Embarrassed, I buckled my seat belt and decided to keep my mouth shut until I was needed for something. Moments after wheels-up, a flight attendant served me orange juice and handed me a couple pills.

"These will help," she said in heavily accented English as she moved off to another task. *Aspirin? Ibuprofen? Something to help with the pain, exhaustion and shock of all of this?* I took the pills without thinking too much about it.

No one said it, but I had the feeling that everyone aboard the jet was Israeli Air Force, undercover and in plain clothes. Besides looking Israeli—dark skinned and dark eyes—everyone operated with the mechanical precision that usually comes with military training. It was a clockwork operation. The pilots, flight attendants, and even the ground crew worked together in an orchestrated symphony of directed movements. Each knew their part, and each played their instrument to perfection. Within two hours of seeing Jessica wrenched from our Escalade, we were in the air, giving chase. If Aaron was indeed with the Mossad, it all made sense.

I had read enough books and seen enough spy thrillers to know a little about Mossad, the Israeli counterterrorism and intelligence agency. Although I don't think they use the word "agency." That's an American phrasing, like Central Intelligence Agency or CIA. To the Israelis, it's "the Institute;" at least, that's the English translation of the name. If movies and rumors were true, Mossad was responsible for some of the most daring, well-planned covert missions ever executed.

Just recently, I had read about the death of Muhammad al-Zawahiri, known to Israel's security groups as "The Engineer," in Tunisia.[12]

---

12 "Report: Hamas operative known as 'The Engineer' assassinated by Mossad in Tunisia," *The Jerusalem Post*, December 16, 2016, https://www.jpost.com/Israel-News/Report-Mossad-assassinates-Hamas-operative-in-Tunsia-475625

It seems al-Zawahiri was a ruthless man, an upper echelon member of Al-Qassam Brigades, the militant wing of Hamas. The assassins were able to corner him, riddle his body with something like twenty bullets, erase surveillance footage of the event from surrounding cameras and escape without a trace. Mossad has never claimed responsibility, but everyone else gives them credit or blame, depending on which side of the argument you fall, for the assassination.

Probably one of the most famous cases undertaken by the Mossad was a plan called *Operation Wrath of God* or *Operation Bayonet*.[13] Steven Spielberg even made a movie about the event in 2005, called *Munich*. The events happened before I was born, but after watching it, I wanted to know the real story behind the movie, so I did a little research.

In 1972, the world watched as eleven members of the Israeli Olympic team were taken hostage and eventually killed by a militant Palestinian unit called Black September. They were aided by members of the Palestinian Liberation Organization (PLO). Outraged, the Israeli people called for revenge. Over the course of something like twenty years, each of the terrorists who had been involved were assassinated, killed violently in different and unique ways. The first terrorist was shot eleven times in his apartment in Rome. Each of the eleven bullets a deadly memorial to the eleven athletes killed, one bullet for each athlete. One terrorist had his head blown off by a bomb placed in his bedside phone. One terrorist was pushed in front of a bus. The reason I remembered the story so vividly had to do with the fact that several hours *before* each assassination, each target's family received flowers with a condolence card reading: "A reminder we do not forget, we do not forgive,"[14] and that's pretty hardcore. In all, eighteen terrorists associated with the

---

13 "Munich: Operation Bayonet,: *BBC News: BBC Two, This World*, January 18, 2006, http://news.bbc.co.uk/2/hi/programmes/this_world/4605414.stm
14 Gordan Thomas, "We Know Where You Live," *The Sydney Morning Herald*, January 14, 2006, https://www.smh.com.au/news/world/we-know-where-you-live/2006/01/13/1137118970193.html?page=1

deaths of the Israeli athletes were killed. As I was reading about it all, I remember thinking that I never, ever wanted to get on the bad side of the Mossad.

But the Mossad is more than just a counterterrorism unit. They are also leading the world in their intelligence gathering efforts and have been for some time.

My first *real* introduction to the Mossad happened shortly after the terrorist attacks in New York City in September 2001. Like everyone else, I was glued to my television set and was scouring the internet and newspapers for information. Only a few days after 9/11, a report was released indicating a high-ranking law enforcement official had "leaked" information hinting that the Mossad had tried to warn the United States about an imminent attack. I remember reading something like, "FBI and CIA officials were advised in August, a month prior, that as many as 200 terrorists had been moving into this country and were planning 'a major assault on the United States.'"[15] The Mossad had tried to warn the United States, but the news had either fallen on deaf ears, there wasn't enough time to do anything with the information, or we just didn't have the infrastructure to seek out the potential offenders. Regardless, the Mossad definitely had an ear to the ground, and if they were this involved with Jessica and her research, this was definitely big. I just didn't know what *this* was.

It was roughly 9:30 p.m. when Aaron finally finished whatever he was working on and moved to the seat across from me. The adrenaline dump had passed, and I was sitting in what had to be the most comfortable airplane seat I had ever flown in. A drowsy feeling began to wash over me.

I took a deep breath, tried to steady myself and said, "I'm sorry I'm just a bother and keep getting on your nerves and in the way. I am

---

15 Richard A. Serrano and John-Thor Dahlburg, "Officials Told of 'Major Assault' Plans," *Los Angeles Times*, September 20, 2001, http://articles.latimes.com/2001/sep/20/news/mn-47840

really trying to understand what's going on, Aaron. I don't get it. Why is the Mossad involved with Jessica? What was she working on that would get her kidnapped? What information does she have?"

Aaron nodded. Finally, in a gentler tone he said, "We have plenty of time to talk about this. The flight to Haifa is about ten hours long, and we will have to hit the ground running as soon as we land." He looked at me and smiled. "I can tell the pills the flight attendant gave you are working. Don't fight it. You should sleep now so the jet lag doesn't slow you down in the city."

I started to ask him again about the information, the problems and the chase, all of it. My mind was running a million miles an hour. I needed to know! But all that came out of my mouth was, "Not alone."

The last thing I remember was hearing someone say, "He'll sleep for several hours," and then the darkness as my heavy eyelids slowly came together.

Chapter Four

Bzzzz. Bzzzzz. Bzzzzz.

Sunlight was turning the inside of my eyelids a peculiar color of red. I gently, cautiously, opened my eyes and realized I was looking down at a cloud, sunlight shining and being reflected directly into my face. The jet engines droned on in an unchanging hum. The airplane window was small, but the shade was open, and I was beginning to wake up. Still super drowsy, I rolled back into a more conventional sitting position. The activity of the crew from the night before was non-existent now.

Across the aisle and facing me, Aaron was sitting at a table, reading something on a laptop. He must have sensed me stirring and looked up at me. A smile, two perfect rows of white teeth, crossed his face.

"Did you know you talk in your sleep?" Aaron asked. "Actually, it's more like a mumble. You mumble in your sleep."

"Only when I'm drugged," I shot back at him. I wasn't in the best of moods, but I was also surprised by how my voice sounded. "My throat is *so* dry, and my voice is almost gone. Is it the processed oxygen in the airplane? Am I that dehydrated?"

At this, Aaron laughed like I was the funniest comedian he had ever heard. In between hearty laughs, he was able to say, "Your adrenaline really must have been pumping last night. Later on, when you tell your kids this story, you'll want to leave this part out. Okay?" The laughing continued. "You don't remember it, but you screamed a high

pitch scream—you sounded like a teenage girl at a Harry Styles con-
cert—pretty much nonstop from the minute you got in the chase car
with me, until the minute I slapped you at the airfield. I'm sorry about
that, by the way, I truly am." Then he was off into hysterical laughter
again. "The only time you weren't screaming like a schoolgirl was when
you were praying. That was the only relief I got from it!"

I guess that explains the look he gave me as I was quoting the 91st
Psalm. I was going to try and defend my actions, but because of the
condition of my voice, when I went to protest, the sound that came out
of my mouth was little more than a *honk*. Aaron looked me directly in
the eyes and saw the confused look on my face. At that point, we both
started laughing. It was the perfect tension breaker and I began to feel
better…about my situation, Aaron, and even the likelihood we could
rescue Jessica.

"A merry heart doeth good like a medicine,"[16] indeed.

I noticed Aaron seemed much more like a person than the rugged
secret agent from the night before. He was just a normal dude. He had
changed clothes and was now wearing a navy-colored shirt and dark
jeans.

"When I get scared, I always seem to end up quoting the Bible, either to myself or shouting it at somebody. Sorry, man," I said.

Bzzzzz. Bzzzzz. Bzzzzz.

After a few moments of thought, I asked, "So what's really going
on? Why did those guys kidnap Jessica?"

"I'm not a scientist, and our information is still extremely limited.
Dr. Adams hasn't published the details yet, so last night was going to be
the big unveiling of her life's work. Here's what I know. She discovered
something and it led to an invention of sorts. Basically, your friend, Dr.
Adams, Jessica, has discovered a way to locate subtle *vertical* cracks in
the Earth's surface *and* mantle, and by using those cracks somehow, she
invented an inexpensive way to harness the Earth's geothermal energy,

---

16 Proverbs 17:22

tapping into the Earth's core. Our scientists have been working on this for years, with little success. Your friend solved the problem.

"The implications are enormous. It's a completely self-sustaining power source that will never be exhausted. It is completely clean energy. Think about it: electricity for everyone on the planet. Heat in the winter for everybody. A cheap way to power irrigation in the desert, which means vegetation anywhere, crops and food for the entire planet. No more hunger. No more starvation. And people will have to build her machines. Others will have to plant the crops and harvest them. The job creation will run into the thousands or hundreds of thousands. It will revolutionize the global economy. It really could solve most of the world's poverty problems, all at once. The implications are on a massive scale, and we've only begun to break the surface of what might possibly be accomplished."

I sat there in stunned silence, mouth open.

Aaron gave me a few moments to let the news register and sink in before adding, "And this is just the beginning. Those are just the initial implications of her work. It could have far-reaching effects. You know, once a new technology arrives, it becomes the foundation and so many different things grow from it. This really will change *everything* as we know it. I'm surprised she hadn't told you any of this." He began clicking on the keyboard of his computer.

Bzzzzz. Bzzzzz. Bzzzzz.

That stung a little bit, but I knew Jessica had signed several non-disclosure agreements over the years. I had stopped even asking about her work because every time I did, it was the same story. "I want to tell you, Matt," she would say, "but because of my contracts, the different governments I work with, I can't tell you anything. One day I will. One day we'll share it together, I promise." I guess last night was going to be our "sharing it together" moment.

Defensively, I popped off at Aaron. "I listened to, well, I sort of listened to Jessica as she was practicing her speech last night. And we even talked about it. She didn't say anything about geothermal energy. In fact, the stuff she talked about was super boring, 'Transition Zone' stuff," I said. I realized it came out a little too harsh. Softening my tone, I added, "She said that this was going to be a big night, not that it was going to change the energy industry, but that it was going to revolutionize the theory of evolution, thoughts about the dinosaurs and their extinction and that it had implications about the Big Bang. It's almost like you've got the wrong Dr. Adams, or maybe the kidnappers do."

"I don't know the answer to that, Matt. I don't know why she would say that or why the part of her speech you heard didn't say anything about a new revolutionary invention. All I know is that this technology is on the cutting edge, several players are willing to do anything to have control of it, and your friend holds the key." He went back to typing.

That's an interesting way to put it... "holds the key."

Bzzzzz. Bzzzzz. Bzzzzz.

"I think you've got a voicemail or a text or something," Aaron said, looking in my direction. "You keep buzzing. Haven't you noticed it?"

"Oh. Actually, I hadn't. What are you working on over there?" I asked as I fumbled in my pocket for my phone.

"I'm getting a head start on all the paperwork that will be involved with last night's incident. I have to make note of everything that happened because my country will be responsible to pay for the damages, any injuries and the stolen car, all of that stuff. I'm trying to get it on paper and submitted before I forget any of the details and so that I don't have to do it later."

About that time, the flight attendant stepped out of the back, from a door behind me, walked toward Aaron and spoke something in another language to him.

Was that Hebrew? How in the world do you learn to speak that language?

A short conversation took place between the two of them, and the flight attendant ducked out of sight again.

"By the way, what time is it and how much longer until we land?" I asked him as he was diving back into his work.

He looked at his watch and said, "We'll be landing in a little less than an hour," and got back to it.

I finally fished my phone from my front pocket. It would have been easier to get to it if I had unbuckled my seat belt, but after the events over the last few hours I was clinging to any amount of safety that I could find. I hit the numbers 5-3-7-7 to unlock my phone. I had a couple of missed calls, but no voicemails. My battery was almost dead. I guess that's what ten hours of international roaming charges will do to the battery life of a phone.

Aaron nonchalantly asked, "Who was it?" as he typed away on his keyboard.

I recognized the numbers. "A coworker and my mom, both calling, I'm sure, to see how the night went. One is interested in the presentation, the other in my love life, or lack thereof. You decide which. Boy, are they in for a shock when I tell them about what actually happened last night." Aaron shrugged.

I continued, "By the way, I know you've been really busy and might not have really thought about it, but aren't you upset that you might miss your son's birth?"

Aaron looked at me with a question written on his face but didn't say anything.

"Last night, you took a call from your pregnant wife. Does she know that you're flying to Israel now?" I asked.

"Oh, that. That wasn't my wife. I'm not married. That was the security team waiting for us at the fundraiser, checking to make sure I had secured the two of you and we were on our way. The wife and pregnancy bit was just a cover story."

The flight attendant showed back up and made her way next to me. She was holding a server's tray and said, "Here, these will help."

Bzzzzz. Bzzzzz. Bzzzzz.

I gave her a sideways look as she handed me a few pills and a steam-
ing cup of liquid. She smiled, sensing my hesitation.

"Vitamins and electrolytes to help with your energy. Hot tea with
honey to help your voice. Here is a toothbrush and toothpaste, a hair-
brush and some deodorant. If you would like to freshen up, please step
into the back washroom. I have set out some clothes that I think will fit
you: blue jeans, tennis shoes and a dark button-up shirt. Breakfast will
be served in a few minutes."

I downed the pills and had a few sips of the tea before standing
and making my way toward the back of the airplane. I stepped into the
washroom. It was a decent space for the size of the jet, much bigger
than a commercial airline bathroom. I looked at myself in the mirror.
Thirty years of looking at my reflection only made the disheartening
information that I now knew that much worse.

Bzzzzz. Bzzzzz. Bzzzzz.

Aaron is much *better looking than me, and now I know he's single.
I know where this story is going. I'm in the friend zone with Jessica, but
Aaron is a dashingly handsome man. High cheekbones and good genes.
A super spy as well. We* will *save Jessica, but* Aaron *will end up with the
girl. I'd like to smack* him *in the face and see how* he *likes it.* My shoul-
ders slumped a little.

I knew it was just jealousy and my being selfish. It was that simple
and I recognized it. A Bible verse came to my mind: *Don't be selfish;
don't try to impress others. Be humble, thinking of others as better than
yourselves. Don't look out only for your own interests, but take an interest
in others, too.*[17] From the moment I met Jessica, I had always tried to be
humble and think of her interests before mine. I needed to do that now.

*Lord, I'm sorry. Please forgive me for thinking so poorly of Aaron
and thinking about him in that way.*[18] Again, I sensed a quiet, negative
nudge as I continued my prayer. *For the eyes of the Lord are over the*

17 Philippians 2:3–4 (New Living Translation)
18 I John 1:9

righteous, and His ears are open unto their prayers: but the face of the Lord is against them that do evil.[19] *I thank You that Your eyes are open for me and Your ears are open to me and my prayers. Help me find my friend and turn Your face against those who are doing this evil. God, You are our salvation; I will trust, and not be afraid: You, Lord Jehovah, are my strength and my song; You are our salvation.*[20] *I put my trust in You and You will save us both. Thank You, Lord. In Jesus' Name, amen."*

I slipped off the tuxedo pants and dropped them on the floor. There was a pair of blue jeans, wrapped in plastic with a sticker on it. Measurements for waist and inseam length were printed on the sticker, and I was more than just a little impressed. The flight attendant was pretty spot on. I opened the bag and slid the jeans on. They were the correct length, but the waist was a little big. Tucked inside the tennis shoes was a belt that was also wrapped in plastic. She had thought of everything.

Bzzzzz. Bzzzzz. Bzzzzz.

The vibration came from the floor and was slightly amplified on the aluminum tiling.

Wait. Why am I still buzzing? I already checked my voicemails and text messages.

I fished into the front right pocket of the tuxedo pants and pulled out the cell phone Jessica had given me. It was *her* phone that was buzzing. If it hadn't been for the fact that I was only halfway dressed, I probably would have said something to Aaron about having Jessica's phone. It had totally slipped my mind with everything that had happened. The lock screen showed twelve missed calls, from several different numbers, a few texts and one voicemail.

The texts were from what I supposed were friends and colleagues asking about how the evening went. Numbers labelled as "Work," "Lab" and "Nuria Melamed" had all called but didn't leave any messages. One text asked where she was and why she hadn't shown up to the dinner.

19 I Peter 3:12
20 Isaiah 12:2

That person genuinely seemed concerned. The texts were all pretty mundane, nothing relevant to her current situation. There was one voicemail from a 'restricted number' that had called four times. This was Jessica's phone and it already felt like an invasion of her privacy looking at the unread texts. It would feel even worse listening to her voicemail, but maybe it would contain a clue.

Several months ago, the last time I had seen her before this trip, Jess and I did something that I am extremely grateful for now. We were standing on the pier in San Diego, when I received a text message. I entered my four-digit PIN to unlock my phone, hiding it, instinctively, so Jessica couldn't see it. Jessica pulled out her phone, unlocked it and made a big deal as she reset her PIN to 6-2-8-8, right in front of me, where I could see it.

She said, "I don't want there to ever be anything hidden between us, Matt. You want in my phone, you know the code."

"6-2-8-8? Where'd you come up with that?" I asked, trying to deflect the conversation.

"6 is an 'M'. 2 is an 'A'. 8 is a 'T'. 8 is another 'T'. My PIN is *your* name, MATT."

I was a little starstruck with her at that moment. I said, "The text was from my mother wanting to know how it was going with you. I was a little embarrassed that my mom was texting me. That's why I hid my phone. And I'm a little ashamed now. Here, I'm going to change my passcode too," and with that I changed mine to 5-3-7-7. "That spells JESS, in case you were wondering."

Jessica flashed me the most beautiful smile I had ever seen. Took my hand and off we went.

"Don't be embarrassed about having a good relationship with your mom. I love that about you. I love that you have always honored your father and mother. That means you're going to live a loooooong time!"[21] She was referencing a Bible verse in Ephesians that I had known since

---

21 Ephesians 6:2–3

childhood. I remember both of us laughing about the singsong way Jessica had said 'loooooong time.'

Now, standing in the confines of a jet washroom, I was struck with the decision: listen to her voicemail or not. I decided she would forgive me if I listened and unlocked her phone. I mean, that's why she gave me her PIN. Accessing her voicemail, I listened.

"Oh, Matt," the voice quietly whispered. I had trouble even hearing it over the quiet roar of the jet engines. "I hope that you're okay and you've still got my phone. I hope you're listening to this." It was Jessica and she sounded scared, like she was hiding, rambling on, "Uh, I've got your number stored in my phone and I don't actually remember it. Uh, if you get this, uh, if you're listening to this, please *be careful.*" Placing heavy emphasis on the words. "*Don't trust anybody* and please hold onto my stuff. That is my *favorite* tube of lipstick. I would be lost without it. I'm a virtuous woman, Matt, I really am. *Don't lose my lipstick,*" she said adamantly. "Oh, here they come," and with that, she clicked off. The voicemail was over. I stood there for a few seconds, the phone still pressed to my ear, waiting, hoping there would be more to the message.

Bzzzzz. Bzzzzz. Bzzzzz.

Her phone was still buzzing in my hand, pressed to my ear. But why? I had checked her texts and now her voicemails. It didn't make any sense. And then, as I was looking at it, the phone died. While the phone was set to silent, the vibration must have been a low battery indicator.

I finished getting changed, brushed my teeth and hair, gathered all my belongings from the tuxedo and stuffed them into my pockets. I had a decision to make. Jessica had instructed me not to trust anyone. Did that mean even Aaron? The guy leading the charge to rescue her? There it was again, gut feeling or nudge, that still small voice was back, and I decided to keep this information to myself.

Chapter Five

By the time I made my way back to my seat, Aaron had put his computer away and was just beginning to eat his breakfast, eggs, pancakes and coffee. He motioned for me to sit down at the table with him as he swallowed the food in his mouth.

"Coffee smells good." I said and almost on cue, the flight attendant was there placing a plate of food in front of me. "Thank you, and coffee for me too?" I asked. The flight attendant smiled and hurried off. I noticed that my voice was beginning to sound better. I looked at my watch and it said it was 5:30 a.m., but it seemed much later than that. I asked, "What time is it?"

Aaron looked down at his watch and said, "12:30 p.m., Israel time. You probably want to change the time on your watch. You don't want to try and do the calculation every time you look at your wrist. We've got a little while before we land. Eat up."

I was famished. I realized I hadn't eaten anything since lunch yesterday and I had been looking forward to a $500 dinner, so that lunch had been light. I cut a bite of pancake that was dripping in syrup and placed the whole thing in my mouth. It was too much for one bite, but somehow, I managed to get it all in. I made it work.

"Hey, you never told me why we're going to Israel. Why would they take Jessica there?" I asked, struggling to keep the pancake in and the words discernible.

"Our intelligence unit is confident that Jessica didn't have her research with her last night. So, they, whoever *they* are, have *her*, but not her technology, her research and all of that. The next logical step for them is to make their way to her laboratory, get her to give the information to them, and then use it for whatever they have planned," Aaron said, as he was finishing up his breakfast. "Didn't you hear her scream 'Eli' as she was being pushed in the Humvee last night?"

I nodded. Thinking back, I did remember hearing her scream that name as she was shoved in the truck. It gave me a horrible feeling thinking of her trapped with those people.

"Obviously," Aaron continued, "Eli is your friend's boss, Dr. Eli Kaplan. We think she was telling you, instructing you with her last free breath, to go find Dr. Kaplan. He must have the information, or controls access to the research, the schematics, the plans, etc."

"That makes sense, but don't you think that they have already raided the facility or covertly snuck in or whatever you spy people do? I mean, it took us at least two hours to get airborne last night after they had flown away," I said.

"Did you see what type of airplane they were in? That was a C-130, propeller driven cargo plane. The *top* speed for that type of aircraft is somewhere in the neighborhood of 590 kilometers per hour. Our aircraft is a Cessna Citation X, and we have a cruising speed in excess of 950 kilometers per hour. Even if they were able to get Dr. Kaplan's whereabouts from your friend, immediately after takeoff, and went directly to the lab, we should be well ahead of them," Aaron said confidently.

"Great. Great," I said. "Okay, then, do you have any clues who 'they' are? Who are these kidnappers? What are they planning to do with Jessica's research and invention? And more importantly, what will they do with Jessica if they are able to get it? Will they let her go?" The question sounded stupid even as it was coming out of my mouth.

"I think you know the answer to that one, don't you, Matt? The information is valuable because she is the only one who has it. If they manage to steal it, and she is left alive, there's the risk of her duplicating the work, so they will want to eliminate that option. Right now, we don't know who these guys are. The working theory is that they are a mercenary group that has been hired by a rival research firm or energy consortium. Honestly, we just don't know, but we think that the group behind the kidnapping is in it for the profit. It makes the most sense. With her work and invention, there is the potential for billions and billions of dollars in profit. Consider the oil industry and how much money is generated by the countries with the oil fields. Think about the Saudi princes, the luxury and opulence, the priceless cars, jewels, mansions, airplanes, and all of that which comes from oil production. Now, imagine that all of that excess could be *yours*. That's the kind of money we're talking about. Maybe now you understand the lengths these people will be willing to go to get what they want. We're talking billions of dollars. Billions, not millions. Do you understand the difference in billions and millions?"

It seemed like a simple question, and I nodded that I did.

Aaron shook his head and said, "No, I don't think you really do. The true difference in one million and one billion is astronomical. We have a hard time to even quantify it, especially since the two words rhyme. That is truly unfortunate. Here's an easy way to begin to fully realize the difference between million and billion. One *million* seconds is equal to a little over eleven days. One *billion* seconds is equal to a little over thirty-one and a half *years*. Do you understand how much money we are thinking? Do you understand the ramifications and why people are trying to steal Jessica's research? Not only is there an astronomical amount to be made by the people who control this energy source, there is also an astronomical amount of money to be lost by the people in the other energy fields. Think of the coal power plants, the nuclear power plants, the wind, hydroelectric plants; they will all go out of business."

"Jessica's in real trouble, isn't she? Be completely honest with me. Do you think we can actually save her?"

Aaron didn't hesitate. "Yes, Matt. I do. We just need to put our heads together and get one step ahead of them. That's what we're about to do. Once we touch down, we're going to be headed to the Azrieli Sarona Tower, in Tel Aviv."

"Azrieli Sarona Tower, Tel Aviv," I said, making a mental note.

Aaron continued, "Jessica's lab is located on one of the top floors. We get there, talk to Dr. Kaplan and get the information. Once the enemy knows the information is no longer exclusive, hopefully, they will release your friend, Dr. Adams, or be willing to swap your friend for the information. We'll gladly swap the research and her information to get your friend returned safely."

I started to lose my temper and said, probably a little louder than I should have, "If Dr. Kaplan has access to the information, why don't we just call him and get him to email it to us or something? Surely there could have been an easier way to accomplish this than flying all the way over here and meeting with him face-to-face. This is ridiculous. Jessica's safety is at risk, and you're making me fly halfway around the world when a phone call would have worked."

Aaron was cool, didn't miss a beat. "Kaplan doesn't know us. Why would he agree to help us, the Mossad, if we just barged into his lab, demanding that he give us this ultra-valuable information? Is he going to trust some random guys with badges? Don't forget, he is going to get rich off of this invention too. This isn't the United States. Even if we had a warrant, like what you would use, it doesn't mean he is going to turn over the correct information. He might not even have it. We honestly have no idea what we are looking for and wouldn't have a clue what we're looking at. We need his *cooperation*. That's where you come in, Matt."

"Where I come in? I've never met, never even *talked* to Dr. Kaplan. How am I supposed to help?"

"The guys in the think tank are sure, based on the length of time of your relationship with Dr. Adams, that she has spoken about you over the years. The two of you have traveled together, and more. Kaplan will be familiar with who you are. And even if he isn't, you know enough about her that he could quiz you and you'd know details so intimate that he could be assured you and Dr. Adams were friends."

"How in the world do you know we've traveled together? How could you possibly have that information? I know the Mossad has surveillance techniques that I can't even begin to imagine, but you and I just met a few hours ago and we've been on an airplane this whole time." I felt like I was interrogating him now.

Aaron just smiled and opened his laptop. He said, "The jet has Wi-Fi capabilities. The laptop has internet access." He typed a few keystrokes and swiveled the computer screen to face me. "You have a Facebook profile page with dozens of pictures of the two of you in different locations. Super surveillance technique, huh?" He might as well have added "you idiot," but I'm glad he didn't.

I wonder what the Hebrew word for moron *is. Aaron might start using it as my nickname.*

The flight attendant reappeared and began clearing the dishes. In my mind, her timing couldn't have been more perfect. I didn't know how else I was going to get out of that moment with Aaron. She asked if we would like more coffee. I nodded enthusiastically.

Aaron turned to me and said, "I see from your pictures that you and Jessica have traveled to several different places together, but you can only tell so much from pictures. What's your, um, status? Are you a couple?"

I knew this was coming. It was clear to me from the moment I stepped off the elevator the night before that Aaron was interested in Jessica, even though he was a few years older than us. I did my best to control my jealousy, my anger, my embarrassment, my low self-esteem. I had a physical reaction before I could put into words the reality of our relationship. Aaron must have picked up on it and before I could answer, he interrupted my thoughts with another question.

"How did the two of you meet?"

The flight attendant returned with a small pot of coffee and poured it in my cup. She left the pot sitting on the table and made her way toward the back of the airplane.

"How did the two of you meet?" Aaron asked again.

"We met in an airport. I don't know how to tell this story without sounding like a complete wimp, but if you know the circumstances behind my actions, it might help you understand. A few years ago, I was flying home from my Dad's funeral. I was in line to get some coffee and it was taking so long, I was getting angry. I could literally feel my temperature rising. Why can't people decide what they want before they get to the person taking orders? Am I right?"

Aaron nodded.

"Anyway, I was looking at my watch, trying to will the time to pass, when I heard an angel speaking in my ear. She said, 'You're not alone,' because she was thinking the line was taking forever, just like I was. But what I heard was an angel telling me that even though my dad had died, I wasn't alone in this world. I can't express the feeling that washed over me at that moment, and I broke down in tears. Not the manliest thing to do, right? But that's what happened. Jessica sat with me in the airport for several hours, talking to me, listening to me tell her about my father and our relationship. I told her stupid stories and fond memories. Five hours seemed like five minutes and it always does when we're together. If she hadn't said those three simple words, 'You're not alone,' I probably would have done something stupid in the coffee shop, lost my temper, yelled at someone who didn't deserve it, and I definitely wouldn't have one of the most special women in the world in my life."

Aaron just sat there, staring at me. There was something in his eyes. Sadness? Anger? Pride? Jealousy? Determination? After a few moments, an admittedly awkward few moments, Aaron asked, "Do you remember the last day you spent with your dad?"

"I do," I replied.

"Tell me about it."

"It was Christmas. I'm not sure if you celebrate Christmas in Israel, but in the United States it's a pretty big deal. Hey! I just realized this is my first trip out of the country! Talk about unique circumstances… Anyway, I went back to the house I grew up in to visit my parents for Christmas. I was there for the weekend. My aunts and uncles came over one night, and I got to spend some time with my cousins like we did when I was young. On Christmas morning, we opened some presents and my mom even cooked a turkey."

"But do you remember the last *day* you spent with your father?" Aaron asked, interrupting my thought.

"Yeah, I guess," I said. "It was the day after Christmas, and Dad and I watched some NBA game on television, ate some leftovers and that afternoon, he drove me to the airport. The last time I saw my dad alive was when I said goodbye at the airport. We actually hugged on that day and my dad told me he loved me. I remember that. He told me he loved me. My dad was too young. He should still be alive."

Aaron sat there quietly, something in his look, his eyes.

"What's going on, Aaron? What are you thinking?"

Moments passed as Aaron gathered his thoughts and was finally able to put into words what he had been sitting there thinking about.

"My father was too young when I lost him too. When I was very young, 1978, I said goodbye to my father for the last time. I remember everything about that day. My dad is my hero and I've spent my whole life trying to be like him, to follow in his footsteps, to continue what he started. My dad made a difference in this world and for my country. I found out later that he died in the line of duty," Aaron finally said.

I asked, "Do you remember your last day with him?"

"Vividly. My last day with him was a Wednesday and I woke up to get ready for school. My mother came in and told me that I didn't have to go to school that day. She told me I was going to spend the morning with my father. I could see the sadness in her eyes but was too young to really understand. Excited, I left my bedroom and went to our kitchen where I found my father. That was unusual. Not because my parents were separated, but because of his job. He was rarely home at all. He cooked me scrambled eggs, adding cheese like he always did. He called it his secret recipe. All these years later, I have the clearest picture of what he looked like when he turned around to greet me because it was so unusual. He was wearing brown corduroy pants and a striped t-shirt, typical seventies dress. But the thing that stands out to me was his face. It was the first time in my young life that I had seen my father's face. He had always worn a thick, long beard that was black as ink, but that morning, standing in the kitchen of that little house, I saw my father's clean-shaven face. It startled me at first. I didn't even recognize him."

Aaron turned and looked out the window, lost in his thoughts, his memories of his father from long ago.

I said, "I'm sure he was a truly special man, and I'm sure he loved you very much."

Continuing to look out the window, Aaron said, "My dad loved just a handful of things. He loved me and my mother, of course. He loved his country and he loved football—ah, what you call soccer, in America. On that Wednesday morning, Father took me to the park, and we played football together. I'm sure we played it together at other times, but I only remember that one day. I could tell you every detail about that day. I even remember the smallest details, like the way my dad's cheek had a dimple when he smiled, how his breath smelled like coffee when he hugged me, even the scent of his aftershave. I remember the details because after that day, everything was different. That's the day my life changed forever, and the course of my life was set."

For the very first time since I met Aaron, I felt some sort of a bond with him. At that moment and for that instant, we were equals. No longer were we "handsome-super-spy" and "confused-dinner-date."

We were two men who had been shaped by the loss of their fathers. His father died in some heroic fashion. My father died of a heart attack. Both men were too young and taken from us too early. And in very different ways, our father's deaths had altered the path we were walking on. Aaron's path became immediately clear. He decided, that day, to follow in his father's heroic footstep. After my father's death and my meeting Jessica, I gradually realized I needed to grow up, dedicate myself to my spiritual growth and develop my relationship with God, become a man who would make my father proud, the man he trained me to be. The catalyst for change for both of us had been the deaths of our fathers.

Aaron continued, "After my father's death, the political leaders thought it would be best if my mother and I relocated, citing safety concerns. We moved to England. That's where I learned English. I traded sunny days in Israel for wet winters, fog and cold in jolly ole England."

I could taste the sarcasm in his voice.

"I traded football with my father, someone who loved and cared for me, in the neighborhood park for football with the English lads, kids who teased me relentlessly, in Hyde Park."

"Well," I said, "I guess that explains your English accent. How long did you live in England and how did you get connected to Mossad?" I poured myself another few sips of coffee, not even half a cup.

"Like I said, I was very young when we moved. We actually bounced around to several places along the way before finally landing in England. Once we were finally in London, we found a community that accepted us, and we began to fit in. It wasn't home, but to my mother, it began to feel more like a community. I went to primary school and then went on to university on a football scholarship. My mother still lives in London."

The flight attendant returned and cleared our remaining dishes. She told us to prepare for landing. We would begin our descent in a few minutes.

"Okay. Matt. Time to get your game face on. We're landing in Haifa, and then we'll have about an hour drive to get to Tel Aviv and to the Azrieli Sarona Tower."

"Why aren't we just landing in Tel Aviv?" I asked, suddenly confused. "Isn't there an airport located in Tel Aviv?"

Aaron nodded coolly and said, "Logistics. Ben Gurion Airport, the largest in the country, is located in Tel Aviv. It's also the busiest with commercial airlines, which makes it harder for us to squeeze in our landing. Logistically, it is better to land in Haifa and drive. Relax. We're going to get her back."

"You mean Mossad can't get flights rearranged so they can land where they want to?"

"If Benjamin Netanyahu was on board the flight or some other government official, then yes. We could. If this was a diplomatic mission, then yes. Of course, we could get flights changed. This is a kidnapping of an unknown scientist. It's just not as high of a priority. Besides, landing in Haifa will actually allow us to get to the Azrieli Sarona Tower easier and possibly quicker than if we landed in Tel Aviv. It will be a quick landing and a quick walk to our waiting car. We will encounter very minimal traffic. It is better to land in Haifa. Trust me. We know what we're doing."

The airplane began a marked descent, steep and unexpected. I think he saw the confused look on my face, and Aaron shrugged and buckled his seat belt. This wasn't his first military flight. Glancing out of the window, I watched as we dipped below the clouds and rushed toward the ground.

Chapter Six

The landing wasn't an easy one. I wasn't a pilot, but I had flown commercially numerous times in my life and this landing felt like we were coming in extremely too fast. *Maybe that's how military pilots were trained? Or maybe it was because the jet was so much smaller than the commercial airline flights I had taken, and it just seemed like we were moving incredibly fast?* Most likely, it seemed like we were about to crash-land because I was on hyper-alert from everything that had happened over the last few hours and the thought of what I was being asked to do.

The wheels slammed down hard on the runway and the light-weight jet bounced a few times. The tires squeaked and squawked as the brakes were engaged. There was a rapid momentum change. In an instant, we went from flying free to being held by the confines of tires and asphalt. I was pushed forward in my cushioned chair and the seat belt pulled tight across my lap. I audibly grunted as the seat belt pressed into the bruises on my stomach and hips, caused from the car accident last night.

Was that just last night? It seems like forever ago.

Even before we came to a stop, Aaron was up and moving about the cabin of the plane, gathering his belongings, his laptop, into a backpack. I looked at him questioning, mouth open, without saying anything: *Should I bring my stuff?* And Aaron seemed to sense my meaning.

"Your belongings are in my report. My country will repay anything that has been lost. You are welcome to carry your things with you, but when we repay, it's always with something better. Up to you," Aaron said. With that, my stuff was quickly forgotten.

The Cessna jet taxied for a few short minutes and at a much quicker pace than I was accustomed to moving at an airport. We lurched as we came to our final resting spot and the engines seemed to power down. I was looking out of the window and found it odd that there wasn't any ground crew anywhere around. I guess we didn't have luggage to unload, so it must not be that unusual. The flight attendant emerged from the rear and what I guessed was the copilot emerged from the cockpit, and began the process of opening the door. I noticed Aaron, and the rest of the crew were armed.

The door opened with a *schnauk* noise as the suction was broken. It unfolded outward, dropping like I imagined a castle drawbridge must have. The stairs that faced us inside the cabin were now available to descend. Quickly, the copilot and flight attendant were down the stairs. The engines hadn't even been fully disengaged. Aaron was right on their heels. They seemed on edge, tense, ready. The next step of the mission was about to begin.

The pilot was still sitting in his seat, working on what I guessed were final shutdown procedures. The copilot, flight attendant and Aaron had already stepped onto the pavement, just as I stepped into the doorway. The bright afternoon sun was in my eyes, and I put my hand up to shield them from the sudden brightness. I was still in the door when I heard the first *thwap* and saw an intense glint of light just outside of my peripheral vision. That was followed closely by several more *thwap, thwap… thwap, thwap* sounds. I was still standing in the doorway of the airplane, confused, when I felt the aircraft lurch forward. I looked down toward Aaron and he wasn't there. Gone. The flight attendant was lying in a quickly spreading pool of blood. The copilot and Aaron had taken up covered positions with their guns drawn. It took mere seconds for my eyes to locate them and realize what was happening.

Gunfight. Thirty seconds was all it took from start to finish.

We were surrounded on all sides by men dressed in black tactical gear. It looked like they were using suppressed weapons. They had long cylindrical tubes attached to the ends of the barrels of their guns, what most of the world calls *silencers*. This would account for the *thwapping* sounds I was hearing. I immediately moved back into the cabin and fell flat on the floor of the jet.

Thwap, thwap, thwap. The men continued to fire. It started slowly and then, like a bag of popcorn in a microwave, began to slowly intensify. Aaron and the copilot began returning fire. *Blam! Blam! Blam!* The unsuppressed weapons blasted through the air. Ducking behind cover, only slipping out to shoot, Aaron and his counterpart fought back. I saw the copilot run from where he was hiding, behind a small stack of cargo boxes, toward a large airplane hangar. It was a short run, but there was no cover for him along the way. Surprisingly, he made it, without a problem. It didn't even seem like anyone shot at him. That's when I realized *my* trouble was increasing exponentially.

The airplane was moving, and I was rolling away from the gunfight. That was a good thing, a great thing, except that when the enemy saw it, they began concentrating all of their firepower on us. I laid there, not daring to move, with my hands and arms covering my head. My distraction, the jet rolling away, must have given the copilot just enough room to run free.

"You, O Lord, art a *shield* for me; my glory, and the lifter up of mine head!"[22] I found myself screaming, but I was also now lifting my head, trying to see what was going on.

The jet engines began to pick up speed. Lying flat on the floor, I saw Aaron follow his copilot and also run for cover, both of them seeming to momentarily break free from the confines of the gunfight.

---

22 Psalm 3:3

Suddenly, the airplane jerked and turned quickly, abruptly to the right. Before we started moving, the airplane had been parallel with the gunfight, giving seventy-five feet of target to the mercenaries. Once we started rolling, we shortened the angle they had to fire at us, and now that we had turned ninety degrees away from them, we seemed to be a much smaller target. Not only that, we were gaining speed and putting distance between us.

Are we going to try and take off? Should I try and close this door?

The pilot's cockpit was only a few feet away from where I was lying. I could tell it was unlocked as the door stood open, swinging as we bumped along. I screamed to the captain, "Should I try and pull the stairs up and close this door? Are we going to take off?" And then, "What do I do?" But I didn't get an answer. The whole time, bullets were popping around me, crunching pieces of metal, breaking glass. I crouched and extended my arm as far as I could, pushing the captain's cabin door open. I shouted again, "What do I do?" Still no answer.

Maybe he doesn't speak English. Maybe he thinks I'm one of the mercenaries who has boarded his airplane.

I slowly crawled forward, saying the only Hebrew word I knew, "Shalom! ... Shalom! ... Shalom!" and pushed the door completely open. I could see all of the panels, screens and instruments, and for the first time I could see through the windshield. I could see exactly where we were headed.

"Are you *crazy?!*" I screamed as loud as my still raspy voice could. We were headed directly for the terminal. I could see pandemonium through the concourse glass as frightened airline passengers and airline staff saw what was going to happen and began running for cover. I shouted again at the pilot, "Stop, stop, stop! Turn *now!* Turn! Turn! *Turn!*" but when I looked over at him, he was slumped across the steering wheel, blood oozing from both sides of his head. A bullet hole through one of the pieces of glass windshield showed the trajectory of the bullet that smashed through both sides of his head.

"Lord, I need Your help!" I screamed. The next instant, I knew what to do. I jumped back into the main cabin area and crawled under one of the tables, knees up and head tucked just like a tornado drill from when I was in middle school; one of the benefits of growing up on 'Tornado Alley,' if you can call anything about being on Tornado Alley a benefit.

The plane shuddered against the impact with the building. Glass exploded, sheet metal groaned, and people screamed in a symphony of sound. It was a violent impact, and within seconds alarms were sounding in the terminal. There was smoke and I heard the sprinkler system engage. I sat there, under the table, assessing the damage to me and to the plane. The interior cabin was virtually unrecognizable, being almost totally destroyed. Lights blinked and alarms wailed. Wires were exposed and oxygen masks hung from the ceiling. On the other hand, I was completely fine. I had been protected, staying safe in the midst of the storm. "He has given His angels charge over me,"[23] I whispered as I crawled from under the table.

I knew the mercenaries would be on me in seconds. I had to get out of there, but I had no idea where Aaron was or if he was even still alive. I made my way to the still opened door of the aircraft. The stairs had been ripped away, but it was only a few feet to drop to the floor of the concourse. At high speed, I joined the crowd of people running away from the smoldering ruins inside the concourse. I'm sure all of those people would be called to witness what they had seen, but my plan was to be long gone before any authorities arrived. But then I realized that Aaron might still be trapped, pinned down from the machine gun fire. I couldn't let him die that way. I couldn't let his father down in that way. I was torn.

Go back for him? I'm not armed. I don't know if I could even find him and for all I know, I'm the only person on this mission who's still alive.

---

23 Psalm 91:11

Someone has to beat the mercenaries to Tel Aviv. Someone has to make this mission a success. Aaron's sacrifice has to be worth it.

To myself I said, "I've got to get to Tel Aviv."

It was chaos in the airport. Alarms were sounding. People were running. The minimal police and military presence on duty at that moment was trying to get organized, and it was pretty simple for me to slip by them. I ran outside and flagged down a taxi. I opened the door and said, "Do you speak English?"

The heavyset taxi driver nodded and said, "Little."

That was a relief. That meant I wouldn't have to make small talk to him, who I was, why I was visiting the city and all that, as we made the drive.

"Okay, will you take me to Tel Aviv?"

The cab driver nodded his agreement. I guess the hour-long drive wasn't a big deal to him.

"Great. Do you take credit cards?" He again, nodded in approval. I dropped into the back seat and shut the door.

The driver asked, "Luggage?" but it sounded more like, "Lukhetch?" He didn't realize anything had happened at the airport and thought I was a normal disembarking traveler.

I shook my head and said, "None. One-day trip." That seemed to suffice. He shrugged and off we went.

I could hear sirens in the distance. I tried to act indifferent to what was going on. I looked at the cab driver in his rearview mirror as he started pulling into traffic, and he wasn't paying any attention to the noise. He turned the knob on his radio, raising the sound of the techno music playing through the speakers.

Unreal. Just another day in the life of an Israeli.

Chapter Seven

"Tel Aviv. Where go?" the cab driver asked me as the city was coming into view over the horizon. His question broke my train of thought. I was trying to understand the weight of what had happened to my friend, Jessica, and then what had happened to the people trying to save her. I was scared and I was on my own, alone in a foreign country. The incident at the airport was the first time I had ever been near a shootout, and it was the first time I had ever really had my life threatened in any way. I had grown up hearing my dad tell stories of the shooting incidents he had been involved with during his time in law enforcement. The difference then was that it was a single shooter with a revolver who was trying to escape from him, not a group of heavily armed mercenaries, professional soldiers, with automatic weapons intent on killing or capturing him. My hands were still shaking as I thought about the staccato sounds of the rapidly firing weapons. I tried to put it all behind me, but twice in less than twelve hours, people had been shooting at me and I didn't really even know why.

Why were they waiting for us? Why were they shooting at us?

What was worse, I didn't even know who the mercenaries were. I mean, if they weren't wearing black, carrying guns and hidden by masks, I wouldn't even know they were the enemy. If they ever faced me wearing jeans, with a concealed weapon, I was toast. It gave me a newfound respect for my dad and his law enforcement days and for Aaron's father, who had somehow died in the line of duty.

Instead of focusing on the past few hours' events, I started looking forward, to the task at hand. I knew I had to reach Dr. Kaplan and get his help, and I had to do it before the mercenaries arrived there. It might be the only way to save Jessica. The quiet drive gave me the time I needed to figure out what I would do next: I'd find Dr. Kaplan, explain what was going on and get him to take me, and Jessica's research, to a Mossad office. There, we should both be safe. I knew that Jessica's lab was on one of the top floors of her building, so with just a question or two, I should be able to find him. Hopefully.

As my thoughts turned back to Dr. Kaplan, I realized there was something else tugging at the back of my mind, a tiny storm cloud off in the distance. Aaron had a pretty good plan, and I was still following it as best I could as a civilian with no support. The plan all hinged on finding Dr. Kaplan and if I accomplished that, the next phase of the plan hinged on his cooperation, giving me or Mossad Jessica's highly valuable research. The storm cloud of doubt, of uncertainty, revolved around the possibility that I couldn't find Dr. Kaplan or the possibility that he would be unwilling to share the research. That line of thinking led to a darker storm cloud: *What if Dr. Kaplan was somehow involved in this plot? Or what if he was behind it to begin with? What if his plan was to steal the research, develop the technology in shadow companies and keep all the profit for himself?*

I was starting to see conspiracy theories everywhere. I resolved right then to follow the Lord's leading, to be sensitive to His direction. Under my breath, I whispered, "This is all pretty new to me, Lord, but please guide my footsteps.[24] Talk to me like You talk to Jessica. I'm calling on You, and I'm depending on You to answer and show me the things I don't know.[25] Have Your Spirit to guide me and show me the things to come.[26] Please keep me safe and keep Jessica safe. Place a

---

24 Psalm 37:23
25 Jeremiah 33:3
26 John 16:13

hedge of protection around us both.[27] Thank You, Father. I ask these things in Jesus' Name."

I tried to put all those thoughts, the conspiracy, the shootouts, the death and destruction out of my head. I decided to put my trust in God and rely on Him. Then, something Jessica had said the night before popped into my mind and diverted my attention.

She said that her discovery would… what? Would…? Something about changing the way people thought about evolution, dinosaurs and the Big Bang. I, personally, had always had a hard time reconciling evolution and all the scientific facts with the creation story found in the Bible. I mean, I'm an educated guy. College degree and all. I've studied science since I was in school and I mean, it's science. It's fact, right? But on the other hand, I love the thought of an all-powerful, intelligent creator, designing each animal, each leaf and flower petal, the water cycle, the living cells. With an artist's master stroke, painting the blue sky and green grass, the fall leaves in their autumn tones, placing the stars in the night sky. Those were just romantic thoughts, religious dreams, right? Because of science, right? I mean, it's science! What did Jessica discover that could possibly change any of that?

I looked out of my window, first looking at the road we were on and the traffic all around and then realizing I was missing the bigger picture. I was missing the beauty of Israel, the *wonder* of God's creation.[28]

The drive was absolutely magnificent. Throughout the entire journey, there was a large body of water, with sandy beaches, peeking in between the buildings to my right. I had been wondering if that was the Mediterranean Sea, but I didn't want to disturb the blissful silence I was enjoying. The drive had given me some time to calm down, clear my mind and think.

"Thank You, Lord, for Your peace that passes my understanding."[29] And at least for the moment, I did have a peaceful feeling. With as

---

27 Job 1:10
28 Psalm 77:14, Exodus 15:11
29 Philippians 4:7

many contrary nudges, those scratchy gut feelings I had encountered, for the first time in a while, I was experiencing the opposite. It was a silky-smooth, peaceful feeling on the inside. *Is this how God is speaking to me?*

The cab driver's question snapped me back into the moment. "Tel Aviv. Where go?" he asked again.

"Azrieli Tower," I said in response.

"Which?" grunted the cab driver.

I sat there in terror. There was more than one Azrieli Tower? "There's more than one? Um. Ah. I'm not sure. Hold on."

Think, Matt, think.

Even though the cab driver didn't speak English very well, it was easy for him to understand that I didn't know exactly where I needed to go. He shrugged and asked, "Azrieli Trihankle? Azrieli Rundt? Azrieli Scoore? Azrieli Sarona?"

It took me a minute to realize he was asking me about different buildings, naming them by shape. "Azrieli *Triangle?* Azrieli *Round?* Azrieli *Square?* Azrieli *Sarona?*"

What shape is a Sarona?

"Sarona! Azrieli Sarona Tower!" I blurted as I recognized the name. The taxi driver chuckled, changed lanes and off we went.

In just a few minutes, the cabbie started pointing and said, "Der," which I understood as, "There," as in, "There's your building."

Within a couple miles, I started seeing directional signs, written in Hebrew and English, that stated Sarona is a neighborhood, not a shape. We were entering the Sarona neighborhood.

The Azrieli Sarona Tower is a beautiful expanse of mirrored glass. Rising from the ground, it twists as it soars into the sky, and from our angle it looked like it pierced the clouds. You can see it for miles and miles. Looking at it, it definitely looks like the newest, tallest building in the city and even if it's not the newest, by a far margin it is Tel Aviv's most beautiful building. It truly is breathtaking. From the ground, it looks like two split towers spiraling toward heaven, reflecting the beauty of God's chosen country for all to see.

We passed along one side of the ground floor of the building where shops and several places to eat were located, and rounding a corner we turned onto Begin Road. I said to the cab driver, "That's a weird name for a street. Begin Road? That sounds more like instructions than a proper name. Like 'start the road here' or something."

The cab driver said, "Road named after Menachem Begin. He were Prime Minister before."

"Oh, it's named for someone. A former Prime Minister, Menachem Begin. Understood. That makes more sense," I said as we came to a small arcade, with two unobtrusive entrances.

"Here go, you," the cab driver said in his broken English.

"How much?" I asked, trying to pay my fare.

"470.49 shekel," he said.

The big number startled me, but I had no idea how much that would be if it was converted to American dollars. Whatever the cost, I didn't really have a choice. I pulled out my wallet, selected my credit card and handed it to him. He placed it in his machine and in a few moments, there was an electronic beeping sound. It didn't sound good. The cab driver removed the card and placed it in his machine again. For a second time, there was the same electronic beeping sound. It was the same sound, but to my ears, it was worse the second time.

"No take," he said and handed the card back to me. "Need card new."

My card had been rejected and the taxi driver still needed to get paid. I handed him a second card; this time it was my debit card, but after two unsuccessful attempts, the cab driver got the same result: angry beeping.

Oh no! Have the mercenaries accessed my ID online? Have they frozen all of my accounts? What am I going to do? My brain was working overtime. *No, not that deep. I'm in a different country! Security measures placed on credit cards! None of my cards are going to work until I call them or get back to the United States! Where's my phone? My cell phone is dead too!*

"Lord, please help me," I whispered.

Panic must have struck my face because the cabbie, who had been watching me in his rearview mirror, put his right arm on the passenger-side seat-back and turned to look at me more directly. He did not look happy.

How much cash do I have on me? That's not going to work, either. All I have are American dollars and not very many of them. What am I going to do?

Deep on the inside, I heard a 'still, small voice' say, *"Jessica's wallet."*

That's right! I still have Jessica's wallet, and all of her cards will work because she spends half the year living here.

I pulled out Jessica's small wallet, found a credit card and handed it to the cabbie. He never looked at it and just stuck it in his machine. He obviously didn't care *who* was paying him as long as he was getting paid. The machine chimed, much friendlier this time. The cabbie grunted, "Mazal Tov,"[30] as he handed me the card back including a receipt, and I got out. Finally, something had gone right.

"Father God, that was so cool! Thank You for talking to me and reminding me of Jessica's wallet," I whispered to myself.

As he again pulled into traffic, I yelled to the cabbie, "Yo, Homes, smell ya later!" A nod to the Fresh Prince, and then I began making my way toward the entrance of the building. I looked down at my watch. It was 3:30 p.m.

---

30 Hebrew for "Congratulations"

Chapter Eight

I entered the lobby of the hulking commercial tower. Glass windows, twenty feet tall, let the natural sunlight in the airy and spacious lobby. The whole space was decorated in shades of tan and grey, accented with reflective metal. In the middle of the gigantic room there was a rounded, white desk, large enough for twenty people to staff. At the moment, the desk looked unoccupied. Far to my right, there was another entrance to the lobby from the outside and beside it, there was what looked like a directory. I made my way to it and realized that it was a digital directory with a touchscreen. Modern technology. I was in luck: the directory was written in Hebrew letters and also gave an option for English letters. It looked like there were fifty-three floors in the building with several floors belonging to a hotel. After a few unsuccessful minutes of searching, I remembered something Aaron had said while we were still together on the airplane. Aaron had told me that Jessica's lab operated on one of the top floors, so I set the directory to search by floor number instead of occupant's name, and off I went. I found a "Laboratory Nedaviah"[31] located on the forty-seventh floor.

"This has to be it," I said under my breath as I turned from the directory.

Being as sore, tired and bruised as I was, there was no way I was walking up forty-seven floors. I moved from where I was standing to get a better view and started trying to locate the elevators. That's when

---

31 Hebrew for "Generosity"

I saw the security guards sitting in a security booth. While the desk in the middle of the room was large enough to seat twenty, the security booth would have felt crowded with four or five men. I'm sure there was a main security office or security floor somewhere in the building, but at the booth here in the lobby there were only a couple guards on duty.

I heard a *ding* and saw a stream of people emerge from around a corner beside the security booth. I surmised, with all of my deduction skills, that the elevators must be there.

I'm a regular Sherlock Holmes, I thought, pleased with my deductive reasoning. I made my way toward the elevators and as I was about to turn the corner, I heard a sharp, authoritative voice, speaking something in Hebrew. Since I don't speak Hebrew, I continued walking, never looking back. Again, the voice boomed, almost a shout. This time I turned to see what was going on.

A security guard, a hulking beast of a man, was following and speaking to me.

"I'm so-rry. I don't speak He-brew. Do you speak Eng-lish?" I asked. I said it very slowly and very loudly, subconsciously thinking that the speed or the volume would help him understand me.

"Yes. I. Speak. Eng-lish," he said in a mocking tone. "I was born in New York City." Then changing his tone, he asked, "Where do you think you're going, pal?"

Surprised and a little relieved, I said, "Oh, my friend works here, up on the forty-seventh floor at Laboratory Nedaviah. Can I go up or what?"

"Yeah. No problem."

I could recognize his New Yorker accent now.

"We've got some new security measures we're working on. You just need to sign in and get a visitor's pass, yeah? The pass lets you control the elevator, yeah? When you get in the elevator, place the pass on the pad above the numbers and it will give you the ability to select a number, yeah? Hang on to your pass and return it to me when you're finished. If you lose it, you'll have to pay for the pass. Capisce?"

"Sure thing," I said. "Where do I need to sign in?" but he was already handing me the pass and a clipboard with a list of names and floor numbers.

"Don't forget to bring the pass back to me when you're finished, yeah?" he said as I was walking toward the elevator.

"You got it, bro!" I said in his direction, almost adding a sarcastic *"Yeah!"* along with it.

I made my way around the corner and pressed the *up* call button for an elevator and thought to myself, *That guy was huge. I bet they call him Hulk around here, New York Hulk.* Moments later I was standing in the elevator, pass pressed to the pad and selecting the forty-seventh floor.

The elevator ride was incredibly smooth and surprisingly quick. It was closer to closing time than opening time, which meant people were heading down to the lobby, not up to their offices. I rode nonstop to the forty-seventh floor. I stepped off of the elevator praying that this Laboratory Nedaviah, was the correct place. I looked for some sort of marker to identify if this was the right stop when two ladies wearing lab coats walked up to the elevator. It wasn't the sign I was looking for, but I would definitely take it.

"Excuse me," I said, "I'm looking for a friend of mine, but I'm not sure that I am in the right place." Both of the women looked at me curiously.

"Ani lo mevin,"[32] one of the women said.

"Ata yakhol lakhzor al ze?"[33] said the other.

"Oh no," I said. Again, I said the only Hebrew word I knew to them, "Shalom," and waved them on their way. They smiled, gave a slight chuckle and the two lab coats stepped onto the elevator.

---

32 Hebrew for "I don't understand"
33 Hebrew for "Could you repeat that?"

This might be harder than I thought. I wonder if the New York Hulk downstairs might agree to be my interpreter. I'm going to have to explain things to him. Maybe that won't be a bad thing. Maybe the building's security should know what's going on.

A million thoughts a second were passing through my brain when I heard, "Excuse me. Oh my gosh, this is going to sound so weird, but are you Matt Davenport?" I had the silkiest, velvety feeling right at that moment.

"Yes, I am and right now, I'm totally confused. Who are you, and how do you know who I am?"

Before I knew what was happening, the young woman hugged me. Speaking quickly, she hit me with several questions all at once.

"I'm so glad you're here! Is Dr. Adams with you? What happened to your face? How did it go last night? Hey, why are you back so soon? I thought you guys were going to visit Philadelphia over the next couple days."

"I'm sorry," I said. "You're talking faster than my ears can listen. Please, slow down and let's start at the beginning. You know me, but who are you?"

I was looking at a young woman, incredibly, unusually thin, unhealthy thin, with skin so white it seemed translucent. She was wearing dark-rimmed glasses with decorations at the corners and her long hair was pulled back from her face, tight, and hung in a ponytail. By the looks of her, she was in her early twenties, had spent her life in front of a computer or tablet, and had never seen sunlight. She was wearing a dark-colored dress but paired it with flats. Professional and comfortable. She was pretty, in a nerdy sort of way.

"Oh, I'm sorry. I get ahead of myself sometimes," she said. "My name is Nuria[34] Melamed.[35] I'm Dr. Adams' assistant and programmer,"

---

34 Nuria - Hebrew name meaning "The Lord's light"
35 Melamed - surname, from the Hebrew for teacher, referring to an ancestor who was a teacher

and stuck out her right hand to shake mine. "Is Dr. Adams here with you?" She was answering questions, but her pace hadn't slowed a bit.

A wave of relief washed over me. Finally, someone who could help. I said, "No, there's been a problem. Is Dr. Kaplan around?"

Nuria replied, "Dr. Adams talks about you all the time. You're her best friend, maybe her only friend in her life outside of work. I never thought I'd actually get to meet you! Especially here, in Israel. I know what you look like from the pictures."

"The pictures?" I asked.

"Yeah. She's got framed pictures of the two of you sitting all over her desk. You want to see her office?" Nuria asked.

"Yes. Definitely. But not right now. Is Dr. Kaplan here?" I asked for the second time.

"No, Dr. Kaplan went to hear Dr. Adams' speech, didn't he? He's been gone for several days, maybe a week or two. I don't see him here much anyway, but I heard some people talking about how excited he was to see Dr. Adams' presentation and that he was preparing to go out of the country."

"What does that mean?" I asked, more to myself than Nuria. Then to her, "He told Jessica that he was sick and couldn't attend her presentation. As far as we knew, he never left Israel."

In a split second, everything in my plan had fallen apart.

What am I going to do now?

I had intended to get Dr. Kaplan and go to the authorities with the research and technology. Dr. Kaplan's absence left some big questions to be answered. The timing of his disappearance was very conspicuous. Did he have a part to play in the kidnapping? Was he truly sick? Had he also been kidnapped? At least, for the moment, I didn't feel the danger of mercenaries tracking me down. Without Kaplan here, the reason and possibility of them coming to lab was small.

Nuria must have seen the inner conflict raging inside and asked, "What's going on, Mr. Davenport?" I could hear the genuine concern in her voice.

"Nuria, is there someplace we can talk, privately?"

"Of course. Come this way," she said and turned away from me. Her ponytail swung side to side as she led me down a hallway toward a small conference room with an incredible view of the city.

We each took seats at a conference table and I saw a phone charging cord resting there, plugged into a power port in the center of the table. I remembered I had Jessica's phone in my pocket. The battery was dead.

I asked Nuria, "Do you mind if I plug a phone into this charger while we're here?"

"If it fits in your phone, you can use it. Quit stalling, Mr. Davenport. Tell me, what's going on? And, what happened to your face?"

Nuria was right; I was stalling. I plugged Jessica's phone into the charger. After a few seconds, the screen lit up and an illuminated battery symbol with a sliver of red showed on the screen. I loved her new phone. Her battery charged so much quicker than mine did.

I was trying to think of a way to begin telling Nuria the events that had led me here and finally said, "There's just not an easy way to tell you this, but Jessica is missing. She's been kidnapped. That's basically what happened to my face."

I let that hang in the air for a moment and then began telling Nuria everything that had happened in the last twenty hours.

Chapter Nine

"Wait. What are you talking about?"

Nuria and I had spent the past few minutes getting her caught up on the events of the past day, but now she was asking me questions.

"What are you talking about, 'she's invented a way to harness geothermal energy?' No, she hasn't. Did she tell you that?"

"Hold on," I said. "She hasn't invented anything? What do you guys do up here?" I was thoroughly confused. "No, the Mossad agent, Aaron, filled me in on what you guys have been developing. He said that Jessica had found a way to locate vertical cracks in the Earth's crust and mantle..."

"That's right," Nuria interrupted.

"And that she has found a way to access the Earth's natural heat through those cracks, and that it could be turned into a natural energy source by accessing the Earth's core somehow. Right?" I finished.

Nuria just sat there confused. "No. Not at all. Do you even know what we do here? Do you know about the Genesis Project or the Genesis Machine?"

"Clean energy?" I tried one last time, grasping at details and hoping my friend had been working on such a noble task.

"No, it's just not possible here. Besides, we're a research organization, not an energy development company," Nuria said.

"Then what is the Genesis Project and the Genesis Machine, if it's not some sort of energy production tool?" I asked.

Nuria just looked at me, unsure of how to proceed. I could see her debating whether to tell me anything at all and so in an attempt to interrupt her train of thought, I said, "And to answer your question, no. If it isn't already completely obvious, I have no idea what you do here, what you're working on, anything. Can you help?"

I didn't want to say it out loud and in any way influence Nuria, but Jessica never would tell me anything. She always cited the non-disclosure agreements she had signed and so I never really pressured her about it. Nuria seemed willing to help, and I didn't want to remind her that she had also signed those same non-disclosure agreements, if in fact she had.

"Please, Nuria. I'm just trying to help rescue Jessica," I pleaded.

After a few more seconds of deliberation, Nuria asked, "Have you and Dr. Adams ever talked about the first book in the Bible, the book of Genesis? Specifically, the first eleven chapters of Genesis?"

"Not really. I mean, we do Bible studies together, and we've referenced different verses located in Genesis and some of the stories, but she never specifically talked to me about the first eleven chapters. What does the Bible, Genesis, and those first eleven chapters have to do with your scientific research?"

"Has Dr. Adams ever mentioned any of her colleagues, histo-geologists or other scientists in her same or similar fields of study? Has she ever talked about Dr. Walter Brown, Robert Carter PhD, Nathaniel T. Jeanson PhD, Andrew Snelling, PhD, or perhaps even showed you some of the documentaries from people like Dr. Del Tackett or Ken Ham?" Nuria continued peppering me with questions.

I was shaking my head the whole time, answering, "No, I've never heard of any of those people. What do they have to do with anything?"

"I'm going to explain it all to you. I'm just trying to see where I need to start. Dr. Adams really never shared anything with you about her work, did she?"

"No, she only asked that I be patient with her and that at some point, she would share everything with me. She promised it would be special and that I would understand all the hard work, time and personal sacrifices she had made. So, I guess that I really don't know anything about anything she was working on."

"No problem," Nuria said with a gentle, caring smile, then added, "Here, look."

Sitting on the table in the small conference room was a wireless keyboard and mouse. She wiggled the mouse and a large, flat-screen TV that was hanging on the wall sprung to life. The flat-screen was the monitor to a computer hidden somewhere out of sight. Nuria opened a web browser, typed something in Hebrew into the search engine and a few moments later, she had a website, the Hebrew version of YouTube possibly, pulled up. Again, she typed something into the website's search function this time, and a list of video clip choices appeared vertically down the screen.

Nuria said, "I'm looking for a certain video from a scientist explaining something. I really should bookmark the video when I find it. Anyhow, this is the guy that kind of started it all. His research gave us the idea for the Genesis Project and the Genesis Machine. He'll be able to explain his theory in a much easier and more concise way than I can. His name is Dr. Walter Brown.[36] Do you know who he is?"

I shook my head. "Should I?"

"No, I don't guess there's any reason you should, but I didn't know if Dr. Adams had ever mentioned him to you. I'm sorry. I was just thinking out loud." She continued, "Dr. Walt Brown is brilliant. He's a graduate of West Point Military Academy and received a PhD in mechanical engineering from the Massachusetts Institute of Technology. You know, MIT?"

"Yes, Nuria. Finally, a question I know the answer to. I know what MIT is!"

---

36 "Walter T. Brown," *Creation Science Hall of Fame*, February 1, 2012, https://creationsciencehalloffame.org/piece/walter-t-brown

Smiling she said, "Okay, I was just making sure. Anyway, Dr. Brown was a National Science Foundation Fellow at MIT. Over the course of his career, he has done it all. He was an Army Ranger and paratrooper and he *also* retired from the Air Force as a full colonel. He has taught college courses in physics, mathematics, computer science, and he's the one who developed a new thought in the history of plate tectonics called the hydroplate theory. If you couldn't tell, he's kind of a hero around here."

"Forgive me," I said, "but I don't remember what plate tectonics is. I know I've heard that term before, but can you refresh me on it?"

"Oh, sure. Plate tectonics is pretty simple. Plate tectonics is the theory that Earth's outer shell is divided into several plates that glide over the mantle. The mantle is the inner layer above the core. The theory is all but 100% accepted as true within all fields of science, not just geology."

I nodded in understanding. "I remember now. The different continents are on different plates. They rub against each other and cause earthquakes, right?"

Nuria smiled and nodded, "That's right. Well, that's part of it anyway."

As a way to justify myself, I felt the need to explain what I remembered. "It seems like all the continents were connected in one big landmass at some point in history and over the millions of years since the Earth was formed, the plates and continents have shifted. They rub up against each other, sometimes causing earthquakes, sometimes pushing mountains up higher and higher. Am I closer now?"

Nuria was giggling. "Yes, Mr. Davenport. Outstanding! Except for one detail, you were right near perfect. I'll get to that in a few minutes."

"Okay, what about that Dr. Brown guy? Is he still alive? Does he work here too?"

"No, he doesn't work here, but he is still alive," Nuria said. "I don't think he even knows about us, but I know that during the first portion of Dr. Adams' speech last night, she was planning to acknowledge how helpful his theories have been and give him credit for setting her on the path of discovery.

"In a nutshell, Dr. Brown developed a theory that *rejects* the generally accepted viewpoint of the scientific community in regard to plate tectonics. He studied the Earth, the mantle and core materials, and then hypothesized about the Earth's geological development. While he accepts the theory of plate tectonics, he rejects one part of the conventional interpretation of it. Dr. Brown asked a simple question: What if it didn't take millions of years for the continents to separate? He then decided to see if it was possible that something else, something other than millions of years, could cause the continental separation. If there was another cause, what was it and how long would it take? His findings, discoveries and resulting theory is a brand-new approach to geology—completely different and almost universally rejected—but it fills in most of the gaping holes that are created by the current prevailing theories. Dr. Adams, with Dr. Kaplan's encouragement, decided to start from the assumption that his theory was true and worked to prove it. Most of the scientific community decided to start from the assumption that his theory was false and worked to discredit it. Because they haven't been able to disprove it, the scientific community's only weapon is to try and discredit him or his work. Okay. Enough of my gabbing. Here, watch."

With that, Nuria pressed the big white triangle in the middle of the video player and the movie sprang to life. She then clicked a little square icon in the corner of the frame and the movie filled the whole of the flat-screen hanging on the wall.

"This video is from the early nineties, so forgive me. The info is good, though, so pay attention," Nuria said, treating me a little like I was in middle school.

The video began with a short introduction to Dr. Brown and his accomplishments, which included heading one of the Department of

Defense's major research and development laboratories, before moving to an interview with the man himself.

This guy really has done it all.

In the video, Dr. Brown looked to be around forty-five to fifty years old; his hair was jet-black and cut short. He stood in what looked like a home library, surrounded by books. The graphics unfolded, in a very eighties way, giving his name and the title, *Professor Emeritus – Physics.*

He began by saying, "We can see on our planet, twenty-five major features that can now be systematically explained as a consequence of a cataclysmic global flood, whose waters erupted from subterranean chambers with an energy release exceeding the explosion of thirty trillion hydrogen bombs."

The screen changed and showed a graphic of exactly what thirty trillion looked like with the fourteen zeros scrolling after a three until it hit the thirty trillion mark.

30,000,000,000,000 hydrogen bombs.

I looked at Nuria questioningly and she just nodded. She paused the video and said, "It's a little shocking at first, isn't it? Global flood with erupting waters. Give him a minute and he'll explain more." She clicked the mouse and the video began again.

"This explanation, a cataclysmic global flood, shows us just how rapidly major mountains formed. It explains the coal and oil deposits and rapid continental drift. It explains why on the ocean floor there are huge trenches and hundreds of canyons and volcanoes. It explains the layered strata and most all of the fossils and even the frozen mammoths, the 'so-called' ice ages and major land canyons, especially the Grand Canyon."[37]

---

[37] "Hydroplate Animation Walt Brown PhD, Scientific Explanation of a Global Flood," *YouTube,* April 27, 2009, https://www.youtube.com/watch?v=KQUpFAcc3FM. *Special note:* All information presented by Dr. Walter Brown in this book, was taken from interviews he has given and books and articles he has written, compiled and placed in this piece of narrative fiction.

The video shifted away from Dr. Brown and showed a spinning globe. It was almost completely covered with land, not looking anything like the way we recognize Earth today. One giant landmass filled almost the entirety of the globe. I was realizing, thankfully, that the brief speech Dr. Brown had just given was only an introduction, and he was about to explain in more detail how a cataclysmic global flood could explain mountains, fossils, canyons, oil deposits and even ice ages.

Brown continued speaking, "The modeling of this theory shows that the pre-flood Earth probably only had one exceptionally large supercontinent, and it was covered with lush vegetation. There were seas and major rivers, but the mountains were smaller than what we see today, the tallest being only about nine thousand feet high. By comparison, Mount Everest is over twenty-nine thousand feet tall."

Nuria paused the video and asked, "Are you following this so far?"

"I think so," I responded. "This guy says that almost all of the geological anomalies we see today can be explained by a global flood. Is he talking about what I think he's talking about? Is he, don't laugh when I say this, is he talking about *Noah's* flood?"

Nuria smiled and hit the play button again. Dr. Brown continued his explanation.

"According to the hydroplate theory, the pre-flood Earth had a lot of subterranean water. About half of what is now in our oceans was once deep underground. This water was contained in interconnected chambers forming a spherical shell, about half a mile thick, perhaps ten miles below the Earth's surface."

Nuria paused the video again and said, "Do you like pepperoni pizza?"

It caught me off guard and I laughed and nodded, not knowing what that had to do with what we were watching.

Man, I'm hungry. I wish I had some pepperoni pizza!

She continued, "Think about a pizza. Starting from the top down, you have the pepperoni, then the cheese, some tomato sauce and the dough. Now, think of the Earth like a pepperoni pizza. The pepperonis are the continents and instead of being spread all over the pizza, they are all sitting together in a group in the center of the pie. The layer of cheese is the upper layer of the Earth's mantle, and the pizza sauce is the layer of water that Dr. Brown is talking about. The pizza sauce layer is the most important part of this video. Listen to what he has to say about the water below the mantle."

She pressed the play button, and again Dr. Brown continued explaining hydroplate theory.

"Ten miles worth of heavy rock in the Earth's crust was pressing down on that layer of water. Then, heat from the Earth's core continued to increase the temperature of the water layer. Both factors resulted in increasing pressure. Increasing pressure in the subterranean waters stretched the crust, just like a balloon stretches when the pressure inside increases."

The screen, which had been showing Dr. Brown, flipped back to a shot of a cross section of the globe. There was a large blue section representing water that was being crushed by the weight of the Earth's crust pressing down on it. The water needed a place to escape.

Dr. Brown continued, "Failure in the crust began with a microscopic crack which grew in both directions at about three miles per second. The crack, following the path of least resistance, encircled the globe in about two hours. As the crack raced around the Earth, the overlying rock crust opened up like a rip in a tightly stretched cloth. The subterranean water was under extreme pressure because of the weight of ten miles of rock weighing down on it. So, the water exploded violently out of the rupture. All along this globe encircling rupture, fountains of water jetted supersonically almost twenty miles into the atmosphere."

I looked at Nuria; she paused the video and I said, "I think I followed it, but give me the pizza version of what he just said."

Laughing, she said "The pepperoni and cheese layers were pressing down on the tomato sauce layer. As heat caused the pizza dough to swell, the pressure on the tomato sauce increased. Suddenly, a crack formed in the cheese layer and the tomato sauce exploded out, forming a crack across the entire diameter of the pizza. Tomato sauce sprayed up, covering everything, even the inside of the oven. Did that make more sense?"

"Yep. I'm with you, and I wish I had a slice of pizza to eat while we were watching this. I'm famished."

Smiling, she again clicked the mouse to hit play and Dr. Brown continued.

"The spray from this enormous fountain produced torrential rains, such as the Earth had never experienced before or after. The Bible states that all the fountains of the great deep burst open on one day, and it describes these events that occurred about five thousand years ago. We can now tie it all together, scientifically."

I said, "Tomato spray covered all the pepperonis and all the cheese, right?"

"Yes," Nuria responded. "Now, here come the effects of having all that tomato sauce spraying everywhere. In the real world, water was being expelled from underneath the Earth's surface at a super high velocity. Listen to what Dr. Brown says the consequences were. Don't worry, I'll give you another pizza lesson after this part too, if you need it." I heard her click the mouse again.

The now familiar voice of Dr. Brown began again, "Some of the water was jetted high above the cold stratosphere, freezing into super-cooled ice crystals that produced some massive ice dumps; burying, suffocating and instantly freezing many animals, including the frozen mammoths of Siberia and Alaska."

The screen again changed and showed water being sprayed high into the atmosphere, being supercooled and dumped in different places instantly freezing the animals it engulfed. The image on the screen then changed as Dr. Brown continued talking. The new image showed a large crack in the crust and water spraying out of it.

"The high-pressure water jetting out eroded the rock on both sides of the crack and produced huge volumes of sediment. These sediments trapped and buried plants and animals very quickly, forming the fossil record. The fossil record supports rapid formation as the plants and animals show no decomposition. Now, this erosion, caused by the water jets, widened the crack in the Earth's crust. Eventually, the width of the crack was so great that the compressed rock beneath the subterranean chamber sprung upward, giving birth to the mid-oceanic ridge that wraps around the Earth like the seam of a baseball. The continental plates slid downhill away from the rising mid-Atlantic ridge and gained speed. Where the plates met resistances, they warped and crumpled, giving rise to very tall mountains where they bucked upwards, and in other places, deep trenches where the plates buckled downwards.[38] This is why the major mountain chains are generally parallel to the oceanic ridges from which they slid. All major mountains we see today were formed in a matter of hours."

"Let me get this straight," I said as Nuria paused the video. "The tomato sauce sprayed up, violently covering all of the cheese and pepperoni. In some places it totally engulfed animals, burying them and/or freezing them where they stood. That's where we get fossils. Does he think that's when the dinosaurs went extinct? During the flood or just prior to it? Don't answer that yet. Let me get the rest of this out, and then you can answer me and correct anything I have wrong. Fossils were formed by rapid tomato sauce burying the animals. The whole time the tomato sauce was spraying out through the crack, it was spreading the cheese layers out, which gave the dough a place to rise up as well. That's the ocean ridges he's talking about, right? When the spray, the crack and the ridges formed, it shifted the pepperonis away from their comfortable resting place together in the center of pie. Some

---

38 "Scientists Just Detected What Appears to Be a Whole New Layer in Earth's Mantle," *ScienceAlert.com*, May 25, 2017, https://www.sciencealert.com/scientists-just-detected-what-appears-to-be-a-whole-new-layer-in-earth-s-mantle

of them floated on the cheese away from the dough ridge and some of them were smashed together, making mini mountains and valleys. That's our continents? Is that right?"

Nuria was nodding.

"Okay. I can see it now. That's a pretty good explanation of what originally caused the plates to shift! I mean, if it's true and if it is..."

My thoughts trailed off and then, "Wait. I understand this and it makes surprisingly logical sense. Why don't they teach this stuff in school? Why isn't his theory more well-known? I mean, from the look of this video, Dr. Brown has been talking about it since the nineties."

Nuria was smiling, enjoying the fact I had embraced and expanded on her pizza metaphor.

"That's right," she said. "They don't teach this in school, in part, because if they taught a global flood is the cause for plate tectonics, ice ages, fossils and all that other stuff, they would have to admit the Bible is true. It would have lasting effects on science, including Darwin's theory. The scientific community doesn't *want* this to be true."

I didn't see what one had to do with the other. "How does Dr. Brown's theory have anything to do with Darwin's theory? He's the evolution guy, right?"

Nuria nodded and continued, "If a sudden flood caused all of this and caused it very quickly, then all of those other effects, the fossils, ice ages, the mountains, the valleys, the large oceans, if they happened or were created immediately, then it couldn't have been done over millions of years. Darwin's theory of evolution is predicated on the theory of small, subtle changes that occur *over time.*" She heavily emphasized the words "*over time*" and continued, "Like a *long* time. In his theory, *millions and millions* of years are required for single cell organisms to appear, and then *more millions* are required for those organisms to evolve into bacteria. We need *more millions* for the bacteria to evolve into an animal and even *more millions* of years before you get man evolving from a monkey, and on and on and on until you need *billions* of years! If Dr. Brown's flood theory is true, Darwin's theory of evolution falls apart because there's simply not enough years. You can see why the heavily atheist-prone scientific community has been so averse to Dr. Brown's theory, can't you?"

"You know," I said, "I have a minor in chemistry. Now, it's been a long time, but one thing that I do remember is one of my professors had a mantra he repeated over and over each time we went to the lab. He said, 'If an idea is not testable, repeatable, observable, and falsifiable, it is not considered scientific,' and that's always stuck with me. I guess that means none of these theories are scientific, right? Because Darwin's theory of evolution, the theory of the big bang, and now I guess Dr. Brown's flood theory or hydroplate theory or whatever he calls it aren't observable, re-peatable or testable. You can't observe or duplicate any of these theories. You can't test them. I don't think the 'this just makes more sense' argu-ment will work to get the textbooks changed either."

"I can see why she's in love with you," Nuria said. "Look, Matt, you left one out. If a theory is falsifiable, then it's not scientific. The flip side to that is, if it's not falsifiable it *is* scientific, right?"

"Who's in love with me? What are you talking about?" I stuttered.

"Yep. She said you were pretty clueless about that too. Evolution and the Big Bang aren't repeatable, observable or testable, right? Can we prove them? Not really. Until we have some evidence that proves them or disproves them, they are just *theories*. People give way too much credit when something is just a theory. Theories are just ideas, not facts or laws. But what if we could prove Dr. Brown's flood theory? Wouldn't that invalidate the competing theories? Wouldn't that disprove them?"

We sat there in silence as I tried to wrap my head around the ram-ifications of what Nuria had just asked me. "Can... can you prove... Wait, can you prove Dr. Brown's theory? Have you then *disproved* Dar-win's theory of evolution and the big bang theory?"

Nuria shook her head, "Not me. Your friend, Dr. Jessica Adams did. *That's* what the Genesis Project is all about."

Chapter Ten

It was getting late in the afternoon as Nuria and I stepped out of the conference room. I forgot Jessica's phone, charging on the table, and had to go back in and get it. I unplugged it and dropped it in my pocket. The laboratory, which had been bustling with activity when I first arrived, now moved at a much slower pace. The hallways were empty and lights in offices were turned off. Nuria walked down the hallway in front of me and stopped at a corner office.

"This is Dr. Adams' office. Want to see it?" She smiled, like she was showing off a new puppy. It dawned on me that Nuria was the first person I had ever met who knew Jessica. They were friends, of sorts, and I became suddenly excited. I had a lot of questions to ask about Jessica.

"Of course, I do!" I quipped.

Nuria switched on the lights and stepped back, out of the way. I walked into the office and immediately saw how spacious and elegant it was. A mahogany desk being the main focal point of the room, my eyes drifted around the space. There were wooden bookshelves along two walls and the other two walls were glass windows from floor to ceiling. Jessica had placed framed pictures in different locations around the room. Desk lamps illuminated the room, operated by the switch on the wall. I was struck by how organized everything was. Books on their shelves had their spines aligned in perfect rows. Her pens and pencils were spaced evenly and exactly in order on her desk. The one thing that looked out of place was Jess' laptop, which sat on the side of her desk, locked down by some sort of metal cage.

"Is it okay if I sit down, look around, see if I can find some clues? I don't want to break any rules or even Jessica's trust, but I need to find something that can help me find her. Do you care?"

She shook her head and said, "No, I don't care. I've got a couple things to wrap up in my office before I go home. Feel free to do your thing. Be sure to check out the pictures and stuff. I'll be back in a couple minutes and we can walk out together, okay?"

"Cool," I said, but Nuria had already walked off. I sat down in Jessica's desk chair, a large leather thing that felt like a throne on wheels.

Was this going to be like the movies? Could I open a drawer and find a clue that would lead me to her location? Probably not. Okay, then. What's my next step? Let's start looking.

Nuria had been correct—there were a lot of pictures of Jessica and me sitting around her office, but there were pictures of others as well. I picked up one of the frames, the one closest to me, and saw a photo of Jessica as a young child, maybe five years old, in a pastel green-colored Easter dress. She had an Easter basket on her arm and was holding the hand of an adult man, who I guessed was her father. Young Jessica was smiling at the camera, squinting in the sunlight, with her head tilted to her right, toward her dad. Her dad wasn't looking at the camera but was instead looking with intense love at his young daughter.

Another photo, one on the bookcase, seemed fairly recent and showed Jessica standing with a thin, older gentleman. His round-lensed reading glasses sat on a nose that was slightly too large for his face, and his thinning grey hair was styled in a spikey fashion. He looked like a grandfather trying to be cool. He also had a big smile on his face, like a teacher thrilled with a student's accomplishment. They were both wearing lab coats, he had his arm around her, and Jessica was holding some sort of award.

I turned my attention away from the pictures, hoping to find some sort of clue. Jessica's desk was a massive, impressive thing. There was a middle drawer, above my knees. I pulled it open and it contained pens, pencils and some blank sticky notes. To the right and to the left of where I was sitting were rows of drawers on either side of me; three on the left and three on the right. At first glance, I missed it, but there was a fourth knob on the left-hand side of the desk, directly at the top of the drawers. I pulled the knob and it revealed an extra writing space. It had initially looked like a drawer, but it was just a flat surface where I found that Jessica had a handwritten letter, taped to that piece of her desk, where only she could see it. It was written in her own handwriting and said:

Dear Jessica,

He who finds a wife finds a good thing and obtains the favor of the Lord.[39] So, this is who you are and who you aspire to be, a virtuous woman. Never forget it:

A good woman is hard to find, and worth far more than diamonds. Her husband trusts her without reserve, and never has reason to regret it. Never spiteful, she treats him generously all her life long.

She shops around for the best yarns and cottons, and enjoys knitting and sewing. She's like a trading ship that sails to faraway places and brings back exotic surprises.

She's up before dawn, preparing breakfast for her family and organizing her day. She looks over a field and buys it, then, with money she's put aside, plants a garden.

First thing in the morning, she dresses for work, rolls up her sleeves, eager to get started. She senses the worth of her work, is in no hurry to call it quits for the day.

---

39 Proverbs 18:22

She's skilled in the crafts of home and hearth, diligent in homemaking. She's quick to assist anyone in need, reaches out to help the poor.

She doesn't worry about her family when it snows; their winter clothes are all mended and ready to wear. She makes her own clothing, and dresses in colorful linens and silks.

Her husband is greatly respected when he deliberates with the city fathers.

She designs gowns and sells them, brings the sweaters she knits to the dress shops. Her clothes are well-made and elegant, and she always faces tomorrow with a smile.

When she speaks she has something worthwhile to say, and she always says it kindly.

She keeps an eye on everyone in her household, and keeps them all busy and productive. Her children respect and bless her; her husband joins in with words of praise: "Many women have done wonderful things, but you've outclassed them all!"

Charm can mislead and beauty soon fades. The woman to be admired and praised is the woman who lives in the Fear-of-God. Give her everything she deserves![40]

I immediately recognized the verses she had written, familiar with the book of Proverbs, but I didn't know what translation it was from. I had grown up hearing that I needed to find a "virtuous woman," a reference to Proverbs 31 in the Bible. I pulled out Jessica's phone from my pocket and snapped a picture of her letter. I figured once things were back to normal, I could text it to my phone; kind of a neat reminder of the time I was in her office.

---

40 Proverbs 31:10-31 (The Message Translation)

"Wow! How long have you been in here, and you've already found it!?" Nuria asked.

How long has she been standing there?

"Oh, you startled me!" I said. Laughing at myself, I continued, "I guess so! I just liked that Jessica had written a portion of scripture to remind herself what God says she can be. It reminded me of my friend, and so I snapped the picture. I hope that's okay."

Nuria nodded and I continued, "While you're standing there, I've got a few more questions for you, like, do you know anything about this picture?" I handed Nuria the picture of Jessica and the slight, older man.

"Oh, yeah! I took that picture! That's the day Dr. Kaplan, that's him in the picture, that's the day he promoted Jessica to project leader. It doesn't sound like much, but that's a great big jump in responsibility... and pay, especially for someone so young," Nuria said. "Um, Matt, it's getting close to closing time, and I don't think I can leave you here by yourself."

Still looking at the picture, I asked, "Do you know anything about *keys* Jessica might have? The Mossad agent said something like, 'She holds the keys.'"

Nuria thought about it a moment and I noticed her attitude changed. Maybe it was the fact that I wasn't leaving yet, but maybe it was more.

She said, "It's funny you should ask that. Dr. Adams has a saying that she mumbles sometimes, 'I will give unto thee the keys of the kingdom of heaven.'" [41]

"Yeah, I've heard her say that as well. I always thought it was kind of cute," I said.

Nuria continued, "One day, I asked her about it. She just laughed, lost in her thought, and said she had the key in her heart. I'm not exactly sure what she meant. I just figured it had something to do with

---

41 Matthew 16:19

you, like you had the key to her heart. I guessed she had just finished a phone call with you. She was always smiling whenever you called."

I found myself blushing at that comment. I never thought about Jessica's reaction to one of our phone calls. I guess I just took them for granted. Then, Nuria did this little throat clearing thing. I took the hint, stood up, grabbed Jessica's phone and put it back in my pocket.

"I've got a couple big questions to ask you, Nuria. I'm going to put you in a tough spot, but it's for the absolute best of reasons. Number one: will you give me Jessica's research, or will you get Jessica's research and take it with me to the Mossad?"

"If I could, I would do it; in a heartbeat I would. I have no idea where her research is or how to access it. I don't even know how to log into her computer. I'm sorry."

"Okay. Question number two: do you know where Dr. Kaplan lives?" I asked. "I'd like to stop by his house, see if he's there, if he's sick, and all that. Maybe see if he can give me any information that might help me find Jessica."

"I'm not supposed to give out personal information like that, but because of who you are and the circumstances and all that, I'll get it for you."

We walked to the office next door, a much more conventional office space, and Nuria sat down, clicked a few keys on the keyboard and then started writing down information on a small sheet of paper. She wrote Dr. Kaplan's address on one piece. She wrote a phone number down on a second piece of paper, then on a third sheet, she wrote her name, address and phone number. She handed them to me and said "When you get in a cab, just hand them this sheet of paper. They'll take you to Dr. Kaplan's house. This second piece of paper is his phone number, just in case. This third piece of paper... Do you have a place to stay tonight? If you need a place to crash, call me or stop by. I'll cook us some dinner and answer any questions you have about Dr. Adams." She smiled.

A wave of relief washed over me. I hadn't given any thought to where I would go after I saw Dr. Kaplan; I just figured I'd go wherever I had to go to save Jessica. But if I needed it, this would be a great place to rest for a while and have a hot meal.

"Thank you, Nuria. I hadn't given any thought to where I would be going next. I'll definitely keep you in mind. It's so generous. Thank you."

"One last thing," she said. "I want to call Dr. Kaplan and just see if he answers his phone. I can tell him to be watching out for you." She pressed a button on the phone on her desk and I heard a tone. We were on speaker. She dialed a series of numbers, and after a moment or two there was a beeping on the line. I knew from watching movies that outside of the United States, phones didn't *ring* like we were accustomed to. In other countries, it is a monotone beeping noise or a double beeping sound. The line beeped a few more times and then voicemail clicked on. I heard the gravelly voice of Dr. Kaplan, speaking in Hebrew and then a final tone. Nuria responded in turn, leaving a message in Hebrew to Dr. Kaplan. She finished, pressed the button that ended the call, turned to me and said, "Okay. I told him that Dr. Adams is missing, you're looking for her, and you'll be stopping by to see him."

"Thank you. Thank you for everything." I turned to leave and then a second of panic set in. "Does Dr. Kaplan speak English?"

"Yes. I should have left the message in English so you could understand it. I'm sorry," Nuria said.

"It's totally not a problem. Thanks so much, and I'll let you know about dinner too."

"You're welcome, Mr. Davenport. Let's get out of here."

I nodded and said, "You can stop with the Mr. Davenport stuff. Please, call me Matt."

"Oh, thank goodness! Jessica and I are pretty informal, and I didn't know how much longer I could keep that up with you!"

Both laughing, we made our way to the bank of elevators.

Chapter Eleven

The Tel Aviv traffic was horrible. Nuria and I had left the laboratory and made our way down to the lobby exit where Nuria had helped me flag a cab. After she leaned in and spoke to the driver, she turned to me and said, "His English is rather good. You'll be fine. Call me," and turned to walk away.

"Thanks!" I shouted as I was getting in the taxi.

I gave the driver the address, and I spent the time in the car trying to learn some basic Hebrew with him. Rafe[42] was great. He was the perfect host, probably because he was trying to earn a bigger tip, but I didn't mind. I was trying not to get nervous, but I was alone again, in a city I didn't know, in a country I didn't live in, without a passport, and people had been trying to kill me since last night. Talking with Rafe was helping.

"Okay, how do I say, 'Thank you very much' in Hebrew?" I asked.

He gave me the Hebrew words back slowly 'To-da ra-ba' and 'You're welcome' sounds like 'Al lo da-var.'"

Simple phrases were given like this over the course of the next hour as we slowly made our way across town in the bumper-to-bumper, rush-hour traffic.

"Here's something you'll probably need," Rafe said. "Ta-ken be-va-ka-sha et ha-ta-u-yot she-li be-iv-rit. It means, 'Please correct my Hebrew mistakes,'" he said, laughing like it was the funniest thing he had

---

42 Hebrew for "God has healed"

ever heard. "Okay, okay. Here's one you'll really use. 'A-tah med-a-ber an-glit?' It means, 'Do you speak English?'"

He was right. That was something that I needed to remember.

'A-tah med-a-ber an-glit?" I said it in what sounded like slow motion. "How was that?"

"Not bad, buddy, not bad," Rafe said. "Hey, we'll be at this address in a couple minutes. It's just down this next street on the left."

I had that negative nudge again.

Trust it.

"Rafe, do you mind letting me out here? I'll walk the last little bit. Stretch my legs some before I see my friend."

"Ken," Rafe said, which I now knew meant "yes" in Hebrew.

"Toda raba," I said, thanking him in my newfound tongue, adding, "Ka-ma ze o-le?" Which meant, "How much does it cost?"

He laughed and said, "You're welcome. You picked this stuff up pretty quickly. That'll be 105.42 shekels."

It was turning early evening as I pulled out one of Jessica's credit cards and handed it to him. He inserted it into the machine, and there was a delightful little beeping noise as it was accepted. He handed me a receipt with a place to mark a tip, something my first driver hadn't done, and I wrote 100 shekels on the line. I didn't know how much it was, but I would repay Jessica once she was safely home.

"Toda Raba!" Rafe said, almost yelling when he saw the amount.

I guess that was more than he was expecting. I hope Jessica isn't reaching her credit limit.

Rafe drove off and I was left standing on the sidewalk, alone. My senses became heightened as I suddenly realized the enormity of what I was about to ask of Dr. Kaplan and the position I was going to be putting him in.

I walked to the end of the block as the sun was beginning to hide behind the tops of the houses, casting a long shadow in my direction. A guy riding a motorcycle was making his way down the cross street ahead of me. This was a residential neighborhood, in what looked to be a very nice part of town. Most of the automobiles, parked in driveways and on the curbs of the tree-lined roads, were luxury vehicles, Lexus, Mercedes, Tesla, Range Rover and the like.

Dr. Kaplan's got it going on! There must be some serious money in the science business! Or does that mean he's been taking some money on the side somehow?

My view of the street was partially obstructed because of the trees on either side of the road. I knew that I should turn left at this cross street, because Rafe had told me, but I didn't know exactly how far down or which side of the street the house was on. I pulled out the piece of paper that had Dr. Kaplan's address on it and found his house number, 316. An even number, indicating his house would be on the left side of the street, the side where I now stood. The first house I came to had the number 338 on the door, so I knew I needed to walk farther down.

I continued down the street, my view still obstructed by trees, until I made it to 316. The guy on the motorcycle had turned around and was heading back down the street in my direction. Kaplan's house was a beautiful, modest home, but it was completely dark, no lights turned on outside or inside. Frustrated at my search's apparent lack of progress, I marched up to the front door when some motion caught my attention. The front door was framed by two ornate glass windows. Inside, I could see some motion, shadows, moving behind the glass. It struck me as odd because it was obvious that whoever was there hadn't turned on the lights. It was like they were trying to stay hidden.

I went to ring the doorbell, when from behind me, I heard a whispered, "Hey! Matt-Matt!" Startled, I turned to look but didn't see anyone. "Psst. Over here."

Directly down the sidewalk's path from the front door, I could see the street. There were two cars parked and a tree that looked to be directly between them. I knew it was just the angle I was viewing it from, that the cars were on the street and the tree was in between them, but on the side of the road. It created a little pocket with perfect cover on three sides for someone who was spying on the house, trying to stay hidden.

"Psst. Matt-Matt. Don't ring that doorbell."

It was Aaron tucked away in the pocket. I had walked right past him and never saw him in hiding. I had been so close we could almost have touched.

"Just walk away. Slowly. Quietly."

I started making my way back toward Aaron, when the motorcycle guy came tooling back down the street. He wasn't driving extremely fast or extremely slowly. He was just riding, up and down the road.

He must have just bought that thing, or he's trying to practice his riding.

As I got close to Aaron, he said, "Don't look in my direction. Just keep walking. Turn right at the next block and wait for me there."

I was happy to see him, unsure of how he found me or what was going on. I followed his directions, walking to the next block and turning right. I found a small ledge of a retaining wall to sit on, partially hidden from passing traffic. I sat there for around fifteen minutes waiting on Aaron while I watched the motorcycle guy ride up and down the street every few minutes.

Finally, Aaron showed up and we moved to a more concealed hiding place. He said, "I have been watching that house for over an hour. Nothing has happened. It looks deserted, but something just doesn't feel right. That guy on the motorcycle has been riding up and down the street the whole time I've been here. Up, down, up, down, up, down, trying to look inconspicuous. I thought he was going to see you, but somehow you managed to walk up to the door at the perfect time so that you were shielded by trees at each angle when he might have been able to catch a glimpse of you. Then, I thought he was going to see me as I raced from my hiding spot to try and stop you from ringing the doorbell. I *think* we narrowly avoided disaster. I *think* the mercenaries are here, somewhere. Did you see anything when you were up close to the house?"

"How did they find us? How did they know to come here?" I asked, incredulous. I sat there a moment, stunned, then remembered Nuria's voicemail. "Can they tap somebody's telephone lines?"

Aaron nodded and said, "Yes, and they probably have had Kaplan's lines tapped for some time. Why?"

"I went to the lab where Jessica works and her assistant, Nuria, was there and recognized me. We talked for a while before she gave me Dr. Kaplan's address, and then we called him to let him know I was on my way. We left him a voicemail. We might as well have just said, 'Hey bad guys, go set me a trap, I'm on my way to walk right into it!'"

"It's a good thing I showed up when I did," Aaron said with a glint in his eye. "So, you made it all the way to the lab, by yourself? And you actually spoke with your friend's assistant. I'm impressed. Did you learn anything valuable?" He seemed slightly taken aback with what I had done.

Negative nudge.

I tried to gloss over the details and not reveal too much information. I said, "Not really. It seems as if Nuria thinks of Jessica like some kind of rock star. There might be a little hero worship going on. She gave me some of the basics of the scientific research they do at the lab, but she didn't seem to know anything valuable other than Kaplan's address," I said, hoping it would suffice. I made no mention of Project Genesis or the Genesis Machine.

Shifting his attention, Aaron asked, "Did you see anything unusual when you got close to the house?"

"Now that you mention it, beside the front door are two ornate glass panels. I couldn't see through them, and I'm sure you can't see through them from the inside either, but I sensed... movement... like a shadow moving behind the glass, or maybe I heard a slight scuff or something. I don't know how to say it other than I *sensed* movement inside."

Aaron said, "We need to get out of here. It's too dangerous to be here right now. They've obviously got Kaplan, and they've probably got the research as well." Aaron turned to leave.

"No, they don't," I said. "They have *either* got Kaplan *or* the research *or* neither, but not both. And there's something else." Aaron turned back to look at me. I continued, "Have you considered that Dr. Kaplan might actually be in on this?"

Aaron just sat there, looking at me with a conflicted expression on his face, his mind racing, contemplating repercussions.

I continued, "So, we have several scenarios. But let's just take Kaplan's involvement out of the equation for the minute. If those are the mercenaries in there, they either have Kaplan and they are searching for the research, or they *don't* have Kaplan and they are waiting on him. There's no reason for them to be waiting for me if they have Kaplan *and* the research. And to be honest, we don't know who is in there. It could be Kaplan trying to be stealthy, hiding from the mercenaries himself. What we need to do is call for backup. Get some more of your Mossad buddies here. Surround the place. Finish this up once and for all."

Aaron slumped subconsciously and said, "That's some pretty sound logic, Matt, but we've got a problem. After the screwup at the airport today, I have been suspended, pending an inquisition and review board hearing. I'm just here, on my own, trying to see this thing through. It's what my father would do. He saw things through to the end. I can't call backup, especially if we don't know who is in the house."

"I've got an idea. Let me see your phone." Aaron was hesitant to give up his phone, but I said, "Trust me. You'll like this. I'm starting to get the hang of this spy-thing you've got going on."

Aaron reluctantly gave me his phone. I opened the web browser app and after a few clicks found what I was looking for. I clicked a link and his phone app opened with the number already dialed for me. I pressed the green *call* button, stepped a few feet away from Aaron and began a conversation.

"A-tah med-a-ber an-glit?" I tried my Hebrew again, then followed quickly, pleadingly with, "Please say you speak English!" I couldn't explain what I wanted in Hebrew. For this to work, it was important that they speak English.

Chapter Twelve

The young man parked his car on the street close to where I had spilled out of Rafe's taxi. He looked young and athletic, muscular, wearing dark pants and a dark long-sleeved shirt. In one hand he had his keys, and in the other, a brown paper bag. The bag looked heavy, like it was full, and the edges were rolled together, closed at the top, creating a semi-handle for the man to carry it. He rounded the corner, turning left and did just like I had, checked the address of the first house on the block. He realized he needed to walk a bit further and continued down the street.

Aaron and I had taken up positions so that we could better see the house we were surveilling, but still giving ourselves enough distance to feel safe from detection.

"Watch. The party is just about to start," I said, as I noticed the man walking toward the house.

"Who is that?" Aaron asked as he saw the darkly dressed man in the dark of the evening. "One of the mercenaries? Looks like he's got something heavy in the bag. More guns? Ammo?"

The young man made his way toward the house, finding the correct address. He turned onto the sidewalk and cautiously made his way to the still, very dark house. Stepping up on the front porch, he leaned in, getting his ear close to the front door, searching for activity. He raised his hand and knocked on the door, three quick, quiet raps, and stepped back expectantly.

Out of nowhere, the motorcycle guy came tearing down the street, engine pressing hard. The wheels screeched to a halt as he whipped it sideways, flipped the kickstand down and jumped off of the bike. From somewhere, he pulled an automatic pistol and had it trained on the young man's back, running at him full speed. At the exact same time, coming from behind the house, around both sides, men in black tactical gear, balaclavas and machine guns appeared. They squeezed inward toward the house's front door. Instantaneously, the front door sprung open and men dressed in the same gear jumped toward the man with the bag, screaming in Hebrew, grabbed him and threw him violently to the ground.

From the safety of our lookout position we saw it all happen. These guys were good, organized and extremely well informed. I turned to Aaron and said, "They must not have the information yet. Otherwise, they wouldn't have jumped that dude."

Aaron just sat there, stunned at what he had just seen. For the first time, he looked scared.

"Uh, yeah. You must be right," he stammered.

"We need to get out of here, and I know just the place to go." I handed him the piece of paper that Nuria had given me with her name, address and phone number on it.

Within just a few short moments, the mercenaries had taken the young man somewhere inside of the house, closed things back down and reset the house as if nothing had happened. Motorcycle guy began his lazy stroll up and down the street again.

"It won't take them long to figure out what happened. Call your Mossad guys and get a team over here." I added, "You and I should go see Nuria. Maybe she's thought of some additional information that will help us, or maybe you have some other questions that might spark her memory."

Aaron still sat there, confused and amazed. He said, "What just happened? Who was that guy?"

"I told you that I'm figuring out this spy-thing you've got going on," I said. "When I borrowed your phone, I found a local Chinese delivery place and ordered a meal. I had Kaplan's address and played it like I was a friend visiting Israel. I told them, in English, that I hadn't eaten enough at dinner and my elderly host had gone to sleep. When the delivery guy showed up, the house would look like everyone had already gone to bed, but I would be waiting on him. I told them not to ring the doorbell, but to tap quietly on the front door and I would meet them."

Aaron said, "Matt, that's brilliant," and with that he pulled out his phone and made a call. He spoke entirely in Hebrew, but I presume it was to the Mossad agents that would shortly be showing up. He turned to me and said, "We should go see this Nuria person. Chances are, since she left the message for Kaplan, she might be in danger as well. Let's go. Quietly."

Unsure of how much surveillance was being used, Aaron and I took our time, scuttling along, staying hidden for several blocks. We finally reached a small, light-colored, foreign-made SUV. It had a dark canvas top and clear plastic windows. Aaron jumped in the driver's seat, and I made my way into the passenger seat. Aaron clicked two exposed wires together that were dangling from underneath the steering column. I was a little shocked to see Aaron driving a stolen vehicle and he must have noticed my confusion.

"I stole it from long-term parking at the airport a few hours ago," he said. "I was trying to escape the ambush and needed a ride. Figured whoever it belongs to won't be missing it for a while. I've been following leads and chasing you all day and haven't had a chance to go get my car." That's when I noticed that Aaron's window was open, except that it wasn't open. It was gone. He must have cut the plastic away to get in the SUV.

I said, "When did you get suspended? Weren't you at the station or whatever?"

"Oh, no. They did that by phone. Pulled my credentials and everything. Didn't have enough guts to face me, I guess," he replied.

"How did those guys even know we were going to be at the airport?" I asked.

Aaron shrugged. "I don't know. I haven't been able to figure that one out. My only thought is, and I hate to even *think* this… We have a mole."

Chapter Thirteen

I struggled with the ramifications of what Aaron had told me. A mole. In the Mossad. We had been riding in silence for what seemed like an eternity as we each pondered what that would mean to us and the possibility of rescuing Jessica. Having a mole complicated an already complicated situation.

Maybe that's why Jessica instructed me not to trust anyone in her voicemail. Did she know?

I asked Aaron, "Do you know where we're going?"

He responded, "Kind of. Vaguely. When we get a little closer, I'll turn on the GPS in my phone. Here, input the address for me, will you?" He unlocked the phone and handed it to me.

I opened the map app and started typing the address. After just a few keystrokes, the address pre-filled for me.

Has Aaron already been to Nuria's house? Was that just predictive type? I'm totally overthinking this. Just chill out. Just chill out. Aaron's on my side. He just kept me from knocking on Kaplan's door. That could have been me, being slammed down on the sidewalk.

We followed busy, well-lit roads most of the way, but we seemed to be driving slower than most of the surrounding traffic. It was noisy in the small SUV with the wind whipping through the torn window and the flapping of the canvas top.

"Hey, Aaron," I said, almost shouting to get over the noise, "why don't you speed up a little? You're driving like a grandma over there. Put it in gear, man!"

Frustrated, Aaron shot back, "The car is stolen. I don't want to give the authorities any reason to pull us over. Getting to Nuria's house two minutes earlier isn't worth the risk of being detained by local law enforcement." It was an odd way for a guy in the business to talk about the cops, but maybe he was just trying to make a point.

It had been a long day, I guess, for both of us.

"Oh. My bad. I wasn't thinking. Do your thing," I responded to him. We slowed to a stop at an intersection where there wasn't any traffic.

"No, I'm sorry, Matt," Aaron said in the suddenly quiet SUV. "It's been a stressful couple of days, and it seems like all I have done is screw up. I lost the person I was supposed to protect, your friend, Jessica. I lost members of my team in the ambush at the airport. Those were good people, good operatives, but not only that, they were my friends. Then, I lost you and really only found you because you stumbled right over me. I've been suspended and there's a good possibility they think I'm the mole. There's something else to add on top of all of that too. Up until today, I felt like I was living up to my father's legacy. He died for what he believed in and for the right and just cause. Over the course of these twenty-four hours, I feel like I've just let him down, let his legacy down, over and over and over again. I'm just tired."

I didn't know how to respond to that, so I just sat there quietly. I felt a tinge of sadness for Aaron, imagining how hard it must be to live in someone's shadow like that. I wondered if there were people he worked with who still remembered his dad, people who had worked with him. Or did Aaron work with people who had been on the same mission when his father died? It must have been a heavy weight to deal with. I always tried to live up to my father's expectations, but it was different than what Aaron was dealing with. I knew my dad loved me and was proud of me. He might not have seen the man I have become, but he knew the path I was walking, and he knew the direction my life was moving. Aaron was never able to show his father any of that. He was living in a dead man's shadow and I could tell it was difficult. As we sat there in silence, I again began to notice my surroundings, the beauty of this *Holy* Land.

Even in the darkness of the evening, Israel was beautiful. I tried to get a bearing on where we were and where we were going. I tried to soak it all in, each road, each building, each landmark. It helped keep my mind from wandering down paths I didn't want to take. After what felt like an extended period of awkward silence, we came to a suburban area, neighborhoods nestled gently away from the hustle and bustle of the city.

Aaron said, "Fire up the GPS. We're pretty close."

It took the phone and GPS map application a few moments to pinpoint where we were located and plot a course to our destination. Finally, a little map with a highlighted route displayed on the screen. Everything, including the directions, was written in a different language, so I couldn't understand it, but the route was short, so I knew we were close. The phone spoke the directions in that same foreign language and on command, Aaron made the turns. Seven minutes later, we pulled up to the front of a quaint, yet beautiful one-story house. It had a covered front porch made entirely out of stacked rocks and the outside light was on. From where we were sitting in the car, the front door looked closed, but the house seemed alive with activity, the exact opposite of how Dr. Kaplan's house had appeared earlier. My mouth was beginning to water thinking about Nuria's cooking. I hadn't eaten since breakfast, before we made our landing this morning.

Aaron parked the stolen SUV on the street, a little farther down from Nuria's house. I said, "Let me go first and tell her what's going on, tell her about you. I don't want to startle or scare her or anything."

Aaron nodded his agreement. "Go for it. On your way!"

I was walking quickly, light-spirited for the first time since I left Jessica's lab, toward the welcoming home. Up the sidewalk onto the porch, I was almost whistling to myself. I stepped up to knock on the door and that's when I noticed it: the door was open, only a fraction, but enough to notice it as I got close. I was instantly quiet, motionless. I listened hard, trying to detect any life inside the house. Peering closer at the door frame, I could tell entry had been forced.

In a flash I could tell what happened: the mercenaries rang the doorbell. Nuria thought it was me and came to answer it. When she asked, "Who is it?" through the wooden door, they forced their way in, hastily trying to close the door behind them. I frantically waved Aaron over to where I was standing and showed him what I was looking at. He put two and two together. From behind his back, he pulled out a pistol that had been concealed in his belt and slowly pushed the door open. Slowly, he stepped into the doorway and I was right on his heels. The house was warm and inviting, food smells filled our nostrils, but there was an unnatural silence in the house. It felt empty.

Aaron and I started clearing the house, room by room, making sure it was empty. We entered into a living room space with a couch, chair and television. The chair was on its side. That room shared space with a kitchen, being divided by a half-wall with a countertop sitting on it. The kitchen contained a door that led toward what looked like a hallway. We cautiously stepped into the kitchen and saw Nuria, lying there, bleeding. She had been beaten. From where I was standing, I couldn't tell if she was unconscious or dead, but nothing was going to stop me from finding out. I peeled around Aaron to check on her, getting down on my knees to check for a pulse.

Aaron leaned down and whispered, "I'm going to clear the rest of the house. If it's empty, I'm going outside to check the perimeter. It looks like these guys were just here. If she's alive, find out what she told them," and off he went.

Nuria had a pulse, but her breathing was ragged.

I'm not a doctor; I don't know what to do! Think, Matt, think.

I tried to catch Aaron, doing a whispered shout, but he was already gone.

I took Nuria's hand in mine and her eyes popped open. It startled me, and I just about jumped out of my skin. She looked at me and said, "Matt. Oh, my God, Matt. Oh, my God," and started crying.

I whispered, "It's okay, Nuria, we're here." In a split second, the first three words Jessica ever spoke to me sprang to life and I whispered, "*You're not alone.*" I added, "We'll get you some help. You're going to be okay. Where are you hurt?"

She coughed a few times, congested, liquid-filled coughs and said in between more fits of coughing, "Kaplan called me. He got our message." More coughs. "He's trying to find you." Coughs. "He's with Mossad. *You* have Jessica's key now." More coughs. "Go to Moho Magnetic Machines."

I had a million questions at that moment, but immediately my thoughts went to Jessica's phone. I had forgotten that I still had it. I slammed my hand into my pocket. There was other stuff in my pockets, but her phone was still there.

Was her phone the key? Had she stored the information there? Where was Aaron?

Nuria looked as if she was going to slip back into unconsciousness so I whispered to her, "Stay with me, Nuria. You're going to be okay. We're going to get you help."

She started a fit of coughing and her eyes widened, filled with panic, terror. Blood shot out of her mouth, spraying liquid, covering her chest and stomach, down to her waist. She started choking on her own blood.

I rolled her over on her side, but it didn't help. She looked up at me, scared, and whispered through choking sounds, "Don't…trust… Omar."

She made a few more gurgling sounds and then lost consciousness again. Her body began to convulse, thrashing violently on the kitchen floor. I tried to help, but I didn't know what to do. After several moments of this, she got very still. I saw her body go limp, totally relaxed, and I sensed it as her bowels released.

I sat there in stunned silence. Nuria was dead. I had never been with someone when they died. I didn't know what to do and the feeling made me queasy. I inched slowly away from her body, scooting backwards across the floor.

Her last words had been, "Don't trust Omar."

What did she mean by that, and where was Aar—?

It took me about that long to put it together. Omar was Aaron. Aaron was Omar, and Nuria's last, dying breath had been to warn me about him. But Aaron had been with me for the past couple of hours.

He's been helping me this whole time, since Jessica was kidnapped. He couldn't have done this. Who did it, and where is Aaron now?

I stood up, deciding to do *something* rather than waiting on whatever it was to come at me. I walked through the kitchen and into the hallway, pausing to listen. It was quiet. If Aaron was in the house, he was hiding. I searched each of the rooms but didn't see him anywhere.

What did he say? He was going to search the house and then check the perimeter. He must have gone outside. Can I trust him?

I opened the back door and stepped silently into the yard. Someone close, in the neighborhood, was grilling. I could smell their food and hear their laughter. I slowly, delicately stepped further into the yard, away from the door, in an attempt to locate Aaron.

The yard was small and outlined with trees, but I could tell it was a well-cared for space. There were flowers in pots and flowers in gardens placed strategically around the yard. Nuria had left some of her yard work equipment on the stone patio. It was apparent that no one was in her backyard. I knew I didn't have a weapon of any sort, so I picked up one of Nuria's gardening shovels and carried it like a baseball bat, gripped with both hands.

To the right of Nuria's house, there was a neighboring home, very close, forming a narrow corridor between the two houses. It was only large enough for two people walking shoulder to shoulder to fit, but there was an air-conditioning unit, so at one point both people would have to walk single file if they were going to use the corridor to get to the front of the house. On the other side of Nuria's house, the left side, there was an expanse, an unfinished lot, that looked like a jungle in the moonlight.

I decided that I would check the corridor, using it to walk around the house toward the front yard. From the front yard, I would then make my way to that jungle looking area. After quickly getting through the narrow and poorly lit corridor, I slowly and cautiously rounded the corner toward the front yard. It was evident that Nuria had been working in her yard this afternoon, as there was a rake and several small piles of leaves scattered around the side of her front lawn.

Standing there in the darkness, I was reminded of a prayer King David had prayed some three thousand years ago: *Blessed be the Lord my strength which teacheth my hands to war, and my fingers to fight.*[43] God was speaking to me by reminding me of the words in the Bible.

I whispered a quiet prayer, "Teach me the ways of *this* war, Lord. Teach me how to fight this battle. Help me, Father. In Jesus' Name." A flash of comfort washed over me, and another Bible verse came to mind: *The snare is laid for him in the ground, and a trap for him in the way,*[44] and an idea sparked in my head.

I had the shovel in my hand, but I leaned it against the house and picked up Nuria's rake. I quietly made my way back down the corridor and placed the rake across the alleyway. I was able to wedge the rake between the air-conditioning unit and some stones of the adjacent house, so that it created a knee-high or maybe thigh-high hurdle, almost invisible in the dark of the evening. I tested it and it looked like it would hold.

I again traveled down the corridor to the front of the house and rounded the corner, scanning, looking and listening for Aaron. The front yard was empty as well. Finally, it was time to check the vacant lot

---

43 Psalm 144:1
44 Job 18:10

neighboring Nuria's house. I made my way, seemingly tiptoeing toward the unkempt lot. Easing into the woods, I took my time, careful to be as quiet as possible. That's when I heard it: whispered voices, angry voices. They were close, awfully close, only a few feet away. I tried, but I couldn't understand them. It was in another language. I did, however, recognize one of the voices. It was Aaron. I froze where I stood.

What do I do now? Who is he talking with? A neighbor? No, he wouldn't be talking to a neighbor in this mess of woods. Is he on the phone? He wouldn't be whispering. No. Someone is with him. Someone is responding.

Then in a twist I never saw coming, the loudest *quiet* noise ever, sounded in my pocket.

Bzzzzz. Bzzzzz. Bzzzzz.

Jessica's phone began to vibrate. It was the low battery indicator, like earlier in the day. I had charged the phone while I was sitting in the conference room with Nuria at Jessica's lab, but that was hours ago. The timing was right for the battery to die, but the timing couldn't be worse for me.

Chapter Fourteen

As a little boy, my parents had what I remember as a Biblical ency-clopedia. I would sit for hours, looking at the pictures, reading the stories, the information, the miracles the book contained. I have vivid memories of reading about how God had miraculously performed for people in times of need. He had saved the Israelites from the hands of the Egyptian army, opening up the Red Sea[45] for them to travel to safety. God instructed Joshua[46] how to defeat the city of Jericho so that the Israelites were kept from harm. I read about Jehoshaphat,[47] who sought God's direction when three enemy armies were preparing for war against him. At the Lord's direction, Jehoshaphat sent his musi-cians ahead of the army and when they arrived at the battlefield, the enemies had been destroyed. There were so many instances where God miraculously delivered His people. I can remember trying to put my-self in their shoes, getting to see the deliverance of the Lord firsthand.

How incredible would it have been to see the Red Sea split in front of me? To walk across on dry land and then see the waters crash upon the army of Pharaoh? What would it have been like to march around the city of Jericho, watching the walls fall flat and then destroying the city? How would it have been to walk out toward the battlefield, fol-lowing the singers—people praising God—to find your enemies slain

---

45 Exodus 14
46 Joshua 6
47 2 Chronicles 20

before you? These were just a few of the multitudes of stories I read, imagining myself in them.

The problem, I now realized, was that I was reading these stories, placing myself in them, with an outcome that I already knew. Of course, it would be easy to march toward the Red Sea, knowing it was going to open for me and swallow my enemies. Of course, it would be easy to march toward the city of Jericho, a fortified city full of enemy combatants, knowing that the walls would fall. Of course, it would be easy to march toward the battlefield where *three* kingdoms had their armies waiting on me, *because I knew the outcome.* I always knew it would be incredible to be a part of one of God's stories because I knew the *ending* beforehand, that part where the Lord delivered His people. The piece I never considered was that the people played a part at the *beginning.* They didn't know what the outcome was going to be. They had to trust God. He delivered them, but they still had to march toward the ocean, march around a walled city, march toward the enemy armies. God couldn't have delivered them if they hadn't been in the right position.

That was then. This was now.

I stood there, frozen, for an eternity. The buzzing in my pocket had stopped, and it would be a minute or two before it buzzed again. I tried to remain as still as possible. I don't know if I even breathed. The whispered voices had stopped. Had they heard the buzzing? Were they aware I was so close? I started to sense movement, so I tried to make my way back quietly, carefully toward the house.

First step, no problem. Second step, no problem. Third step, no problem.

Almost clear. I'm going to make it. I'll get out of here.

Fourth step, problem. A twig snapped under my foot, and in the silence of the night it sounded like a cannonball crashing in the woods. I heard unrecognizable words, no longer whispered, within feet of me. I took off at a sprint, breaking out of the woods at a gallop.

"Make my feet like hinds' feet,"[48] I said to myself as I ran toward the backyard.

"Matt, stop!" I heard Aaron say, pleadingly, but I kept running, just as fast as my feet would take me. I looked over my shoulder and saw him and the dark figure of another man, spilling out of the woods, running toward me.

"Matt, *stop!*" I heard again, this time a command, no longer pleading. I never slowed my pace.

Through the backyard and into the corridor, I sprinted. The two men were close on my tail. I came to the wedged rake and hurdled it. The men were only a few yards behind me now. I heard the sound of bone on bone contact as my first pursuer crashed into the rake. Both men must have then fallen into one another.

At that instant, time stood still. I was still running, but I heard a voice on the inside say to me, "*Break their teeth, O God, in their mouth: break out the great teeth of the young lions, O Lord.*"[49] I had remembered another of King David's prayers.

Why was that coming to me now?

And then I knew... *That's what God's voice sounds like!*

Time resumed. As I reached the end of the corridor, I grabbed the shovel I had left leaning on the house. I stepped around the corner and out of sight. To whoever continued to chase me, it would look like I had kept running. I could hear the muffled screams of pain from whomever had crashed into my trap, but now I was also hearing footsteps, heavy, running footsteps, still chasing me. I held the shovel like a baseball bat, with both hands, blade at the far end. As soon as I heard the footsteps closing in and saw a glint of movement, I swung the shovel with all my strength. I heard a bone-crunching sound as the flat of the blade made contact with someone's face. Their feet went high in the air in front of them as the momentum from the blade and the momentum

---

48 Psalm 18:33
49 Psalm 58:6

of their running reached a face-shattering crescendo. Their upper body went backward while their lower body kept going forward. It was a brutal collision, a clothesline of epic proportions. In the darkness, I saw something fly from the man's hand. It tumbled to a stop just a few feet from me. It was his pistol, a Smith & Wesson 1911.

Now, I'm armed.

At that moment, at that exact instant in time, it was revealed to me; I understood how the Israelites felt crossing the Red Sea, how they felt as the walls of Jericho crashed down, how they felt when Jehoshaphat's army saw the enemy vanquished before them. This was what God's deliverance felt like. I had been delivered from the hands of the enemy, who even provided me a weapon as I escaped.

God is so good.

I decided to enjoy God's deliverance from a different place, a place where people weren't trying to kill me. I didn't figure either man would be following me any time soon, but I didn't want to stick around and find out. I had paid attention on the drive to Nuria's house and so I was decently familiar with my surroundings. I started running.

Breathlessly I whispered a prayer. "Thank You, Lord, for Your gentle guidance, for Your Holy Spirit showing me how to escape the evil plans of my enemy. Thank You for talking to me and for Your continued grace on my life."

I was close enough to the city that I could see the glow from the city lights and moved in that direction. I made my way out of the neighborhood areas as quickly as possible while still trying to stay concealed. I reached in my pocket, found Jessica's phone and turned it off. I wasn't going to let it give my position away again. Once I reached a more urban area, I could disappear.

Chapter Fifteen

I made my way out of Nuria's neighborhood and into the city. I used alleyways and even public transportation (thanks to Jessica's credit card) to put some distance between me and Aaron or Omar or whoever he was. Exiting the city bus, I wandered, walking, turning left and right at random intervals so that no one would be able to follow me. I soon found myself in what looked like a not-so-great part of town. For the first time in my life, I wasn't afraid of being alone in a place like this. Somehow, I felt alive. I had faced adversity all day. I had faced people trying to kill me. I had followed clues and I was figuring things out. I was still alive and healthy. It gave me new energy. New life. Being in a shady part of town, even in a foreign country, wasn't going to give me a second's worth of pause.

I think this is what Jessica was telling me about. This is the Lord talking to me, helping me. I'm going to find Jessica, alive, and then I'm going to tell her how I feel about her. Nothing can stop me. I cannot be defeated, and I will not quit.

Even in not-so-desirable parts of town there were hotels; most charged by the hour and they were used to giving a certain level of discretion to their clients. I found one such hotel and approached it, stopping in the light of the doorway to see how much cash I was carrying. Thankfully, I had been planning on spending time with Jessica and I had visited the ATM before I met her. That meant I had a few hundred dollars on me. American dollars. I didn't want to use Jessica's credit card in a place like this. And I might be able to get this place on the cheap if I paid in cash. The question now was if American money would be worth anything in Israel.

I stepped into the slummy hotel and saw there was an overweight, greasy woman sitting behind the counter. She was turned facing a small television that controlled her attention at the moment. She had long frizzy hair that at one point had an obviously dark coloring but had started greying in recent days. From the angle at which she sat, she could see the television, anyone coming in the entrance to the hotel, and the stairway that led to the floors above.

I walked up to the woman and said, "Shalom."

She looked at me and smirked.

"A-tah med-a-ber an-glit?" I asked, hoping she spoke English.

"How long do you want room?" she asked in heavily accented English. She must have seen the question on my face and added, "You walk like American. You look like American. How long do you want room?" I could smell the cigarettes on her breath even from several feet away.

I nodded and said, "All night."

The greasy woman grunted a wheezing laughed and said, "Money-bags over here thinks he last all night."

I shook my head, "No. Just me. No one else."

"Sure, sure," she said. "Lots of men come here, rent room for just man. Later on, woman come visit. I'm sure it is 'sister.'" And another roar of wheezing laughter erupted from the woman, blowing horrible cigarette breath in my face. The laughter quickly turned to a hacking, wheezing cough.

I wasn't in the mood to argue with her, so I asked, "How much?"

She said, "All night, 300 shekels."

I had no idea how much 300 shekels would be in American dollars, so I pulled out a crisp $50 bill, the bill with Ulysses S. Grant on it, and asked, "Will this do?" The greasy woman's eyes had gotten big, but she sensed she could get more out of me and was shaking her head before I even finished asking my question. I put the $50 back in my pocket and pulled out a $100 bill, Ben Franklin staring at her now.

Again, she shook her head. This time she said one word. "Both."

I nodded, handed the $150 to her, and she gave me a key to a room on the fourth floor.

I climbed the stairs to my floor, the top floor, and did my best to ignore all of the sounds that were emanating from the rooms along my path. I found my room and entered it. There wasn't much to see, but it looked clean; the bed was made, and the remote to the television was on the side table. I shut the door behind me, locked the deadbolt and secured the chain.

After a quick shower to wash off the stink of sweat and blood, I rinsed out the shirt I had been wearing and hung it across the bar in the wardrobe to dry. I needed to think.

What do I know? What clues do I have? What's my next step? What were the things Nuria told me?

I found a scrap piece of paper, part of a menu to what looked like a pizza delivery place that must be close by, and wrote down the things I knew:

1. Mercenaries don't have Kaplan or research
2. Kaplan called and talked with Nuria
3. Kaplan is trying to find me (good guy or bad guy?)
4. Kaplan is with Mossad (an agent or just in their custody?)
5. I have the key now (what is it? phone?)
6. Don't trust Omar
7. Go to some place with magnets. What was the name? Mondo? Micha? Metal?

I turned Jessica's phone back on.

Bzzzzz. Bzzzzz. Bzzzzz.

Jessica's phone was again alerting me that the battery was almost dead. When Jessica and I had been together, she asked me to put her phone on silent, and it had been on silent since then. Since the car ride when she had been kidnapped. I hadn't noticed the texts and missed calls from throughout the day. I quickly scanned through the texts, but there was nothing of importance to the mission at hand, nothing that would help me find Jessica. There were several missed calls, but none had left a voicemail.

I decided to play Jessica's message again. I just wanted to hear her voice. I found the voicemail icon on her phone and pressed play. "

Oh Matt," the voice quietly whispered. "I hope that you're okay and you've still got my phone. I hope you're listening to this." It was definitely Jessica, but listening to the message this time, she didn't seem scared. She sounded distracted, or maybe it was her trying to tell me something… in code. The message continued. "Uh, I've got your number stored in my phone, and I don't actually remember it. Uh, if you get this, uh, if you're listening to this, please *be careful.*" I again noticed the heavy emphasis on the words. She continued, "*Don't trust anybody* and please hold on to my stuff. That is my *favorite* tube of lipstick. I would be lost without it. I'm a virtuous woman, Matt, I really am. *Don't lose my lipstick.*" she said adamantly. "Oh, here they come," and with that, she clicked off. The voicemail was over. I dropped the phone from my ear, not letting it buzz pressed against my face like I had this morning.

Was that just this morning?

I knew there were a few things I should check before Jessica's phone went dead again, and I knew my time was running out. I pulled up the web browser and typed in "M," "Magnet" and "Tel Aviv" and 407,000 results flashed back to me in .70 seconds. The third result in the list, under "Tel Aviv Beach & City Souvenir Magnet," and "Tel Aviv to build magnet-powered SkyTran monorail" was a link to "Moho Magnetic Machines." I clicked the link, and it took me to a very basic webpage with a physical address, some pictures of the exterior of the building and their hours of operation. Whatever this company did, they weren't trying to sell anything online. The company had a cool little logo that consisted of an "M" with three sides that formed a cube and the exponent of 3, like M-cubed. I wrote the address down on my scrap piece of paper and then pulled up the map application on the phone. I plugged the address in the search bar and in moments, I had directions to Moho Magnetic Machines, M3. It wasn't far, but I knew that the phone would be dead long before I could use it in the morning to find the building. I tried to draw a quick map of what was displayed on the screen. It wasn't pretty, but I was confident I would be able to follow it in the morning. Morning would be here before I knew it, so I tried to calm my mind and get some rest.

My shirt was hanging on the bar in the wardrobe drying, and I knew I didn't want to sleep in blue jeans. I slipped them off and, following the lead of one of my favorite fictional characters, slipped the jeans between the top mattress and the box springs. In the books, the fictional character, Jack Reacher, was able to keep wrinkles out of his clothes by putting them between the mattresses. I was willing to see if it worked in real life.

As I laid my head on the pillow to try and get some sleep, I began thinking about Nuria and what she had told me. There were two things that were confusing to me. She said that I had the key, *now*. Like, I hadn't had it before, but I do *now*. Is that how she meant it? The other thing that confused me was the "Don't trust Omar" phrase she said. How did she know about Omar?

I never used the name, Omar, when I was talking with her, did I? And, she had never met him. So, she must have heard it from someone. Kaplan? How would Kaplan even know about Omar? If I'm not careful, I'm going to think myself into circles and be awake all night. I need to think on something else. I need to think on something true, honest, and of a good report...[50]

"God, thank You for keeping me safe. You were talking to me, and I recognized Your voice! That was amazing. Thank You for showing me

---

50 Philippians 4:8

what to do to set the trap. Thank You for helping me get away! Thank You for providing me a weapon."

Now, I'm beginning to understand what Jessica has been trying to teach me. She has a relationship with God and they fellowship constantly. I want that too...

I realized I was missing my friend, fighting the thoughts of nervousness for her and what she must be going through. I decided seeing her pictures might make me feel a little bit better, get my mind off of things and help me fall asleep a little faster. I pulled out the phone and opened up the photos application. The last picture in the app was the one I had taken of the personalized letter that Jessica had written to herself.

The photo was so small on the screen that I couldn't read any of the words, but I noticed something that I hadn't seen while looking at the actual letter in Jessica's office. Some of the individual characters, some of the letters, seemed to be written darker, like she had drawn over certain ones more than once. Looking at the tiny screen, I couldn't read the words, but those letters were much clearer. Then, before I could give it any more thought, with the phone in my hand, it gave one final *Bzzzzz. Bzzzzz. Bzzzzz*, and died.

I decided to say a final prayer before I drifted off to sleep. "Lord, please keep my friend safe, give her comfort and let her feel Your presence. Help me find her or help the two of us get to safety, together. And Lord, the Bible says, 'When thou liest down, thou shalt not be afraid: yea, thou shalt lie down, and thy sleep shall be sweet.'[51] I ask You for sweet sleep for Jessica and myself. I ask these things in the Name of Jesus. Amen."

It didn't take long, and the drowsiness came in waves. I drifted to sleep thinking, *Don't trust Omar. Don't trust Omar. Don't trust Omar,* into the night.

---

51 Proverbs 3:24

Chapter Sixteen

The next morning, I awoke refreshed. I was famished, but I was alive and invigorated. I peeled back the covers and checked the time. It was 6:30 a.m., and my head and my heart were ready for what today held. I jumped in the shower again to knock off the sleep and did my best to brush my teeth with only water. I peeled the mattress back and pulled my jeans out. There weren't many wrinkles, that's for sure, but there were a few deep creases. Not much I could do about it now and hopefully, just wearing the pants would work some of them out. I put my day-old clothes back on, my shirt being a little stiff from the air dry, and I worked on my hair, running my fingers through it trying to make it look halfway respectable. My stomach growled, reminding me it was past time for another meal. Maybe there would be a place to get some food as I walked to Moho Magnetic Machines.

"This is the day that the Lord has made and I will rejoice and be glad in it,"[52] I said as I was gathering my belongings and finished the thought with, "Surely goodness and mercy shall follow me all the days of my life."[53]

I walked down the stairs of the now quiet hotel and into the lobby. The greasy woman had been replaced by a balding man with a thinning mustache who looked much too young to be losing his hair. He was wearing a black tank top, smoking a cigarette, and watching the same

---

52 Psalm 118:24
53 Psalm 23:6

TV the woman had been watching last night. I guess this kind of life-style doesn't lead to the healthiest of outcomes. I handed him the key and left. He barely noticed me and neither of us spoke a word.

I pulled out my hand-drawn map, checked some street names and decided that the direction I needed to go was on a diagonal from where I was standing. Instead of walking to the end of the block and turning right, I decided to cut through the hotel parking lot and make my way diagonally through the city block. The entrance to the hotel wasn't exactly in the center of the building, so I decided to walk to the shorter edge and turn left into the parking lot. That meant that I would eventually walk most of the distance around the hotel on the back side. I walked the length of the side of the building and rounded the corner to the back of the hotel, and that's when I saw it. Parked in a semi-hidden spot behind the dumpster was a small silver-colored SUV with the driver's side window gone. In the daylight, it was easier to see what color the SUV was and that the window had been torn away, roughly and quickly. It was unmistakable. This was Aaron's, er, Omar's stolen SUV.

What do I even call this guy? Until further notice, he's Omar. Omar, Omar, Omar. How in the world did Omar find me? It's impossible. I was so careful. Did he track Jessica's cell phone? It wasn't turned on long; there's no way that he could have traced it, could he? How is he here? Isn't his face smashed in?

I cautiously approached the little SUV, in case Omar was sleeping in the vehicle. I put my hand on the gun, which I had tucked inside my belt like I had seen him do. When I got to the SUV, it was empty and obviously unlocked. I had a destination, a map and now I had trans-portation. It was turning out to be a surprisingly good morning. I sat down in the driver's seat and reached under the steering column to find the exposed wires. I had seen Omar do this; maybe I could too. It took me a while, but after a couple minutes, I found the correct wires and had sparked the engine. I was on my way.

I followed my hand-drawn map, only making a couple of wrong turns, and found Moho Magnetic Machines within an hour. Because of my excitement with hijacking the little SUV, I completely forgot to find a place for food.

It was approaching 8:00 a.m. as the logo on the sign appeared in the parking lot. I drove past the building, just in case anyone was waiting for me, then went to the next block and turned away from Moho Magnetic Machines. I went another block, turned right and found a place that was partially obstructed from view. I pulled the small SUV into a parking spot so that the driver's window was parallel and partially hidden by a city trash can beside the street. It would take someone really paying attention to notice the window was gone. If anyone found it, if Omar *somehow* found it, or if the police found it, no one would know that I was at Moho Magnetic Machines, several blocks away.

I threaded my way back to the industrial building and cautiously approached the parking lot. After making sure no one was there, I found my way to the entrance. I walked up to the metal door, turned the knob and pulled, but it was locked and didn't move. There was a doorbell next to the door, and looking up, I noticed there was a security camera monitoring the entrance. I pushed the button to ring the bell and tried to look as innocent and non-threatening as possible. I waved at the camera. A moment later, I heard a metallic buzz as someone on the inside unlocked the door.

I guess I wasn't quick enough because by the time I reached the door, the buzzing had stopped, and the door was locked again. I gave a sheepish grin to the camera, shrugged my shoulders as if to indicate, *"What can I say?"* and waited with my hand on the doorknob for it to buzz again. The second time around, I caught it and opened the unlocked door. I went into the building, feeling a little bit of safety at the thought that anyone who might be following me would have to be buzzed in. The door opened up into a hallway, and following it, I came to an opening with a young woman sitting behind a desk.

"Pardon, me. Umm, A-tah med-a-ber an-glit? Do you speak English?" I asked the woman.

She nodded.

"Most people in Israel, at least in the city, speak English. In fact, we have a lot of people who live in Israel who are transplants from English speaking countries, like America," the young woman said in unaccented English.

"Is it that obvious?" I asked, looking down at the nameplate on her desk and adding, "Rachel."

She laughed. "We deal with a *lot* of Americans here. Most of them catch the door on the first buzz." She laughed again. "And we have a lot of Americans who work here too. What can I help you with today?"

Rachel was a pleasant young woman with a ready smile and a cheerful voice. She was probably closer to thirty than to twenty, but she still seemed young and in love with life. She had the look of someone who had once been an exceptional beauty, but a desk job and lack of exercise had added an extra twenty or thirty pounds. She had bangs cut across her forehead that came to rest just above brilliant green eyes. Her hair was jet black cut short, falling just below her ears.

I said, "I'm not exactly sure. It's a really long story of how I ended up here, but I'm in Israel because of my friend, Dr. Jessica Adams. I don't want to alarm you or anything, but she's missing and I'm looking for her. I went to her lab and spoke with her assistant, Nuria. Nuria told me that she works here sometimes. Is there anyone here who might know my friend who could give me some info that might help me find her?"

I barely had the words out of my mouth when the young woman, Rachel, with concern in her voice, said, "Oh, no! She's missing? When? How? We love Dr. Adams here. Jessica is awesome. She's here all the time. Usually, when she comes, she brings us something healthy, like fruit, to eat for breakfast or to snack on."

I could tell by the slight blush that Rachel was a little self-conscious about her weight, and she quickly changed the subject.

"Oh, I'm rambling. Yes! Yes, you'll want to talk with the project manager she works with. Hang on, I'll get him for you."

With that, she picked up a phone and dialed a number. She looked me in the eye, as the phone was connecting, and motioned behind me and to my left. There was a counter with donuts and coffee. When I turned back to her, she mouthed, "Help yourself," and shrugged a *that's why I'm a little overweight* kind of shrug.

A moment later, someone must have answered the phone because Rachel said, almost shouting in a slow and deliberate manner, "Hey, there's a man here," and turned to me asking, "What'd you say your name is?"

"Matt Davenport."

Then back to the person on the phone, "There's a Matt Davenport, a friend of Dr. Adams, who is here. He says she is missing and he's looking for her. He wants to ask you some questions. Mind coming to help him?" Silence for an extended period, longer than just a yes or no answer, while the person responded and then, "Great. I'll let him know."

She hung up the phone and said to me, "He'll be down in a few minutes. He said they were right in the middle of a test, but it shouldn't take long."

I nodded and said through a bite of a donut, "I haven't eaten anything since breakfast yesterday. I've been working so hard; I haven't slowed down to eat. I'm starving."

Rachel laughed and said, "Eat all the donuts. *All* of them. Whatever you don't eat are going to attach themselves directly to my hips, so *please* eat them all."

She didn't have to twist my arm too hard. I was famished. The coffee and donuts helped and within minutes, I had eaten a half dozen or so.

I asked Rachel, "What do you guys do here? What is Moho Magnetic Machines? What does that…what does *Moho* even mean? Is that like a Hebrew word or something?"

"Good guess, but no, not Hebrew. Moho is short for a man named Andrija Mohorovičić."

"How in the world do you know that?" I asked. "The fact you remembered the dude's name is pretty impressive."

"Yeah, it took me a while to learn how to pronounce that one, let alone remember it. When you're the receptionist at a company named after an important, but pretty much unknown scientist, they require you to learn the basics about him. Anyway, this guy Moho was like the father of modern seismology," she replied.

"Okay, that answers the Moho question. What about the other one? What do you guys do here? Are you in the earthquake detection business?" I asked.

"We do a lot of different things here," Rachel said as she went into an obviously pre-written, well-rehearsed answer. "We research, develop and test equipment for a number of different applications, but honestly," she said, whispering, "I don't know what any of them are. I basically just answer the phones, buzz people in and direct people's calls."

We both laughed and I grabbed another donut, powdered sugar, and started munching on it. My hunger was starting to pass, and the coffee was giving me a boost of energy. I was beginning to feel like my old self again, and I sat down on a small couch to wait. On the table beside the loveseat, there was a copy of a recent newspaper, the *Jerusalem Post*. The date on the paper was July 11, 2018, and the front-page headline was an article almost custom made for Moho Magnetic Machines. I started reading:

"WHEN A MAJOR EARTHQUAKE RIPPLED THROUGH JERUSALEM" [54]

Israel Sits on the Syrian-African Rift and Has Been Experiencing Large Quakes Every 80-100 Years for Centuries.

By Sarah Levi

---

54 Sarah Levi, "When a major earthquake rippled through Jerusalem," *Jerusalem Post*, July 11, 2018, https://www.jpost.com/Israel-News/The-last-big-one-The-July-11-1927-Jericho-Earthquake-562174

Exactly 91 years ago, on July 11, the last major earthquake struck the Holy Land.

This past week, Israel's north has been experiencing a new round of tremors measuring up to 4.5 on the Richter scale. According to experts, it is only a matter of time before the next "big one" hits.

This region has consistently experienced large-scale earthquakes every 80–100 years for centuries. Israel sits along the Syrian-African fault line, which runs along the border with Jordan, part of the Great Rift Valley that extends from northern Syria to Mozambique.

Known as the 1927 Jericho Earthquake, the 6.25 magnitude quake lasted approximately five seconds and rippled from its epicenter in the northern Dead Sea region to Jerusalem, Jericho and Nablus, reaching Ramel, Lod and Tiberias. The earthquake claimed 500 lives and injured an additional 700 people. It also caused massive structural damage throughout the region.

This was also the last time an earthquake caused significant damage to Jerusalem. Over 130 people were killed and some 450 were injured.

I heard a sound that drew my attention from the newspaper, a door softly squeaking open. Looking over the top of the paper, I took my final bite of powdered sugar donut as a short, older gentleman walked into the room.

Is this my guy?

Rachel pointed in my direction, confirming my suspicion. He walked over and said, "Mr. Davenport?"

"Yes," I said with a mouth full of donut, standing, trying to wipe powdered sugar from my fingertips and onto my jeans.

The man extended his arm to shake hands with me and said with a smile, "Hello, my name is Omar, Omar Abdul."

It was all I could do to keep from spewing powdered donut all over him.

Chapter Seventeen

It had been a rough start to meeting Omar Abdul, the man Jessica had, supposedly, worked closely with. Once the initial shock and fear had subsided, once I choked down the donut that I was fighting with, I was able to recover enough to shake his hand. The man was solidly built. Not like a weightlifter, but like someone who did manual labor for a living. He didn't look imposing, but that grip was a death-lock. I guess it came from years and years of turning wrenches or building machinery or doing something with his hands. He was not a very impressive figure, but his grip was. After a few minutes of very generalized explanation about Jessica's disappearance with very few details, Omar had volunteered to show me where he and Jessica had worked together. He didn't seem sinister in any way, but with the events leading up to my introduction to the "new" Omar, I kept my guard up.

Omar was a scholarly looking gentleman who I guessed was around fifty-five years old. He had thinning hair, but a long, full black beard. He was wearing dark blue jeans and an olive green, short-sleeve, button-up shirt that had three pens in the pocket. He had an infectious smile and an incredibly thick accent that took me a moment to process each time he spoke. It was obvious to me that English wasn't his first language. His diction was so bad, I honestly wished I had someone there adding subtitles across his chest so I could follow his side of the conversation easier. He also wore hearing aids in both ears. I began to notice that every time I spoke, he looked at my mouth. He must have been reading my lips as much as listening to me. Sensing it might help, I did my best to speak clearly and with more volume than normal.

We had gone through a door behind Rachel's desk and into an exceptionally large industrial warehouse that had enormous amounts of activity. For all I could tell, they might have been building cargo ships in that expansive space. We walked up a flight of stairs to get to Omar's workshop.

"Are you familiar with magnetic resonance imaging, Mr. Davenport?" Omar asked as we entered his workshop, a thirty-foot by thirty-foot room that looked like it was half chemistry lab and half mechanic's chop shop. One half of the room had sanitary gloves, beakers and chemicals while the other side had machinery and greasy tools. It was quite an unusual combination. The workshop had a wall of windows that overlooked the warehouse area.

"Magnetic resonance imaging?" I asked. "It sounds familiar, but I don't remember from where."

Omar smiled knowingly. "Mr. Davenport, have you ever had an injury like a ligament or muscle tear?"

"Uh. Sure," I said, not knowing exactly where this line of questioning was going. "In college, I blew my knee out, MCL, playing pickup basketball. Had to have surgery, all that. Why?"

"When you went to your doctor, what did he do?" Omar asked, pointing to a seat beside his desk, inviting me to sit. It was an interesting seating arrangement. His desk was placed against the wall, overlooking the workshop so when he sat down and moved his chair under his desk to work, he could look out over the factory workers. But that left an awkward placement for a visitor's chair. I sat down in the chair, with my back against the wall and my right arm resting on his desk.

Puzzled, I sat down and answered about the doctor's visit. "I remember him intentionally trying to hurt me." Chuckling to myself, I continued the thought. "He twisted, pulled, rubbed, popped, moved my knee in all types of painful ways. Then, it seems like I had to make my way to the basement of the hospital where we did some X-rays or something, to see the extent of the damage."

Omar nodded the whole time. He said, "Mr. Davenport."

I interrupted and said, "Please call me Matt."

Omar smiled and continued, "Matt, an X-ray would only reveal if a bone was broken, not if a muscle or ligament was torn. To know that more precisely, you would need to have an MRI done."

"Oh, yeah. That's right. I did have an MRI done on my knee," I said, feeling foolish that I hadn't remembered.

"Tell me about it," Omar said.

Still unsure of the line of questioning, I paused for a minute and just looked at Omar. He must have sensed my hesitation and said, "Bear with me. I'll explain my logic momentarily."

"Okay. Sure. Doing my MRI. I went into the office and they made me take off all of my clothes and put on a hospital gown. They asked me if I was wearing any metal, watch, wedding ring, etc., and wanted to make sure I didn't have a pacemaker. Something to do with magnets in the machine. Hmm. Then I went in the room that had this big, square, plastic looking machine in it, colored in shades of cream and white. The machine had a hole right in the middle with a place where I lay down. The technician came over, adjusted things until he was satisfied I was in the correct position, and then he gave me some heavy-duty headphones. He told me to remain completely still and that I wouldn't feel a thing. He was right; I didn't feel anything."

"Great," Omar said. "What do you remember about the actual process?"

"I remember trying not to move. At one point I needed to sneeze but had to hold it in so I wouldn't mess up the test. The other thing I remember is how loud the process was. Even with the headphones on, it sounded like two jackhammer armies going to war with each other in that machine."

Omar smiled and held up both hands, index fingers pointing to the hearing aids in his ears. "Exactly, my friend. This is what a lifetime of working with MRI machines without protection will do to you."

I was genuinely beginning to like Omar, which made this all the more tricky. Nuria had warned me, "Don't trust Omar," but who was she referring to?

I asked, "Can you tell me a little about what you and Jessica were working on? I'm trying to piece together *what* happened, and to do that I need to know *why* it happened. I think something she was working on has gotten her in trouble with some bad people."

Omar nodded and asked, "How did you find me? What brought you to my workshop?"

It was a fair question, so I answered, "I went to Jessica's lab, Laboratory Nedaviah, to speak with her boss, Dr. Eli Kaplan. Do you know him?"

Omar shook his head in response. "Not really. We've met on occasion, but that's it."

"No big deal. Anyway, Dr. Kaplan wasn't there, but I spent time with Jessica's assistant, Nuria, and she told me to come here to Moho Magnetic Machines, but she didn't tell me who I should speak with. I didn't think to ask." I wanted to add, *I didn't think to ask her who I should talk to because she was dying in my arms at the time.*

My answer must have satisfied Omar enough that he began explaining exactly what he and Jessica had been working on. He began by asking me yet another question. "One last question. Did Rachel, my receptionist downstairs, explain to you about Andrija Mohorovičić?"

"Yes, actually she did," I replied. "She said Moho was the—how did she put it? The father of seismology? But I don't understand what seismology and MRI machines have to do with anything."

"Okay, Matt. Let's start at the beginning," Omar said and then the phone on his desk rang. It was so loud, it nearly knocked me out of my seat. Again, Omar smiled and pointed to his hearing aids again.

"It has to be that loud, or I would never be able to hear it. I had the phone receiver specially made to amplify the sound too. You would probably be able to hear that side of the conversation at the bottom of the stairs," he said with a big grin on his face. Omar pressed a button on the phone and the ringing quit immediately. He said, "They can leave me a message."

"The beginning," he started again. "Andrija Mohorovičić was a scientist back around 1900. He was born and raised in Croatia, a part of Eastern Europe that had a lot of seismic activity. He was a brilliant meteorologist, had degrees in mathematics and physics, but he was always learning. In 1908, he acquired some seismic equipment for the university where he was teaching and in 1909, there was an earthquake nearby. He began to study the effects of these earthquakes. He knew that earthquakes traveled in waves, seismic waves, but what he was able to determine was that these seismic waves acted just like light or sound waves." Omar grinned a big smile and then just sat there.

After a few seconds I said, "I'm sorry. I don't understand what any of that means. You'll need to keep explaining, please."

Omar laughed and said "Ah. I'm sorry. I forget sometimes that not everyone has the same science background," then continued with his explanation. "Seismic waves act and react just like sound or light waves. It will be most easy to explain like this."

He opened a desk drawer and started rooting around inside. That was the first time I noticed the monitor sitting on his desk. The monitor was for the security cameras outside. I had noticed the one camera above the door when I arrived at the facility, the one Rachel monitored and used to buzz me in the building. On the screen, I saw there were four different camera images divided across the screen, one camera view for each corner. There was the camera above the door, two cameras on each end of the parking lot and one camera that I determined must be located at the back of the building overlooking a large loading and unloading bay area.

I turned my attention back to Omar as he finally found the tools he was looking for and began again. "We know that light travels in waves." He turned on a flashlight and pointed it at the desk. "Here, you see? All the waves are hitting the desk at the same moment. Right?"

I nodded. "Okay."

He said, "It looks like white light, but it is really made of different light on the spectrum: red, orange, yellow, green, blue, indigo, violet and so on. They all combine together to give us white light. White light is a combination of all the different colors of light."

I interrupted with, "Roy G Biv," but Omar looked confused, so I said, "Red, orange, yellow, green, blue, indigo, violet? Roy G Biv! No? Nothing? Never mind. Sorry. Please continue."

Omar said, "White light is hitting the desk, but if we place a prism on the desk and shine the light through it, what happens?" With that, he placed a prism on the desk and shone the light through it. A small rainbow appeared, refracted through the prism.

I said, "We get all the colors of the rainbow."

Omar nodded and asked, "Why?"

I just shrugged my shoulders. "Because…science." It seemed like a perfectly logical answer.

Omar laughed and said, "Yes, but let's be a little more specific. When the light waves hit the prism, they are refracted at different speeds. Some have faster, or technically, smaller wavelengths and some have slower, that being larger wavelengths. The different colors of light travel at different speeds after passing through the prism. Are you following?"

I nodded and Omar continued.

"When the light hit a different material, the waves changed and when the wavelengths changed, the colors were separated. Andrija Mohorovičić realized that seismic waves react the same way. When seismic waves hit different material, they change wavelengths, just like the light did in our prism."

"Okay," I said. "So, when seismic waves travel through land, they travel at one speed and when they hit water, they change speeds. Is that it?"

Omar nodded. "In a very, very simplified way, yes. But think of it like this: as the seismic waves pass through any material, they change speeds.

So, we have land that contains granite, limestone, sandstone, volcanic rock and so on. The waves travel at one speed through granite, at a different speed through limestone, then through sandstone at another speed. It's not just solids and liquids, it's each and every material. You following?"

I nodded.

"Now," he said, "let's go back to the MRI machines. MRI machines and seismology are built on some of the same scientific principles. Just like our prism changes the wavelength of the light passing through it, and seismic waves are changed as they pass through different geological material, MRI wavelengths are also changed as they travel through different substances in your body, like fat tissue, bone or muscle."

"I *think* I'm following you," I said.

Omar nodded, paused a minute to think and said, "Imagine it like this." He picked up the flashlight and prism again. He continued, "The flashlight is the MRI machine and the prism is your knee." Smiling, he imitated a banging noise like one of the machines would make and turned on the flashlight. He again shined the light into the prism and the light was refracted, producing a rainbow. He said, "The MRI machine sends a signal, using magnets making those loud banging noises, through your knee and then another portion of the machine reads the resulting wavelengths. The blue color," he said, pointing to the refracted light, "might be fat tissue. The green color," he said, changing where he was pointing, "might be muscle. The red might be bone. Each of the wavelengths represents a different type of material."

"Okay. I'm getting it. The MRI readings are affected by the different substances in our body. Bone shifts the pattern differently than muscle. Muscle shifts the pattern differently than fat. One part of the machine produces the wave, and the other part of the machine reads the resulting wave," I said.

"Well done." Omar was beaming. "Hence the name magnetic resonance imaging. We use magnetic resonance to produce an image. We, Jessica and I and our team have started calling it *pinging*."

"Pinging?" I asked, suddenly confused again.

"Oh. Yes. That's another good way to explain this concept. Have you ever watched a submarine movie? When a ship and a submarine are trying to destroy one another, the ship sends out a *pinging* noise through the water. It's actually called sonar, but the way they represent it in the movies is with a pinging sound. The sound is reflected off of the sea floor, unless it hits something before then, like a submarine. By pinging the water, the boat hopes to locate the submarine. Do you follow so far?"

I nodded.

Omar continued, "MRI machines ping between two magnets and chart the differences they encounter, very similar to when a ship pings between the ship's bottom and the seafloor, looking for differences they encounter."

"That makes sense."

He said, "One last thing. In an MRI machine, the magnetic waves are produced by radio signals and hydrogen molecules. Because I'm trying to keep this simple for you, we don't need all of the details; just know that the radio signals and hydrogen molecules are important parts of the process as well. It will come into play in the next part I'm going to explain. This is the part that your friend, Dr. Adams, and I have been working on for so long. We got our big break while we were in Russia."

Just then, the phone rang, a different sound this time, and I nearly fell out of my seat again. Omar didn't notice the sound but saw me jump.

"Your phone is ringing."

He said, "Oh! Pardon me. That ringtone is Rachel downstairs. I probably need to take that one. There might be someone here to see me or a phone call I need to take. That call a few minutes ago might have been important."

"Sure thing," I said, turning to look at the phone. My attention was drawn to movement out of the corner of my eye. The security camera monitor with the four screens showed something going on in the area of the back door. It was men, so small that they looked like little ants, lots of ants, approaching the loading bay. That's when it dawned on me. These were the mercenaries, in full tactical gear, machine guns swinging as they ran. It was a surprise attack. Their swiftness and coordination were breathtaking. I scanned the other three monitors, but they were empty, save for a single man wanting to be buzzed in the front door.

It only took a matter of seconds for me to piece things together. It went something like this: When I arrived at Moho Magnetic Machines, Rachel called upstairs to Omar, who was conveniently running a test. That 'test' gave him time to call his co-conspirators and alert them to my presence. The rest of this was just killing time until the muscle could get here and deal with me. Nuria warned me not to trust Omar…

I didn't wait until Omar finished his phone call. I wasn't giving him a chance to explain or to keep me hostage or put that death-lock grip on me. I took off. I banged the workshop door open and hit the stairs at almost full speed. I took them three, sometimes four at a time, making my way back toward Rachel's desk. Flinging her door open, I was immediately standing face-to-face with Aaron. Somehow, he had found me. Again.

Chapter Eighteen

This day that had started out so well, a map, transportation and even breakfast, had very quickly devolved into something completely different. I was standing face-to-face with a man that only twenty minutes ago, I thought was trying to kill me. Now, I was simply confused.

Aaron saw me and immediately put both hands in the air and calmly said, "Matt, we're on the same side. I'm unarmed. I will explain everything, but we need to leave, *now*."

I only had a split second to decide, but going with *one* supposedly unarmed man made a lot more sense than being taken by dozens of heavily armed men. I told Aaron, "Okay. Let's go, but know this: if I suspect anything, I will not hesitate to shoot you. I *am* armed."

At that, Rachel, who had been on the phone, dropped the receiver and screamed, standing up and backing into the corner away from us.

Aaron understood and nodded to me. He said, "I've been watching the place for a while. They're approaching from the rear. We need to move, out the front door, right now," and started walking down the hall, toward the front door.

I turned to Rachel and said, "I'm very sorry I scared you. I hope the rest of your day is better than the last two minutes. Thank you for the donuts!" and then I followed Aaron.

Outside, Aaron led me away from the building, crossing several streets, and deeper into the city. After several minutes of running, we reached an abandoned industrial building. There was a tall chain link fence with signs written in Hebrew and English that said, "No Trespassing." The gate to the fence had a long chain and was locked with a padlock.

We made our way around the corner so that we couldn't be seen from the main street, and came to a place where a large section had been cut from the fence, creating a type of doorway where we could enter the property. Aaron had obviously been there before and knew a place to enter the building. Once we were inside and out of sight, Aaron turned, very slowly, and faced me. He again raised his hands, then lifted his shirt very slowly, showing me there was no gun on him.

"You can frisk me if you want," he said.

"That won't be necessary," I said. Honestly, I didn't want to get too close to him so that he couldn't try anything with me.

Aaron said, "Okay. Follow me. I want to be on the high ground, someplace I can see," and led me to a staircase in the back corner of the building. The staircase opened up to a catwalk that led around the perimeter of the building. Along one edge there was a door, but I couldn't see where it led. In the other direction there was a platform, a room without walls, which must have been used as an additional workspace. There were several wooden sawhorses and a few chairs in the open room. Aaron half sat, half leaned on one of the sawhorses. He tried to relax and get me to do the same. He said, "What happened last night? Why did you take off like that?"

I was still on edge about seeing the mercenaries, about Omar, about Aaron *randomly* showing up, about Nuria, about all of it. I said, "No, Aaron. I'm not answering any questions until I get some answers. I'm asking the questions now."

Passive and deferential, Aaron said, "Sure, Matt. Ask me anything."

"Who were you talking to in the woods last night?" I belted. It just came out. "And how did you end up at the hotel where I stayed? How did you make it to Moho Magnetic Machines?"

Aaron quietly answered, "Last night, after the delivery man was snatched by the mercenaries at Kaplan's house, you told me to call and get some Mossad agents to take them down. Remember, I've been suspended, so I called my old partner, the man who trained me, the one person I could trust. I told him to get a team over there and then for him to meet me at the address you gave me. You didn't understand any of that because he and I were talking in Arabic. He arrived at the house moments before we did. He beat us there. He had already found the woman, unconscious, swept the house and was checking the perimeter when we showed up. I didn't know he was there, so I swept the perimeter and then made my way into the woods to make sure they were clear. He saw me in the darkness and thought I was one of the mercenaries. He set an ambush. I'm just glad he didn't kill *me*. You can imagine it was an intense conversation between the two of us. Right then, at that moment, we heard a buzzing noise. We thought it was a mercenary and started quietly searching. Then I saw you running and tried to get you to stop so I could explain. We chased you and I slammed into the trap you set. You should see the bruises across my thighs, but that's nothing compared to Yuseph, my partner. He's in the hospital. Most of the bones in his face are broken."

Negative nudge.

I sat there in silence for a moment. Aaron's answer sounded good, but something, somewhere didn't fit. "Okay, how did you find me last night and again this morning?"

Aaron smiled and said, "I've known where you were every second since you put those clothes on yesterday. Hasn't it crossed your mind that we would put a tracker on you? If we got separated, I could find you. If you were abducted by the enemy, you would lead me to them, to their base of operations. Last night and again this morning, you haven't traveled more than two miles, so it has been pretty easy to catch up to you." Then pausing for a moment, Aaron asked, "Hey, did you steal my SUV this morning? I thought I had that thing hidden better."

"Yeah. I took it. I watched how you rubbed the wires together to crank it and I just followed your example. I figured if you had randomly showed up at the hotel, which would be a statistical anomaly, I could put some distance between me and you by taking your ride. It's parked a few blocks from here, if it hasn't been stolen or towed."

"What happened to make you take off like that, last night? You didn't even give me a chance to explain anything, but now that you've heard it, it makes sense, right?" Aaron asked.

The more he talked the more things fell into place. I began to relax and nodded, answering his question. I said, "Okay. So, last night. I was sitting there checking on Nuria, when her eyes popped open. She told me a couple things and then her eyes got really big and she said, 'Don't trust Omar.' It was the last thing she said before she died. You had used the cover name of Omar that first night when you picked us up at the hotel, and I thought she was talking about you. I went outside looking for you. I made my way to the woods and recognized your voice talking to someone. It freaked me out, and I was just going to ease out of the woods and leave when you guys heard me and started chasing me. If Nuria hadn't told me not to trust you, or Omar, I wouldn't have been so spooked. Sorry about your old partner. I really am."

Aaron asked, "I guess that makes sense, even though I'm the guy who has been doing everything in my power to get your friend back. So, why did you go to Moho Magnetic Machines, and did you learn anything? Wait, what were the things the woman told you before she died?"

"Nuria told me that I had the key, whatever that means; she wasn't making a whole lot of sense at that point. Then she said I needed to go to Moho Magnetic Machines, and right before she died, she told me not to trust Omar. At that Moho place, all I learned was some basic stuff about seismic waves and a little about MRI machines. I think the project manager was just about to tell me some details concerning what he and Jessica were working on when I saw the mercenaries approaching on the security camera. That's when I took off. By the way, the project manager's name is Omar."

"Mm-hm. Did Omar say anything about Russia?" Aaron asked.

"Wait," I said, trying to suppress this horrible feeling, that negative nudge, I had been fighting since yesterday. "I've got a question for you that's been nagging at me. I've talked to Jessica's personal assistant, and now I've talked to the project manager of the program, and neither of them have said *anything* about geothermal energy. Nothing. In fact, the personal assistant flat-out *denied* it. Why do you think that's what Jessica was working on? Where'd you get that information?"

"Did either the personal assistant or project manager say anything about Russia?" Aaron asked again. "They were under strict orders not to, but I have found that you're a little more persuasive than you look and might have learned about it."

I shook my head. "No, nobody has told me anything about Russia. Omar said the word Russia, actually he said something like 'we hit a jackpot when we were in Russia,' at just about the time I was running out of the door, but I didn't get to ask him or hear anything from him about it."

Aaron nodded. "That's when we, Mossad, first became suspicious of your friend, Dr. Adams and her team, including Omar Abdul."

I don't know why, but I was surprised he knew Omar's last name.

He continued, "Any time a group of Israeli scientists travels to a country that is not-so-friendly with ours, we take notice. Their team went to Russia, and we immediately added them to a watch list of sorts. We began tracking their movements, their patents, their progress. We tapped their phone lines. We had to make sure that they weren't an enemy of the state, even an unwitting participant in an enemy's plan. That's how we discovered what they were working on. We have had our suspicions that Omar Abdul was a mole, leaking information. I think, with the presence of the mercenaries today, it has been confirmed."

"Yes, I would say it has. What's our next move? Do we have any leads?" I asked expectantly.

Aaron nodded and said, "Yes. I have a plan, but I don't think you're going to like it."

Chapter Nineteen

Aaron's plan had been simple, but he was right when he said he didn't think I was going to like it. His plan meant exposing myself, again, to the possibility of being captured by the mercenaries. I argued and pleaded, but in the end, he was right. This was the only way it would work. I agreed to his plan on one condition, and I warned him it was an odd condition. My one condition might be just as difficult for him to go through with as the one he was asking me to perform.

Since my conversation with Aaron yesterday in the airplane, I had spent a lot of time thinking about my dad, wondering what he would think of the man I had become, how my life was going.

What would Dad think of the way I had handled the events of the past couple of days?

My dad had a chance to see the direction I was headed. He knew, before he died, that he had raised a quality young man. He had raised a young man in church, with morals, in a house full of love. Even though I had made mistakes, messed things up, been a bratty teenager, my father had the opportunity to see how I was turning out. Aaron's father never had that. Aaron's father was never able to see what direction his young son's life would go. He never got to see the man Aaron had become. But he left Aaron a gift. The only problem was Aaron didn't see it that way. Aaron, from what I could tell, was struggling to fill his father's shoes, to live up to the man that his father was. Aaron felt like he was falling short of what his father would want him to be. In my opinion,

Aaron's perspective was wrong. Instead of trying to fill his father's shoes, he should think of it in a different way. Aaron's father left him a gift…a legacy. Aaron didn't have to live up to anything. He could bask in his father's accomplishment. His father was a national hero. There aren't many people on the planet who can say that. My condition to Aaron was simple: I wanted to know about his father and about his sacrifice.

We had some time to kill. It was still pretty early in the morning, and Omar Khalid wasn't going to lunch anytime soon. Aaron sat there thinking, reasoning before he decided to speak.

"My father was a great man. I've told you that. I've told you he died in the service of his country. I told you he died a national hero. Why do you want to hear more? Why do you want the details?"

"I'm just trying to understand. You've told me a little about your father, and you've told me a lot about how you feel that you're letting him down. You've inferred you'll never be able to carry on his tradition and live up to his memory. I want to know why you feel that way, and the only way I'll know *why* is if I know *what* he did. That's my condition to go along with your plan. Otherwise, we're thinking of something else, a different way," I replied.

Aaron didn't want to talk. That was obvious. He looked away. He said, "I'll be back in a few minutes," and headed toward the stairs.

I watched him as he walked in the large warehouse. He walked around the perimeter of the large facility. At each door he came to, he checked its security, making sure they were each locked, bolted tight from the inside. At each window he passed, he stole glances surveilling the surrounding area. As he walked, he almost looked like he was talking to himself.

What is he doing? Is he praying? He never struck me as a deeply religious man.

After a few minutes he came back up the stairs and found a chair, dragged it noisily on the concrete floor over to where I was and sat down.

"What do you want to know?" Aaron asked, resigned to the fact that he was being forced to talk.

"I saw you talking as you walked downstairs. What were you saying? Were you praying or something?" I asked.

"No. Don't be silly. I was trying to figure out a different plan so that I didn't have to tell you about my father. I was exploring different scenarios. With the different options available to us, with our limited resources, this is the best plan we have, which means I have to tell you about Abee."

"Abee? Who is that? Is that your dad's name?" I asked.

"You're American. I forgot. You only speak English. In other languages, children call their fathers by different names. When you were a small child, you probably called your father Daddy. In Spain they may say Pappa. Here, when we are children, we call our mothers umee and we call our fathers abee." Aaron didn't want to talk about his father, and now the resentment was surfacing.

"Gotcha. Tell me about your abee."

"As you know, the land we are standing on is claimed by several different countries. Currently, and since 1947, Israel is the country that occupies this land. For millennia people have been fighting over this region. Different ethnic groups lay claim to it. Different religions lay claim to it. The Crusades were fought, in part, for control over this territory. Think about that for a moment. The world's three largest religions, the Muslim, Christian and Jew alike, all have a reason to want to control this land. Different factions and countries want control of this land. Invaders are all around and have been, but let's think back to 1947 when the United Nations recognized Israel as a nation. Enemies were exposed. Attacks were immediate. Unless you understand some of the history, you can never hope to understand what my father accomplished."

I nodded and Aaron continued, "By the time 1978 rolled around, Israel had fought many wars. Consider this: the country basically *started* in 1947. One day they weren't a country and the next day they were, and *immediately* had to start fighting. Israel fought a War for Independence, the Sinai War, the Six-Day War, the Yom Kippur War, all before 1973. There hasn't been any real kind of peace since Israel became a nation.

"So, 1978 shows up and my abee is called into action."

Aaron continued, "He had trained. He was a soldier. Had been a soldier longer than I had been alive. But he was also a true believer. They would name the mission he was on *Operation of the Martyr Kamal Adwan*, in honor of someone who died on an earlier mission, a mission from 1973. Looking back, I think my father knew he wasn't going to survive. I think he knew he was being deployed to a suicide mission. I think he saw it as his duty, and there wasn't anything that could prevent him from fulfilling his duty as a soldier, as a fighter for his country. I think he realized the minute the code name to the mission had the word 'Martyr' in it and had the name of someone, a soldier, who died. My abee wasn't stupid. He knew what was going to happen, what he was being asked to do."

"So that early March morning of 1978, my mother came into my room knowing it was the last day that I would see my father. I know now why she had that sadness in her eyes. She knew. He had already told her. She knew he was giving himself for something bigger, for a cause, for a purpose. She knew that's what he had been put on this Earth to do, to sacrifice himself for something bigger than himself. But it wasn't just my father's sacrifice. No, it was my mother's as well. She knew what he was preparing to do, and she let him do it. She didn't fight him. She's as big a hero as he is in all of this. That's why we were sent away. That's why we were protected after his mission. His name will live on in history, and so will mine. I will make her proud because people will remember my name. I will leave a mark on this country. I will make my abee proud and I will see him again one day."

I was beginning to understand the depth of Aaron's passion. I was beginning to understand why he felt like he did.

He continued, "So my abee spent the day with me, like I described to you. We went to the park and played football. We had lunch together. It was a wonderful, beautiful, perfect day. It was a day that I didn't understand when it was happening. I was simply happy to be out of school and with my father. I knew, even at such a young age, it was unusual to spend time out of school and I knew it was unusual to be with my dad. He was gone most of the time. So, we spent the entire day together, playing, eating treats, doing fun things. I realized later, what he was doing was leaving me with happy memories of him. That was his real gift to me. A perfect day with my abee. Perfect memories. That was the last time I ever saw him.

"Now, onto the mission and the events of the days leading up to my father's death. When I tell you this story it might not sound like much to you, but it was the first time something like this had been done in this part of the world and in this current conflict. It was monumental. It was a turning point. Since then, things have grown and strategies have changed, but at that time in history this was a revolutionary mission. You have to remember, we were at war—we're still at war—but this was a secret mission to disrupt a meeting between the leaders of the enemy's army, to take out the leadership, to effect change, forcibly. This was something daring, something that hadn't been done before. For the rest of this history, my father's story, I've only heard it from people who witnessed it, people who lived through it. And the story was told to me much, much later, in bits and pieces, when I was old enough to understand it all.

"The mission objectives were simple: The enemy had planned a strategy meeting of its leadership. In attendance were all of the highest-ranking officers and officials. My father's mission was to be a disruptive force to that conference. If they could eliminate enemy leaders, it would be an added bonus. My father, my *abee*, and twelve other soldiers, thirteen in total, set out on a freighter to get behind enemy lines. After hours of sailing, the thirteen soldiers boarded two Zodiac boats trying to make landfall under the cover of darkness. The freighter stayed in deep waters miles from the shore so as to avoid detection, but that left the team hours' worth of hard riding in the small boats. The waves were boisterous that evening. Before they reached the shore, one of the Zodiacs capsized in the rough seas. Two soldiers were killed. The remaining eleven made their way to shore, but the rough seas threw their timing and their location off. It was morning when they landed and forty miles off, to the north, of their intended destination.

"Once on the shore, the team had planned to blend in and make their way to the enemy's headquarters. However, they were seen, quite by accident, coming ashore and had to fight their way inland. They fought their way to a road where they were able to capture a small enemy transport. They all crammed inside until they were able to eventually capture an enemy bus. They began driving south along a coastal highway where they were able to capture a second bus. Don't ask me how they were able to capture one, let alone two buses full of enemy combatants, but they did. They began to wreak havoc as they drove toward their destination. The enemy knew they had made landfall, so the element of surprise was gone. They chose to be a disruptive force where they *were,* knowing they would never make the meeting of the generals.

"They killed scores of enemies and wounded twice as many more. They drove through town after town along that coastal road killing, throwing grenades, shooting, disrupting life the whole way. The enemy set up roadblocks in several different places, but the bus was able to break through. Eventually, the enemy was able to set up a roadblock and scattered nails on the road. The tires blew out and the bus came to a stop. My father's team was trapped on the bus. They didn't go out without a fight, though. When it was all said and done, nine of the remaining eleven team members died. The other two were captured and imprisoned. My father died that day, on that coastal road in an enemy's stolen bus.

"My father is still considered a hero. There are several roads named after him and even a primary school bears his name. He left his mark on this world and for his country. I will too. Mark my words."

I had planned to tell Aaron that I thought he was looking at his father's death wrong, that his perspective was off. After hearing the story, I decided I needed to process things. Maybe I needed to change *my* perspective.

With as much sincerity as I could, I said, "Aaron, that's an incredible thing your abee did, and he's left you a wonderful legacy. I see why you push yourself so hard and you're so driven. I want to tell you the first three words Jessica ever said to me all those years ago, and I hope that I will be able to prove them to you as we work your plan. Jessica's first three words were, 'You're not alone.' And, Aaron, you might feel all alone having lost your abee, or you might feel all alone because of the circumstances or the past couple days, the suspension and all, but you're not. You're not alone. I'm all in on your plan. Let's do it."

Chapter Twenty

Aaron's plan had been simple, and now that I was in the middle of it, I *knew* he was right when he said he didn't think I was going to like it. His plan meant I risked being captured by the mercenaries. I argued and pleaded, but in the end, he was right. This was the only way it would work. Only a few hours had passed since Aaron and I had escaped from Moho Magnetic Machines and the grasp of the mercenaries approaching the rear of the building. But now, here I was across the street, staring at the building once again, concealed from view by a large green dumpster in an alleyway. The activity in and around the building was minimal, which I guess was to be expected of a warehouse facility. It's not like they were in retail with people entering and leaving all day. There were only a handful of cars in the parking lot, which made it easier to keep an eye on things.

The plan was to kidnap Omar Abdul, take him back to our secret location and find out what he knew. Because Omar and I had already talked, I was to be the bait while Aaron did the grabbing. Our hope was to get him at lunchtime or after work on his way home. If he got in a car, I was to flag him down, get him to stop and Aaron would get in the car while Omar was distracted. If he walked someplace for lunch, I was to make contact and Aaron would approach from the rear. The biggest problem I had with both of these scenarios was that I had to give Aaron my gun. He couldn't coerce Omar to comply with demands without a weapon. Reluctantly, I handed over the firearm and now here I was, hoping an old, near-deaf man would leave for lunch so that I could play my part in his kidnapping. The waiting was the worst part. I thought a lot about Aaron and what he told me about his father.

Finally, at a little after 3 p.m., I saw Omar step from the front door of the building and make his way over to a little, four-door vehicle. The car was so small and so nondescript, it was virtually anonymous all by itself. The only thing that made it unique in any way was how dirty the thing was. It didn't look like it had ever been washed. Omar got in the car, backed out of the parking spot and made his way to the exit. As he pulled into the street, he made a left-hand turn, toward me, and I stepped out of my hiding spot. I raised my hand in a waving manner. Omar smiled and slowed down and rolled to a stop. I walked over to the passenger side window and Omar leaned across to manually crank the handle that lowered it so that we could speak. It couldn't have been more perfect. As he was leaning over, Aaron opened the rear driver's side door and sat down. I leaned into the open window and shouted, "We need to talk" and got in the car. Omar sat back up and saw Aaron, gun in hand, in his rearview mirror and nearly jumped out of his seat. He turned and looked at me with a look of horror on his face.

"Drive. We will show you where," Aaron said.

Nothing happened. We didn't move.

"Drive. We will show you where," I shouted again. Omar obviously hadn't heard Aaron the first time. I turned to Aaron and said, "I told you, he's pretty deaf. You will need to be very loud."

Omar drove the car as we shouted instructions to him. We made our way back to our hiding location and marched Omar inside to begin our interrogation.

Omar tried to ask questions along the way. He tried to explain things along the way. Every time he tried to speak, Aaron forcefully told him to keep his mouth shut. There would be plenty of time for talking in a few minutes. Finally, we made it back to our base of operations.

We led Omar around the corner, through the chain-link fence entrance and into the building. We marched him upstairs and found a chair for him to sit in. As he sat down, Aaron and I walked in front of him so that he could see our mouths. He needed to read our lips as we asked him questions. I looked him straight in the eye and started with the interrogation.

"Omar, you were telling me about seismic waves and MRI machines this morning. You said something about Russia, hydrogen molecules and radio frequencies. I would like for you to continue from that spot. Tell me about Jessica's machine and Russia. Keep it simple. Tell the truth, and we will let you out of here soon."

Omar nodded, and I noticed he was shaking almost uncontrollably. A part of me felt sorry for him, but if treating him this way led to getting Jessica back, it was worth it.

He began, "Your friend, Dr. Adams, is with—," but before he could finish the sentence, Aaron slapped him across the mouth, surprising the both of us.

Aaron said, "You answer only what we ask you. Nothing else. Tell us about the machine and Russia."

Omar wet himself.

It was an awful sight to see a man urinate on himself out of fear. Again, I said, almost pleading, "Omar, tell me about the machine and tell me about Russia. Keep it simple and on point."

"Yes. Simple. On point," Omar said.

It was like having clear instructions gave him some sort of stability.

"Jessica's machine, we call it the Genesis Machine, works like an MRI machine does at a hospital. One side shoots beams, like our flashlight, like waves, through a material and then the other side reads the resulting wavelengths. The difference in wavelengths shows that the beam went through different materials, and we can map those substances. Now, the complicated part." Omar began pleading, "Please don't hit me again, I'll make it as simple as possible."

I nodded to Omar and said, "Keep going."

He continued nervously, "The complicated part is that we are shooting strong magnetic frequencies that charge the hydrogen atoms, and then we use radio frequencies to read those resulting wavelengths. Like I said this morning, you don't really need to know how it works, just that we measure hydrogen atoms and their wavelengths. Here's the genius part: your friend, Jessica, Dr. Adams, discovered a way to use this MRI-like machine to harness the Earth's magnetic fields and use its hydrogen-rich core[55] to map the crust and mantle layers. Just like a ship pings through the water to try to locate a submarine, Jessica pinged through the Earth and then was able to actually *map* it. It's revolutionary. It's the biggest discovery in the last four hundred years, at least since Galileo."

I was not impressed. "All of this, the death, the destruction, the kidnapping, all of it because Jessica discovered a way to map the Earth's guts?"

Omar looked at Aaron, fearful, and then nodded, not daring to speak again.

Aaron said, "Tell us about Russia. Simple and on point."

Omar said, "Yes. Simple and on point. The two deepest holes that mankind has ever dug are over twelve kilometers deep, and they are both located in Russia.[56] [57] These are small boreholes deep into the Earth's crust. Realize, these boreholes are only a matter of inches across. Small, small diameter. As the scientific teams drilled, they collected samples of the materials they were passing through. We have a

55 "Hydrogen in the Earth's core—Water-rich birth of the Earth," *Tokyo Tech News*, November 20, 2014,
https://www.titech.ac.jp/english/news/2014/028845.html
56 Tom Levitt, "The $1 billion mission to reach the Earth's mantle," *CNN Business*, October 2, 2012, https://www.cnn.com/2012/10/01/tech/mantle-earth-drill-mission/index.html
57 Sebastian Anthony, "To the core: How can we travel to the center of the Earth?," *ExtremeTech*, August 4, 2014, https://www.extremetech.com/extreme/187291-to-the-core-how-can-we-travel-to-the-center-of-the-earth

perfectly accurate record of the different strata along the Earth's crust down to a depth of twelve kilometers. We went to Russia to test the Genesis Machine to see if the results we were getting actually matched what was below the Earth's surface. Was it working like we hypothesized it would, and if it was, could it give us data that could be verified by the collected results from the boreholes?"

"And did it?" Aaron asked.

Omar nodded, slowly, as a smile crossed his face. He was proud of their accomplishment. "And so much more. We pinged, and over the next several hours got results back. Our results matched exactly. Then we realized something else: we were able to map not only twelve kilometers down, but thousands of kilometers down. Farther than man has ever, or probably will ever, be able to dig. We were able to tell where the different materials began and ended, the different layers in the crust, mantle and even the Earth's core. We were able to tell between solid and liquid. We were even able to tell when there was a void in one of the layers, empty space."

Aaron followed up with, "If you have a machine and verifiable results, what are you building in the warehouse at your lab?"

Omar responded, "The hardware for bigger machines. The machine we took to Russia has an exceptionally small scanning diameter. Just like the borehole was small, only inches across, so was our MRI reading. It only mapped a very small sliver, barely inches across. That machine was practically handheld. We are building bigger machines, the hardware for them, at least, so that we can map much larger portions, much quicker. Dr. Adams controls the software to the programs."

Aaron's eyes lit up, like he was beginning to understand. There was a moment of recognition, like he was beginning to see the potential.

I asked, "So, why is this the biggest discovery in the last four hundred years? What makes this bigger than Galileo?"

Omar nodded; he was starting to relax a little. He was turning back into the teacher from earlier in the day. He said, "Do you remember what Galileo is known for?"

"The only thing I can remember about Galileo is that he did something with telescopes," I said.

"Yes, that is somewhat true." Omar said. "He worked with and modified telescopes and made many discoveries about our solar system. He found the moons of Jupiter and described in his writings the rugged lunar surface. What he is most famous for is proving or confirming heliocentrism. Heliocentrism puts the sun at the middle of the universe, not Earth. Until 1615, Europeans believed that God's creation, mankind, was at the center of the universe, here on Earth; that the Sun, stars, planets all orbited around us. Galileo proved otherwise. There was no doubt about it. He proved, through science and scientific methodology, that man wasn't at the center of the universe and the church declared war on him."

I guess Omar saw the confused look on my face and continued, "Four hundred years ago, the mindset was different than today. In the church's mind, they felt Galileo was asking the question, 'How could there even be a God, if man wasn't at the center of His universe?' Galileo never intended to do that. The church saw it as an all-or-nothing proposition. So, the church declared war on Galileo, and in doing so, the church effectively declared war on science as well. The pushback was immediate, and science has been fighting back, with a vengeance, ever since. Why do you think most scientists are atheists?"

Confused, I asked, "How does the church declare war on someone?"

"Galileo published a paper in which he promoted heliocentrism—the theory that the Earth and other planets revolve around the sun. This was the time of the Inquisition, and the Inquisition declared that heliocentrism was officially heretical. Heliocentric books were banned, and Galileo was ordered to refrain from holding, teaching, or defending heliocentric ideas. In 1632 Galileo, now an old man, published another paper which implicitly defended heliocentrism, and it was immensely popular among the intellectuals. Responding to mounting controversy over theology, astronomy and philosophy, the Roman Inquisition put Galileo on trial and in 1633 they found him guilty of heresy, sentencing him to indefinite imprisonment. Galileo was kept under house arrest until his death in 1642.[58] *That's* how the church declares war on someone."

Aaron interrupted, "Enough with the history lesson. Why is this the biggest discovery in four centuries?"

Omar, visibly shrinking in his seat said, "Oh, I haven't gotten to that part yet. I'm sorry. I'm sorry. I got distracted. This is the biggest discovery because of what we found next. Our next test was to ping at a place in the undersea mountains of the Indian Ocean. The place where we went is called Atlantis Bank. This is where Henry Dick has been drilling since the mid-1980s,[59] and so we were able to tag along with his research and drilling team. We were blessed. Where we pinged, we got some curious readings. After we returned home, Dr. Adams spent months analyzing the test result data. Finally, the day came when Dr. Adams announced to the team that she believed she had discovered something amazing. She brought us all together, everyone she had been working with, which meant I was also invited. Jessica told us she believed she had found one place where the 'fountains of the deep originated,' and she was convinced she could find many more."

Aaron and I looked at each other and then back at Omar, confused.

"What are you talking about, 'fountains of the deep?'" Aaron hissed.

Omar turned his face and squinted his eyes, waiting for the slap or punch that never materialized.

After a moment, realizing he wasn't going to be hit again, he continued, "In Genesis, the first book of the Torah and in the Christian Bible, there is an account of a righteous man and his family. He is even

---

58 "Galileo Affair," *Wikipedia*, https://en.wikipedia.org/wiki/Galileo_affair
59 Gwendolyn Schanker, "The Quest for the Moho: Between Earth's crust and mantle lies a mysterious boundary," *Oceanus Magazine*, August 8, 2016, https://www.whoi.edu/oceanus/feature/the-quest-for-the-moho

mentioned in the Koran. In the Torah, Koran, and Biblical accounts, his name is Noah and he is remembered for surviving an Earth-encompassing flood. In actuality, there are several other accounts of a global flood, in just about every historic civilization, from the Chinese to the Native Americans. You've probably heard about the *Epic of Gilgamesh*, but there are others."

Omar started veering off course, taking an unnecessary rabbit-trail. "The ancient Chinese lettering has its roots in the flood story. There's a wonderful book called *The Discovery of Genesis,* by C.H. Kang and Ethel Nelson, that you could read if you were interested. There's another book called *After the Flood* by Bill Cooper, where he traces man's roots back to Noah. There are others if…"

"What in the world are you talking about?" I asked, interrupting his thought.

Aaron finally put a stop to the rabbit-trail that Omar had followed. "Enough!" He shouted. "What about the 'fountains of the deep?' What did she find?"

Again, visibly shaking in fear, Omar replied, "There are lots of descriptions of a worldwide flood, but Jessica, as a Christian, always referenced the *Biblical* account of the flood, and she always quoted from the King James Translation. She told us all, each at different points, about the validity of that translation, of how the Puritans and the Anglican bishops had come together under the mandate of King James, to produce a translation of the Bible that was an accurate translation, one without bias. Because of the checks and balances that King James put in place, one of the purest, most accurate translations had been created. Whenever she would talk about it, it was always so boring to me and most of my team, but she was so passionate that we just let her talk."

Aaron made his way to Omar and raised his hand like he was about to slap him again.

"No, no, no. Wait! The King James Version of the Biblical account uses a phrase to explain how the flood occurred," Omar stammered. "It states, 'In the six hundredth year of Noah's life, in the second month, the seventeenth day of the month, the same day were all the *fountains of the great deep broken up,* and the windows of heaven were opened.'[60] See, Dr. Adams believed that the global flood had *actually occurred.* In our mapping of the Earth's crust and mantle in Russia, she found *layers* of water, different bands at different depths in liquid states, miles thick beneath the Earth's surface. Then in the Indian Ocean, she found one of the places where the great deep was broken up. She had found a place where water had escaped from the Earth's mantle and either began or added to a global flood. She had found a way to verify what the Bible said was true. Science was confirming the Bible. Possibly, the war between the two has finally been won."

I stood there with my mouth wide open. Everything that Jessica had said preparing for her speech, everything Nuria had told me while I was at the lab and everything Omar had told us all lined up, perfectly. It was all clear, moving from one point to the next point to the next point.

Finally, able to regain some of my composure, I said, "Omar, you have said several times that at your workshop, you are making the hardware for the machines to do this mapping. What about the software? Do you have anything to do with that?"

Omar shook his head. "No, Dr. Adams and her assistant, they are the only ones who know about the software. The assistant, her name is Nuria Melamed, is a software program engineer, and the two of them built the program so that you need a set of keys to use the machines. My machines are useless without Dr. Adams' software and the software is useless without the keys. It was the way that Dr. Adams kept anyone from stealing her research. The software can only be accessed from her laptop, and it can only be accessed with the keys. I don't even know what the keys are. I've just heard the ladies mention them."

I turned to Aaron and said, "Well, now we know why she has been kidnapped, to get her keys. I asked Nuria about the keys when I was

---

60 Genesis 7:11

there, but she played it off, gave me a wild goose chase to follow and didn't tell me. I guess she didn't know me well enough or didn't feel comfortable telling me about the keys they designed. It makes sense, but it sure would have made things easier knowing Jessica was kidnapped for those keys."

Aaron nodded and Omar said, "But Matt, she hasn't—" But that was all he got out before Aaron slapped him again, the echo ringing through the cavernous space.

Aaron seethed. "Don't say anything unless you're told to. I thought you understood that. Now, tell us about the device to harness the Earth's geothermal energy."

Omar, still woozy from the thunderous slap, said, "I'm sorry. I don't know what you're talking about," and started crying, fearful of more pain.

It was quiet for a moment as Aaron and I pondered if Omar was holding out on us. Was this his way to keep the *real* discovery, the discovery of a way to harness the Earth's geothermal energy, to himself?

In that quiet moment, that's when we heard the noises.

I froze. Motionless, I looked at Aaron who was already holding his index finger up in front of his mouth giving the universal *"shh"* sign, and he already had his gun pulled from his waistband. Omar was smart enough to keep his mouth shut.

Aaron ran, quietly, in the direction of the sound. He looked out of the window and came charging back to me, shouting, "Time to go. The mercenaries are here and are about to breach the building."

Then, pointing at Omar, he said, "He must be wearing a tracker. We've got to get to the airport."

Aaron was running and grabbing my arm, screaming, "We've got to keep you safe, Matt. You're the most important piece to this puzzle now. *Move! Come on! Let's go!*" Pulling me as he went.

Chapter Twenty-One

The mercenaries must have learned from their previous attempt to apprehend me at Moho Magnetic Machines earlier in the day. This time, they had the building surrounded.

Everything happened in a blur. Aaron and I were running at top speed along the catwalk. There was a loud explosion that I felt and heard, much more than I saw. It boomed across the gaping expanse of space. It shook my insides and knocked me off balance. I grabbed the handrail, trying to keep from falling. My ears rang and I was blinded for a split second. Looking down, I saw the mercenaries entering the building from multiple points.

What I thought was a singular explosion was actually a coordinated set of synchronized blasts as all the different exit doors were breached in unison. The doors were big, heavyset things made of iron, and the explosive charge that the mercenaries used to breach each one of them must have been an incredibly large load.

I realized that a breach in real life is nothing like what the movies or television portray. In the movies, the door blows, and all the men come rushing in, each sweeping a portion of the room, killing enemy agents in a frenzied chaos of gunfire. No one ever misses. In actuality, a breach is much more controlled than that. The door is blasted open and one man goes in. Moments later a second enters. Moments later, a third. This makes sense, so that if an enemy combatant is set up and aiming at the doorway, not everyone gets shot at the same time as they rush into the room. I was watching this transpire through multiple doorways below me as the mercenaries entered the facility.

There was an immense amount of dust, dirt and grime in the empty space. The explosion produced an incredible amount of debris that almost instantly obstructed the view from our position. It also created enough of a smokescreen for Aaron and me to run, unseen.

I started down the stairway and Aaron grabbed me, stopping me from descending.

"Quiet now," he whispered. "Come this way." And he led me to the door I had seen earlier. That door led to the place where an elevated bridge had once been. Now, all that was left was debris and a ladder that someone hastily laid across the empty void, connecting the two buildings. As quickly and as quietly as we could, we made our way across the ladder bridge and into the next building. Aaron quietly pulled the ladder to our side of the bridge, effectively eliminating the bridge or the evidence there had ever been a bridge in the first place.

In their haste to execute a successful assault, the mercenaries obviously only had minimal planning time. They must not have noticed the ladder connecting the two buildings, or they would have had a contingency plan. Aaron and I made our way through the neighboring building and down the stairs, far away from the watchful eyes of the mercenaries. We sprinted away from the building and the imminent threat. I had not been in this direction, so I was trying to follow Aaron as he weaved through the tight city streets.

I could feel my heart beating in my chest as we ran hard for another few blocks, knowing that the mercenaries wouldn't give up their search without being as thorough as possible. We also knew they would try to maintain a level of covertness to their operation. They couldn't go running through the streets of Israel waving submachine guns and go unnoticed. After a few minutes of running, things started to look vaguely familiar.

Breathlessly, I got Aaron's attention. "Wait, wait. I know where we are. Come this way." He was not happy having to stop and change directions.

"Where are we going?" he whispered.

Still running, I said, "It's just… it's just… here!" Somehow, miraculously, we had run back to where I had parked our stolen SUV, the one I had stolen from Aaron earlier in the morning. It was still sitting in the same location, parallel parked on the street where I had left it when I went to Moho Magnetic Machines.

Aaron shouted, "You drive! I've got calls to make. I'll show you where to go."

I jumped behind the wheel as Aaron slid into the passenger side. He was pulling out his phone when he saw me fumbling to try and get the engine started.

Frustrated, he said, "Out of the way" and grabbed the wires. Reaching across the vehicle, he was finally able to get the little SUV started. He said, "We need to turn around and head the other way. Do it as naturally as possible. Then, when we're driving, don't do anything crazy. Just take your time. If you see them, just drive normally. Don't even look at them. Hopefully, they won't think to look for us in a vehicle."

Aaron dialed a number on his phone and in a moment, he was speaking to someone, in another language, barking orders. Whoever he was speaking with must have been a subordinate because it didn't sound like Aaron was taking *no* for an answer. Occasionally, he would point in a direction, wanting me to turn or change lanes. The drive took the better part of an hour, through the city. We could have been driving in circles; I couldn't tell. All I knew was Aaron was on the phone almost the entire time.

At one point, Aaron finished a call and sat back, relaxing for a moment. He said, "Everything should be arranged by the time we get there."

"Where are we going? What's the plan?"

"Yeah, look, Matt. Right now, you're the most important piece to the puzzle."

I interrupted, "You said that a little while ago. What does that even mean, and where are we going?"

Aaron continued, "You're the most important piece to the puzzle because you have the key. The mercenaries, the energy consortium, the competitors, whoever they are, they can't access the information on the computer without the key, without you. We need to get you to safety. We need to get you to some place of strength. We need to get you to a place where the mercenaries can't touch you. Once we do that, we can make a trade of some kind. We are headed to the airport to get you out of here. Do you have any idea what the key is? Did Jessica give you something?"

I nodded.

"What did she give you, and when did she give it to you? Have you seen her?"

I remained silent for a long moment.

"Well?"

"She gave me her cell phone the night she was kidnapped. She didn't have any pockets in her gown, and asked me to carry all of her stuff, including her cell phone."

Aaron asked, "And you still have it?"

I again nodded. For some reason, I felt ashamed—either for hiding the information from Aaron for so long or because I was now revealing it to him, effectively betraying Jessica's trust and doing what she told me not to. I couldn't tell.

Finally, we made our way to the airport, or more specifically, we made our way to the smallest airport I had ever seen in my life. It only had one landing strip and a few small hangars. As we approached, I could see several single engine airplanes sitting unattended and a couple helicopters as well. Aaron, again on the phone, pointed out to me where the entrance to the airport was and instructed me to find hangar number three. Everything was written in Hebrew and it was getting dark, so it took me a minute, a frustrating minute, to find the correct place. We drove the little SUV directly inside the hangar and out of view.

What I saw inside the hangar took my breath away.

Chapter Twenty-Two

Since the battle at the airport yesterday, I had felt alone, with only moments of cautious relaxation. Most of the time since that gun-fight, I have *been* alone. I have been dodging bullets, escaping the grip of the mercenaries, basically running for my life. There have only been a few moments that I have had a feeling of relative safety: when Aaron saved me from the mercenaries at Dr. Kaplan's house or when I was in the grimy hotel, locked in my room, alone. I felt safe. But those moments were few and far between. For most of the time since Jessica was kidnapped, I had been on high alert. All of that changed the moment I drove that stolen SUV into hangar number three at the world's tiniest airport.

What I saw inside the hangar was a small army. They were dressed in tactical gear, but not in tactical dress. In other words, they were dressed like everyday citizens except they were carrying machine guns, grenades and different types of armament. It was like Aaron had called his office and all of the agents had dropped whatever they were working on and were now here, to defend me.

As we were pulling to a stop, Aaron said, "Everything will happen quickly because we are trying to get you out of here. We have several missions culminating right here, right now. This has become the de facto staging ground. You and I won't be staying. We will get on a plane with a pilot and leave the country, eventually making our way back to the United States. Once we are safely off the ground, a helicopter team will be sent to Dr. Adams' lab to retrieve her research—they are going to secure her laptop and bring it to us. Now, most of the agents here won't speak English, but it won't matter. We won't be here long, and we won't be talking much."

Just as we exited the SUV, a woman walked up carrying a backpack and tossed it to me. It was heavy and had cords and handles on it. She said, "Mizala"[61] and pantomimed pulling a cord from across her chest and a parachute opening.

I nodded, put the backpack on and secured it with clips in the front, across my chest, and said, "Simple enough." She must not have spoken English because she just shrugged and walked away, on to her next task.

Aaron and several of the agents began, almost immediately, an animated conversation in another language. They were pointing to things, at each other, in my direction, in the direction of the airfield. There was a lot of hand movements and shrugging of shoulders. I didn't understand any of it, but I was engrossed in the dynamic of the conference. Aaron was directing the conversation, explaining or pleading or commanding, I couldn't tell. I was so involved in watching that conversation, I didn't notice the little canister roll into the hangar behind me.

That little canister was what is commonly known as a stun grenade, a flash grenade or a "flashbang." I like the flashbang name the best because it accurately describes what the small grenade does. It isn't meant to do harm, but to impair. When it explodes, the grenade, the flashbang sparks a brilliantly sharp light, temporarily blinding anyone who has their eyes open. That's the "flash" part of the flashbang. The blindness lasts for approximately five seconds. The second part of the flashbang is the "bang," a loud concussive explosion that dazes by causing hearing loss and disturbing the fluid inside the ear, which causes loss of balance and in my case, utter disorientation.

The mercenaries had found us and were beginning their assault.

---

61 Arabic for "parachute"

Maybe it was my lack of training. Maybe it was because I had never experienced a flashbang before. Maybe it was dumb luck at how close to the explosion I had been. Had I not been knocked unconscious, I might have stood there when the assault began. Whatever the case, when I came to my senses, I was lying on the floor away from the activity, and there was a gun battle raging all around me. The mercenaries had entered the hangar after the effects of the flashbang took hold. There were dozens of them already in the hangar. I couldn't hear anything but an intense, high-pitched ringing in my ears, but I could tell that the battle was extreme by the number of shots being fired; I could tell by the small flaming explosions expelled from the gun muzzles with each shot and the number of mercenaries and Mossad agents already lying on the floor, either injured or dead.

I slithered to a covered position behind the SUV and saw Aaron. He was engaging the enemy and tried to communicate with me. I couldn't hear anything he was saying. I tried telling him that, shouting, but I didn't think he could hear anything I was saying.

Aaron looked at me and then, like we were playing charades, mimicked his plan. He pointed to me and to himself and then he used two fingers like he was walking. I nodded understanding that he wanted the two of us to walk or better yet, *run* somewhere. Then he pointed to a side door that was less than ten feet from where I was hiding. Again, I nodded. Then he made a motion like he was flying. I understood; we are going to run to that door, get in the airplane and takeoff. Nodding at each other, Aaron counted down on his fingers, 3, 2, 1 and we started running. Somehow miraculously, we made it to the door.

Running out of the door at a full sprint, we made our way toward a small, single propeller airplane. The pilot was already on board and had the engine coughing to life. My hearing was beginning to return to me, and I could hear the little engine begin to cough to life. I didn't know if there was going to be enough room for the three of us to fit in the little plane's cabin, but before we even made it there, a streak of howling smoke washed passed us and the airplane burst into flames. Somehow from somewhere, one of the mercenaries must have shot it with something, a rocket propelled grenade possibly, causing it to erupt in front of us. There was no saving the plane or the pilot.

Aaron never broke stride. He diverted to the left of the flame ravaged little aircraft, which took us further from the mercenaries' stronghold, toward a waiting helicopter.

The helicopter was a dark color and at first, I didn't even see it. We jumped on board and Aaron and I tried to find a place to sit. The cockpit was big, and a bench seat separated the front from the open back, but the rear of the chopper was full of big plastic crates. We had to shift things around to be able to sit.

Aaron shouted, "Be very careful with these. They go boom!" It was incredibly hard to hear anything he was saying over the roar of the engine and the ringing in my ears.

The blades of the helicopter began whirring faster and faster. Wind whipped us in the cabin and the pilot cautiously took off. Because it was a helicopter, I was expecting to go straight up, vertical, and away from the danger, but that's not what happened. The helicopter pilot lifted off, just feet above the ground, and like he was getting a running start, flew horizontally down the runway, before lifting off, up and into the air.

As this was happening, Aaron handed me some headphones and I put them on. He took another set and put them on. I could see his lips moving; he was trying to speak to me, but there wasn't any sound. He must not have had any sound either as I tried to communicate with him. We couldn't have been more than ten to fifteen feet in the air as Aaron and I began trying to fix our headphones. The pilot was speaking but Aaron and I couldn't hear him either, but he didn't know it. So, Aaron leaned over the front row of seats, adjusting some dial, trying to get a signal so we could all communicate. I noticed he had placed his gun in the rear of his waistband. Again, I had the negative nudge, but it was overpowering me at this point.

"Action. Take action. *Take action!*" The still, small voice was screaming to me.

That's God speaking to me! I know it. What does He mean, "Take action!"?

The pilot spoke and my headphone crackled with life, "As-salam alaykom."

"*Do it!*" I again heard on the inside, only now I knew what I was supposed to do.

I grabbed the gun from Aaron's waistband and turned it on him. Aaron froze. I had only been in this country a couple of days, but I knew that "as-salam alaykom" was not Hebrew. That was an Arabic or better yet, a Muslim greeting and not something two Mossad agents would ever say to one another.

I said, through the headphones, "You're not Mossad, are you?"

Aaron smiled, a devilish, evil smile, and started to move back toward me.

"Don't move, or I will shoot you. Just answer my question."

In a flash, a split second, Aaron shifted his weight back from leaning over the front row of seats and landed directly next to me. His right hand grabbed the gun while his left hand raised to strike at me and then the unthinkable happened. The gun fired.

Aaron's hand was injured, and he howled in pain, but the real shock came from the helicopter itself as it banked at an incredible angle. Alarms began blaring. Deafening sounds as gears wrenched. I looked up and saw that the pilot had been shot, and no one was flying the helicopter. I had the gun in my hand, I had a parachute on and that *still, small voice* said…

"*Jump!*"

…and out the door I went.

Chapter Twenty-Three

My eyes explode open.

It's an unusual feeling, like being torn from a lifelong coma.

My ears are ringing, and my head is pounding, and I have no idea why. Desperate to figure out where I am and what's going on, I try to look at my surroundings, but the pain is unbearable. I gasp as each shift of my weight, each movement, is torture to my body. All I know is that I have to keep going; I must save her. Three words keep running through my mind, relentless, nonstop, pounding like a heartbeat. *You're not alone. You're not alone. You're not alone. You're not alone.*

My face is pressed into sun-bleached pavement. It's a colorless grey and warm to the touch. I can smell dirt and exhaust fumes. Shifting my weight again, trying to roll over, every muscle groans and spasms. I'm stiff from physical exertion, bruises cover my body, and for some reason, there is blood all over me.

I must save… her.

I am finally able to turn to see the sun, hanging low and still in the sky. It's either early morning or very late afternoon, I can't tell which. The air is dry and crisp with no hint of moisture. There is something familiar yet unusual in the air. Sirens are wailing in the distance, an alarm clock call to my stiff, tired body.

You're not alone. You're not alone. You're not alone. You're not alone.

Slowly, I press up onto my hands and knees. The pain takes my breath away. I'm forced to stay in that position to regain my strength, my composure. Each breath in and out feels like it takes hours to inhale and expel. There is no traffic on the street, but I know I need to get out of the road, so I press up to one knee and see more of my surroundings.

On either side of the street, cars line the curb, parked close to one another, bumper to bumper. City parking. Past the cars, there are two-story buildings as far as I can see, framing the street. The bottom levels are littered with shops, not yet open or closed for the evening. The glass windows are barred shut, and there are colorful signs in an unknown language.

The signs hang perpendicular to the buildings, over the sidewalks. The sidewalks act as a boundary to the cars, keeping them several feet from the buildings. The language on the signs isn't English. I can't read it. It's Hebrew or Arabic, unfamiliar. I must be in the Middle East, Egypt, Israel, Sudan, or Iran. This doesn't surprise me and, incredibly, it doesn't scare me.

I'm different now.

You're not alone. You're not alone. You're not alone. You're not alone.

I flex my fingers, roll my wrists and extend my elbows. Nothing seems to be broken or dislocated, so I stand. The pain is excruciating. Immediately, I am supporting my weight, my hands on my knees.

Something in the air reminds me of camping as a kid. S'mores... Stories around the campfire... Smoke... Smoke is in the air! A heavy smell of smoke. Something is burning. The sirens are louder now, closer.

You're not alone. You're not alone. You're not alone. You're not alone.

The city is waking up.

Like me.

I step a few feet toward one of the cars parked along the street, a heavily dented machine, and place my hand on its roof for balance. There is a metallic clunk as my hand touches down. Gripped in my palm is a gun, a Smith & Wesson 1911, .45-caliber automatic.

A feeling washes over me, a knowing. A still, small voice. *I am alive. I am ready. No matter what comes at me, there is no weapon, no enemy, formed against me that can prosper against me.*[62] *Nothing can stand in my way. I am undefeated. I am more than a conqueror.*[63] *I choose to win. I choose to...fight.*

"Heavenly Father, thank You for Your faithfulness. I'm praying now to ask You for Your wisdom and strength. You have not given me a spirit of fear, but of power, love, and You've given me a sound mind.[64] Lead me. Empower me. Give me the strength of Samson and the wisdom of Solomon. Teach my hands to war.[65] In the mighty name of Jesus. Amen."

You're not alone. You're not alone. You're not alone. You're not alone.

A knowing. Somehow, I know to check my pockets. There, I find a couple of cell phones with no power and broken screens, a visitor's pass to somewhere, two wallets—a woman's small wallet and mine, and incredibly, I see that I am also holding a tube of lipstick. I notice my shoulders feel heavy, weighed down, and I realize I am wearing a bulky backpack on my shoulders. It's clipped securely across the front of my chest.

The black smoke billows. It's incredibly close. Something is burning. The sirens scream, incessantly and loud. They are close.

People start spilling from the buildings and into the streets, families, men, women, children. Not American. Not Caucasian. Not happy. I begin to realize I am the cause of all of this.

You're not alone. You're not alone. You're not alone. You're not alone.

Panicked screams fill the air. English screams. A woman's screams. I see her now, running toward me from the opposite direction of the smoke.

---

62 Isaiah 54:17
63 Romans 8:37
64 2 Timothy 1:7
65 Psalm 144:1

"Matt! Matt! Maaaaaaaaaaaaaatt!"

The most incredibly beautiful woman I have ever seen is running toward me screaming my name.

Matt, yes, my name is Matt and her name is Jessica.

I remember it all.

Chapter Twenty-Four

The expression on Jessica's face said it all.

"Matt, are you okay? Are you hurt? Talk to me, please talk to me!" she said breathlessly as she ran closer to me.

Jessica had seen me jump from the helicopter; she just didn't know it was me. She watched a body, a man, me, fall, watching in horror, until she lost sight of me as I landed on the top of a building. She regained her view as my momentum carried me over the ledge. Falling again, I hit one of the shop signs attached to the building, which broke free, and then I seemingly came to rest on the hood of a car. At some point, I rolled off the heavily dented vehicle and into the street.

I stood there just looking at her, a sight more beautiful than any I had ever seen.

Cautiously she smiled, not knowing if I was injured, and very slowly said, "Matt, do you know where you are? Do you know who I am?" and then, "Do you even know who you are?"

"Davenport, Matthew Davenport," I said, in my best James Bond voice. I put my arm around her waist and pulled her tight. Her eyes got big and she started smiling, and then I planted the most passionate kiss on her lips that mankind has ever seen.

The world went silent.

The people milling in the street disappeared.

The smell of smoke was gone.

There were only two people on the planet at that moment, and they were locked in an unbreakable embrace. The world has never known passion like that.

As I came to my senses, realizing what I was doing, I slowly released the kiss and loosened the embrace and I whispered, "I've been waiting my whole life to do that to you."

Slowly, the sights and sounds around us came back in to focus, but it was different than before somehow. The siren's screams were less abrasive. The people looked less dangerous. The bruises hurt less, and I knew, I just knew, *I'm not alone. I'll never be alone. Never again.*

"Your *whole* life? You *waited* your *whole* life to kiss me? Well, what took you so long?" Jessica asked with a relieved giggle.

"In my defense, I've been chasing you for two days!" I said with a smile and kissed her again. "I'm so glad I found you. I never want to let you go. I never want to be further away from you than I am right now, right this instant." And then the weight of everything came crashing down around me and I asked, "Can you please explain *exactly* what is going on?"

"Yes, come with me," she said as she took my hand and slowly led me back to a black Range Rover parked a few hundred yards from where we were standing. She walked slowly because of the limp I had acquired somehow in the midst of the fall.

We crawled in the truck, and I unclipped the harness from across my chest and pulled the backpack, the unused parachute, off my shoulders and set it in my lap.

Jessica shot a confused look at the backpack and I said, "It's a parachute."

"I can see that! Why in the world didn't you use it?" she asked.

"I jumped from the helicopter and had my hand on the cord. I wasn't extremely high and didn't know if the chute would even work. Then, on the inside, I just knew. *'Don't pull the cord.'*"

"You just knew?" Jessica asked.

"Yes, the Lord told me, don't pull the cord. I can't explain why or really even how He did it. The Lord's been helping me this whole time and I knew He wouldn't let me down. Do you understand what I just said? God has been talking to me!"

"Matt, that is amazing! See? God really does want to have a relationship with you. And he obviously has been taking care of you. It is a miracle you survived that fall. You landed at the exact right place, or it would have been a lot worse. We need to get you to a hospital, right now. Who knows how many bones are broken? You look like you were hit by a freight train, dragged for miles and then tossed into a blender for good measure!"

Jessica took her right hand off the gearshift of the idling Range Rover and lightly placed it on my left thigh. We had spent enough time together over the years and we had done enough Bible studies together that I had a feeling of what was about to happen.

She said, "Matt, you know this, but let me refresh your memory. The Bible says that faith comes by hearing and hearing the Word of God.[66] So, let me speak some of God's Word to you. You've listened to Him and have kept God's Word's in your heart. They are life to you and health to your flesh.[67] You did your part, and now you're entitled to *life and health* to your body! Jesus was wounded for our transgressions, *He* was *bruised* for our iniquities and with His stripes we are healed.[68] [69] Jesus told us to lay our hands on those who need healing, to pray for them and they will recover.[70] Matt, Jesus was already bruised for you and He instructed me to pray for you."

Jessica closed her eyes and I did the same. She began praying. "Father in Heaven, Lord of my heart, thank You that hear us when we pray

---

66 Romans 10:17
67 Proverbs 4:20–22
68 Isaiah 53:5
69 I Peter 2:24
70 Mark 16:18

because we're praying according to Your will.[71] You told us in the book of Philippians to make our requests known to You,[72] and You also said that if two of us shall agree on Earth as touching anything that they shall ask, it shall be done for them of my Father which is in Heaven.[73] Matt and I agree and ask; we make our request known now for his healing. I am laying my hands on him and we believe for a quick, supernatural recovery for his body. We thank You that You hear us, and You're working to effect a healing and a cure to him now. In Jesus' Name we pray.[74] Amen."

"Thank you, Jessica. And amen. I agree."

Suddenly, there was something scratching at the back of my brain, something bothering me. "There's something else," I said. "There's another piece of this puzzle… Oh, no! *Drive!* Drive, drive, drive! Back to your lab! Go!" I shouted. It even hurt my ears in the confines of the truck.

Alarmed, startled, almost panicked Jessica asked, "Why, Matt? What's going on?"

"Aaron or Omar—or whatever his name is—is on the way to your lab to steal your research, your laptop. We have to get there first. At this point, he may or may not be the one actually going, but he told me they were going to your lab to get your research. They are going to take your laptop," I said as Jessica put the truck in gear.

"Wait," Jessica said, "Do you still have my stuff? Or did they get it from you?"

I reached in my pocket, squirming to get my hands around the contents and pulled out her half-destroyed phone, her wallet and her small tube of lipstick and said, "I'm the pockets." We both laughed. Jessica

---

71 I John 5:14
72 Philippians 4:6
73 Matthew 18:19
74 John 16:26

breathed a sigh of relief. In the back of my brain, something *clicked…* the key. I still had her phone; therefore, I still had the key.

It felt good to be with Jessica again, but I still didn't know what this was all about.

"Jess, I'm so lost. What's going on? Start with how you even got here, to the airport," I asked.

Jessica said, "My friend, Omar Abdul, the man who has been building all of my machines, the one you guys grabbed today, he told us where you were headed. He's super hard of hearing, but someone shouted something about an airport. There were only a couple of options, so we had a general idea of where to look for you."

I pleaded, "Okay. Now, from the beginning, please tell me what's going on."

The wheels screeched as she did a one-eighty in the street to go back the way she had come. Jessica started, "Two nights ago you were kidnapped."

I interrupted "No, two nights ago *you* were kidnapped."

Jessica smiled. "Two nights ago, *we* were kidnapped by a man named Omar Khalid. He was the one who posed as our driver. When the real driver, a driver from the Mossad unit assigned to protect me, showed up and we were gone, they scrambled. The Mossad are the ones who slammed into our Escalade and took me, but they didn't realize that you were with me, that you were my date. With Dr. Kaplan not attending as my 'plus one,' they thought I would be alone. They just thought you were part of the kidnap team. It's a good thing you didn't try and stop them. They probably would have killed you. It wasn't until we were in flight, headed to Israel, that I finally regained my composure from the accident—I hit my head and had a slight concussion—that I told them you were in the car with me."

I asked, "As they were putting you in the Humvee, you screamed 'Eli.' What was that about if you weren't telling me where to go?"

"Oh, Eli, Dr. Kaplan was in the Humvee. I don't remember screaming that, but I guess it just surprised me to see him there. It was a good thing he was in the truck or I would have fought much harder. It turns out that Dr. Kaplan has been working with the Mossad, behind the scenes the entire time, since we began this research or maybe even before then. I didn't even know about it. I still don't know the exact details of their relationship."

Jessica was driving fast, through the outskirts of the city. My guess was that soon enough we would hit traffic, and she was trying to gain as much ground as quickly as possible before that time.

Confused, I asked, "So the Mossad agents had *you*. Who have *I* been with this whole time? Who is this Omar Khalid guy? What he told me was that he had used the name Omar as a cover story and that his real name was Aaron. He told me *he* was with the Mossad."

"Matt, you are so lucky to be alive," Jessica said.

"It's not luck. I serve the living God, and He has given His angels charge over me and they keep me in all my ways!"[75] I said.

"Amen! Preach it!" Jessica said. "Your angels kept you from harm in a *big* way. It turns out that this Omar Khalid character is a bad dude, worse than bad, bad. He's on the FBI's top ten most wanted list, and the Mossad has been after him for years. He is connected to all the wrong people. He comes from a long line of bad people. Terrorist people, Matt."

We were coming back into the city and the traffic was thicker here. We were still making decent progress as we were going in the opposite direction of the evening flow.

"So, what is he—or what are *they*—after? I have heard two different stories about why you were kidnapped. One story had you pinging in Russia, and one had to do with vertical cracks in the mantle and geothermal energy."

---

75 Psalm 91:11

171

Jessica shot me a look that I don't think I had ever seen her make before. It was a look of total confusion. "Two stories? Geothermal energy? What are you talking about?"

"One story said that you had designed software and a machine that could ping through the Earth's crust and mantle and down through all the layers, mapping it to the Earth's core." Jessica nodded, following along. I continued, "The other story I was told was that you have designed a way to locate vertical cracks in the crust and mantle and have figured out a way to harness the energy created at the Earth's core. This whole escapade, the kidnapping, killing, everything makes more sense if you've found a way to tap this energy source because of the money at stake, the world's economy, all that. So, have you figured out how to do it? Have you really designed a machine to harness the Earth's geothermal energy?" I asked.

"I designed a machine that maps the Earth's crust and mantle down to the core. It maps the Earth's subsurface. It also can locate vertical cracks in the crust and mantle; in fact, it has already. It's a new technology, but there's nothing about geothermal energy with it. It will have lasting effects in the scientific community, but nothing to affect the world's economy. And to be totally honest with you, I have no idea why anyone, Mossad or terrorists, would want my technology or my machines. I really don't know. Maybe Dr. Kaplan will be able to explain it."

I said, "Maybe Aaron, I mean Omar, has gotten bad information. He has been talking about this geothermal energy thing, and that's what he's been after this whole time. He told me about it on the first morning we were together, in the airplane, and then even today, he slapped the good Omar around a few hours ago, trying to get information about it, about your geothermal harnessing machine. Maybe he wanted the machine and the profits from it to fund his terror plans or something?"

Jessica replied, "I don't know. I don't know how anyone would make any profit from my information. Maybe it was just part of a cover story, Matt."

"Okay, fine. But why are they after your technology then? Why has Dr. Kaplan been in touch with the Mossad ever since you started this project? If it's just subsurface mapping technology, what am I missing? This still feels kind of wrong."

"I don't know, Matt. I don't know. We'll ask Dr. Kaplan after we get my research."

"Okay. For now, forget the why. So, what you're telling me is, this whole time, I've been chasing you and you've been chasing me?" I asked.

Jessica nodded, "If we're being technical, you and Omar have been chasing me, and the Mossad agents have been chasing you and Omar. And I've been *so close* to you so many times today."

"What are you talking about?" I asked.

We were coming to places that she was more familiar with, and Jessica was weaving in and out on city streets.

"Today, you showed up at Moho Magnetic Machines and 'my' Omar let us know. The team of Mossad agents showed up shortly after, in an attempt to get you and possibly grab the bad Omar."

"Yeah, I saw them coming on the security monitor on Omar's desk and we bolted."

"I know. I was there," Jess said. "And then, after you grabbed 'my' Omar, the Mossad agents went complete *Call of Duty* on the warehouse where you were hiding, a coordinated breach. But when the dust settled, the only person there was 'my' Omar. How did you guys get away?"

"We were upstairs and there was a place where an elevated bridge had once been. Someone had placed a ladder across to the next building over. We took it, made our way out and then drove a stolen SUV to the airport," I said.

"Right. So, the Mossad agents and I followed you to the airport, after they got the info from 'my' Omar to go there. When the assault on the hangar began, it was much bigger than what the agents were expecting. It turned into a battle. Up until that point, any time we got close, you guys just ran. There were so many terrorists in the building! When the gunfight broke out, my escorts got me away from the action in a mini-caravan, driving just a few blocks away. The agents at the hangar weren't expecting such an intense battle and had to call in reinforcements, including my escorts. So, they all went back to fight. I heard the gunshots and one really loud explosion. Smoke started billowing from that direction. I watched as a helicopter took off, staying just above the rooftops of buildings. That's where I was, alone in this Range Rover, parked on the side of the road, when I saw you fall out of the helicopter."

"Jump," I interrupted. "I jumped. I didn't fall. I mean, I technically fell once I had jumped, but I didn't fall out of the helicopter. I jumped."

"The landing wasn't a pretty one to watch. The Russian judge gave the lowest marks, a 4 out of 10." Jessica laughed.

I tried to laugh, but everything still hurt and sitting still was causing the muscles to tighten up. I tried stretching out each of my limbs in order, right arm, left arm, then rocking my weight to my left side so I could stretch my right leg and then reversing the action, rocking my weight to my right side so I could stretch out my left leg. It was so good to be back with my friend and the excitement of seeing her, kissing her, being with her now while trying to outrun a terrorist organization, had my adrenaline pumping again. Even though I knew it was probably worse than it felt at the moment, the pain was lessening in intensity.

As we got closer to Jess' lab, I was reminded of my time there with Nuria and I didn't know if anyone had informed Jessica. My mood changed.

"Did you know I was here yesterday?"

Jessica responded, "No. I don't even know how you got to Israel. Tell me."

"After you were kidnapped..." I put my hands in the air and did air-quotes as I said *kidnapped*. "Omar told me he was with the Mossad. We stole a car and chased you guys to the airport. We tried to stop you as you were taking off in a big propeller airplane, but we were minutes late. So, we got on board a small, private jet that I thought was being flown by Mossad agents or Israeli Air Force and we flew to Israel, following you guys. As we got close to landing, our pilot made some very radical moves and we landed hard and fast. At the time, I thought it was because of his military training. Now I know it was because they were trying to get on the ground and away from the airport before the Mossad got to us. There was a gunfight and I escaped. Believe it or not, I took a *cab* to the Azrieli Sarona Tower and paid with your credit card. There are a *lot* of incredibly heroic details that I left out just for time's sake, but I'll fill those in another time," I said with a smile.

Jessica laughed and said, "Save them for later, Double-O Davenport. What happened next? Hey! You used *my* credit card?"

"Um, well, yes. I tried paying with mine, but the charge wouldn't go through. I think it had to do with the fact that I didn't let the credit card company know I was going to be here. Heck, *I* didn't know I was going to be here. Anyway, the cab driver did *not* look like someone I wanted to skip payment with. You know?"

Jess smiled. "I'm just giving you a hard time. What did you do next?"

"So, I got to your building, figured out where I needed to go and got stopped by this hulking beast of a man—the security guard—before I ever even got out of the lobby. He's from New York. I've been calling him *New York Hulk*. Do you know him? Never mind. Beside the point. So, I made my way up to your floor and was kind of wandering around aimlessly, looking for someone who spoke English and could help me. Finally, I found these two ladies in lab coats, and was trying to communicate to them, when this nerdy-looking, twenty-something girl gave me this big, 'running-hug,' recognizing me from the pictures on your desk. After a few awkward minutes of 'who are you?' and 'what are you doing here?' type questions back and forth, I figured out that she was your personal assistant, Nuria. She's the one who really helped me while I was at your lab. Then later that night, she saved my life. Her actions last night were very, very heroic."

"Did Nuria tell you that she was my personal assistant? I've told her over and over to stop saying that. She's *not* my personal assistant. What did she do to save your life?"

I interrupted, a little confused, "Then, who is she? Does she not work at the lab?"

"Oh, yes. She works at the lab. It's not that. It's that she's not my personal assistant. She's my colleague, my coworker, and my really good and loyal friend. I couldn't have accomplished the things I have without Nuria. She's brilliant, sweet and incredibly loyal. She's like, my only *girl* friend in Israel. No, she's probably my only *girl* friend, outside of my mother, anywhere. We pretty much tell each other everything. So, that's why I hate it when she says or when she tells people that she's my assistant. She's just not. She's too important. Now, how did she save your life?"

I could tell that either no one had told Jessica that Nuria was dead, or it just hadn't sunk in yet. She was still talking about her in the present tense. I was glad that Jessica hadn't noticed that I spoke of her in the past tense. I decided I needed to make sure that she knew what had happened to Nuria, just in case we ran into a coworker at Jessica's office who might have already been informed. I didn't want Jessica to find out that way, from someone else, especially since I was there, knew the details, and the cause of her death.

Not sure how to broach the subject, I cautiously asked, "Has, um, anyone told you about Nuria?" I tried to ask it quietly and reverently, hoping someone had already broken the news to Jessica about her colleague, coworker and friend's death.

Jessica shook her head and asked, "What about Nuria?"

"Jess, I'm sorry that I'm the one who has to tell you this. I've got some bad, no, some really horrible news to tell you. There's no good way to do it and no way that I can say this that will make the news any less easy to bear." I paused, unsure of exactly how I needed to phrase this.

What will make this the least painful? Should I rip the bandage off quick and fast, just tell her Nuria was killed last night, in her home? Or should I be more delicate, even if that means prolonging the news just a few moments.

"What? You're scaring me, Matt. What's going on with Nuria? Should I call and just ask her?"

I looked down at her phone still in my hand. I said, "Your phone is out of juice, so you'll need to charge it before you call anyone or use it for the keys. But you can't call Nuria at all. I'm so sorry to tell you this, but Nuria was killed last night, in her home. She had given me her address when I was at the lab yesterday afternoon and told me that if I needed a place to stay or a hot meal to stop by. I was the one who found her."

"No, no, no, no, no," Jessica said through tears. She was openly weeping, and her driving was becoming erratic. "What happened? How? Are you sure? Sweet, sweet Nuria. She never did anything to anyone."

"I'm so sorry, Jess. So, so sorry."

We sat in silence for a few moments at a traffic light and I took her hand in mine. Finally, I said, "I think I've worked out the details of how it was done. Omar Khalid called it in. Omar had it done."

"What are you talking about? Weren't you with him? How'd Omar kill Nuria?"

"Were you at Dr. Kaplan's house with Mossad agents late yesterday afternoon? Were you there when the Chinese delivery guy showed up?" I asked Jessica.

"No, I've never been to Dr. Kaplan's house. What does that have to do with Nuria?"

"Omar and I had been separated at the airport. I spoke with Nuria at your lab. I thought my best bet to save you and your research was to go to Dr. Kaplan's house, to try and find him. She gave me Kaplan's address. Then, in a sweet gesture, she gave me her address in case I needed a place to stay for the evening. Sweet Nuria. I went to Kaplan's place and as I was about to knock on the door, I sensed movement inside and went on hyper-alert. Omar, who I knew as Aaron the Mossad agent, was surveilling the house and stopped me from knocking on the door. So, Omar and I were reunited, together, at Dr. Kaplan's house. You have to remember that I thought the Mossad agents were mercenaries who were after your research and your machines. We thought of a way to reveal if they might be on a stakeout, waiting for us inside Kaplan's house. We ordered Chinese delivery and watched and waited. The mercenaries swarmed the poor guy and we knew we needed to get away, find a safe place to go to regroup and plan our next move. I told Omar that we should go to Nuria's house, told him she was your personal assistant and showed him the address. He must have thought she knew something. At this point, I was *certain* he was a Mossad agent. You have to remember that. I was absolutely *certain* he was a Mossad agent. He had an answer for everything."

Jessica just looked in my direction, weaving through traffic, crying. She didn't speak. Just looked at me. Upset and crying. A lot.

"Omar made a phone call; said he was calling Mossad agents to take down the 'mercenaries' at Dr. Kaplan's house. I didn't think anything about it at the time. I mean, why would I? The entire phone call was in a different language. *All* his phone calls had been made in a different language, Hebrew, or so I thought, so this one was no different. What I didn't know, but what I now think happened, was that he was calling another terrorist, sending at least one enemy agent to Nuria's place. I honestly don't know how many he sent. By the time we showed up, Nuria was just about dead. I held her in my arms and told her, 'You're not alone.' The things Nuria told me as she was dying, I know, saved my life. Her last words, literally, her dying breath was, 'Don't trust Omar.'" I paused and looked at Jessica. She was gripping the steering wheel with white knuckles, crying. I added, "I was holding Nuria's hand when she died. There wasn't anything I could do."

"Oh, Matt," Jessica said, openly crying. "They didn't need to kill her. None of this makes sense. What could they possibly be after? Why do they want my research? My technology? My stupid machines? I wish I had never invented this stuff! And I can't believe *you* gave them her address? Why would you *do* that? You're the reason she's dead. Do you know that?"

Through tears, she slammed on the brakes of the Range Rover, rocking us violently forward and whispered, "We're here."

Roughly two hours after we left the airport, we were finally back at the entrance to Azrieli Sarona Tower.

Chapter Twenty-Five

The Azrieli Sarona Tower was an incredibly beautiful building during the day, and I didn't think anything could surpass the initial impression I had of it when I arrived via cab the day before. I was mistaken. The view of the building at night was mesmerizing. In a perfect world Jessica and I would be driving up to this building, in our own Range Rover, holding hands and looking at the beautiful expanse before us. The building stretched 782 feet above ground and at night, with the glass reflecting the city lights, it was probably the second most beautiful thing in Israel. Jessica was, by far, the most beautiful thing, even through her tears, through her hurt, through her pain, through her loss.

Jessica must have seen the way I was looking at her and at the building and said, "I used to love coming here, being here, but now I don't know how I can face being in the building knowing Nuria is dead," and then she added something completely unexpected. She added, "And it's your fault. In fact, I don't know if I can be around you anymore. I think I'm going to need some space. So, let's get in, get the research and then get you to a hospital or to Mossad. I'll figure something else out."

"She's not dead because of me or because of you, for that matter. She's dead because of Omar Khalid. Period," I said, a little too forcefully for the moment.

"You don't know what you're talking about. You're a little boy pretending to play with the grown-ups. This is the big leagues, Matt, and you're not ready for it, and it cost Nuria her life. You stepped up to the plate and struck out and it cost Nuria everything. It cost Nuria her life. I lost my friend because of *you*. You're the one who practically told the bad guys to go to her house, question her and kill her. That was so stupid. How could you be so stupid? I thought I knew you better than that."

Jessica was practically screaming at me. She opened the door of the Range Rover, crawled out and slammed the door, hard. It was loud and the big, boxy truck rocked on its tires.

I already felt horrible. I already blamed myself. I just sat there for a moment, stunned, sad.

Suddenly, the driver's door swung open and Jessica was again standing there. She barked, "Are you coming or are you planning on how you're going to get me killed too? On second thought, wait here." And she slammed the door again.

"Jess, wait," I shouted as I opened the door and tried to get my stiff body working again. I had my hands full, phone, lipstick and wallet, so I put the stuff back in my pockets and realized there was something else in there, in my pocket. With my one empty hand, I closed the door to the Range Rover and tried to catch up. I realized I was carrying the backpack in the other hand. It was cumbersome, so I slung it on my shoulders. Jessica just kept walking. "Please, Jessica, wait on me." But she never slowed her pace.

We made our way into the lobby area and past the electronic directory, with Jessica several yards ahead of me. There was no one, not even the guards at the security desk, but I guessed at this time of night, there were probably very few people here in the building at all. The guards must be doing a routine security sweep. She rounded the corner to the elevators, and I was just a few seconds behind.

I said, "You're not alone. Jessica, we've both lost someone and you're not alone in this."

"Just stop it, Matt. You're only making things that much worse. Just leave me alone. I *want* to be alone. Stop talking."

I pressed the call button and Jessica said, "Dang it. I don't have my badge. We'll need to wait for the security guard to come back, or we can take the stairs." Defeat and agitation rang through her voice.

I said, "Not that it really matters right now, but I'm definitely not in any condition to take the stairs. We could just use my visitor's badge, if it still works."

When I was getting out of the Range Rover, I had felt the visitor's pass in my pocket as I put Jessica's phone back in place. I pulled out the pass I had taken from the building yesterday. It seemed that I had accidentally forgotten to return it before I got in the taxi that Nuria had called for me.

I decided to try and get Jessica's mind off of Nuria while we waited on the elevator, so I asked her, "I keep hearing about the keys. What are the keys, and what do you use them for? Different people have told me that we need keys to access your research; even 'evil' Omar said it a couple times. I was told that *I* have the keys. What are they? Is it something on your phone?"

Jessica, frustrated that I wouldn't be quiet and leave her alone, said, "Did you go in my office when you were here?" I nodded and she continued. "Did you notice my laptop was bolted to the desk?" Again, I nodded. She said, "One of the keys is to unlock the computer from the workstation. It looks like a normal desk, but it's actually a brand new one that Dr. Kaplan recently had installed. It is reinforced titanium and the whole desk is bolted to the office floor. That computer isn't going anywhere unless it's unlocked."

"Wow. Why do you need a reinforced titanium desk and computer holder? And do I have the key? What are the keys?" I asked.

Acting like she didn't hear me or at least ignoring me and changing the subject, Jessica asked, "Do you still have my lipstick?"

I dug into my pocket and pulled out the little silver tube.

She said, "Have you opened it up?"

Trying to lighten the mood, I said, "No, I decided that I wouldn't wear makeup on this trip, so I didn't check to see if that shade was going to match my outfit." I smiled a childish grin and immediately realized that was the wrong thing to do. *The. Wrong. Thing.*

She said, "Well, look, *Genius.*"

I popped the cap off and inside was a normal looking bullet of lipstick, a dark maroon color.

"Twist it," she said.

I twisted the tube and something surprising happened. It turned out that the bullet of lipstick was a perfectly camouflaged key. As the tube was twisted, the key pressed up through the lipstick so that the key was usable.

She added, "When Dr. Kaplan ordered the desk, he also ordered the lipstick key. Both of them are made of titanium. That's why the lipstick looks a lot better than our phones do. Or your face."

I twisted the lipstick closed, put the cap back on and put it back in my pocket.

"Okay. What about the other key?" I asked, ignoring the comment about my face.

She said, "It's a key for the software. I gave you a clue about it in my voicemail. Did you get my voicemail? Did you even listen to it?"

The elevator arrived with a *ding*, and we stepped in. I placed the battered visitor pass on the pad and Jessica said, "You get the next elevator. Get out. I need some alone time, some space." She pushed the button to the forty-seventh floor.

It caught me a little off guard and I was speechless. I started to protest, but instead just nodded and stepped back out of the elevator. I could give her the couple of minutes of peace and quiet it would take for the next elevator to come pick me up. Jessica turned to the wall so she wouldn't have to see me or look me in the eye.

"Killer," I heard her whisper as the doors to the elevator started to close.

Instantly, that made me mad. A fever rush boiled under my skin and I exploded, "I didn't kill her, you..." But by then the elevator doors had closed, and Jessica couldn't hear anything I was saying. It was probably a good thing that I didn't have the opportunity to finish that sentence because it wouldn't have been appropriate. Jessica was in pain and projecting it onto me.

I stood there, stunned and physically hurting. Now I was hurting emotionally, as well. Hurting for my friend and hurting because she was blaming me.

Is this one of those things that would blow over? She's just hurt and venting. Am I going to be blamed for this forever? Are things between me and Jessica, romantically speaking, over just as they are getting started?

I stood there looking at the empty lobby. I had been standing in this same spot yesterday, but things, with me, were so different now. When I showed up here yesterday, I didn't know what was going on, who was after me, where I was going, who I needed to talk to or anything. But it was more than that. I didn't know who I was, what I was capable of. I didn't recognize the power that dwells within me and certainly had never recognized the voice of God as he communicated with me. As I stood there looking at that lobby and bank of elevators, I began to realize what I had become.

Yesterday, I was afraid. Today I am confident. Yesterday I was lost. Today I know where to go. Yesterday I was alone; today I have Jessica again, sort of. Yesterday I thought I was in this all by myself, but as I stand here in the lobby, I've realized that the Lord has been with me this whole time. He is still with me. He sticks closer than a brother[76] and will never leave or forsake me.[77] He continues to talk to me.

I waited a couple of minutes and then pushed the elevator call button and stood there, trying to calm my mind down. After a few minutes, the same elevator that Jessica had taken returned and the doors opened. I stepped in, placed the battered pass against the card reader

---

76 Proverbs 18:24
77 Hebrews 13:5

and pressed the button for the forty-seventh floor. The doors closed and the quick ride was underway.

"Lord, please fix this. I need Your help."

On the inside, deep down I heard the words, a command: *Use your authority.* I recognized God's voice.

I was familiar with several Biblical scriptures where Jesus referenced His authority and different scripture verses where He transferred that authority to those who follow Him. He even said that in His Name He gives us authority to conquer the power of the enemy.[78] *That makes me His authorized representative!* I decided to finally act like it.

Standing in the elevator, I said, "In the Name of *Jesus*, enemy, Satan and strife, leave us alone. I speak the peace of God, proclaim it and demand it in this situation and to Jessica, specifically. The Bible says resist the devil and he will flee from you, so *go!* In Jesus' Name."[79]

Then, again on the inside, deep down I heard two more words, a name: *Terry Mize.*[80]

I was familiar with the name, but then I felt the elevator slowing as I reached the forty-seventh floor. I began to ask the Lord, "What about Terry Mize? What does…" The doors opened up with a *ding*, and I stepped off and turned toward Jessica's office. "…Terry Mize have to do…" To my surprise and horror, I was standing face to face with Omar Khalid.

He had a gun.

It was pointing at me.

Down on her knees, kneeling beside Omar was Jessica, bleeding from the left eye. She had a handprint across the left side of her face where Omar had obviously viciously slapped her. Omar was holding Jessica in place with a handful of her hair, pulled tight from the top of her head. Any movement she made just pulled the hair tighter. It

---

78 Luke 10:19
79 James 4:7
80 See Terry Mize Ministries to learn more: http://www.terrymize.com

looked incredibly painful and with every flinch that she or Omar made, it made her audibly gasp.

"Good to see you again, Madam," Omar said, looking down at Jessica, in a tone mocking his driver cover story from two nights ago. He then barked in my direction, "Don't try anything, or I will shoot the both of you in the kneecaps and leave you here lying in a pool of your own blood. And for your sake, Terry Mize, whoever that is, better not be on his way up." Pointing the gun at Jessica, he continued, "Matt, take out the gun that you stole from me and slowly place it on the floor of the elevator. Then send it back down to the lobby."

I pulled the gun out of my waistband and set it on the floor of the elevator. I moved in slow motion, which was partly due to what Omar had said to me and partly due to how stiff and horrible my muscles were feeling. Leaning in, I pressed the button to the lobby and stepped out of the doorway. It seemed that you didn't need the visitor's pass to send the elevator down, which is why I had forgotten to return it the day prior. I only used it once, when I went *up* to the lab. Not as I was headed back down.

"Omar, why are you doing this?" I asked. "Why are you trying to steal this research? Why? What would your father think? Or was all of that a lie as well? Did your father actually die a hero, or were you just playing me this entire time? I saw the pain as you were talking about him. What would he think of you right now?"

Omar just smiled, gleamed a "knowing" smile and said, "Matt, every word I said to you was true and my father would be pleased with every action I have made, everything I have done the past three days, because these last few days are the culmination of a lifetime of work, two lifetimes' worth of work. I'm not going to be denied. No one can stop us."

Confused, I didn't know exactly what to say so I just stood there looking at him. I felt betrayed on so many different levels. We had shared the pain the losses of our fathers caused and connected in a way that was deeper than surface level. Now, he was telling me it was all true, but it just couldn't be. How could his father have been a hero in this country and now be proud of the actions of his son?

Omar dropped the handful of hair he had been holding and Jessica immediately crashed to the floor. She was crying, tears of pain and tears of remorse.

"Get up," Omar hissed at her.

Omar marched us down a hallway and then, following the exit signs, turned left. We turned the corner and found ourselves in a hallway that was twice as long as the first. This hallway came to an end with two choices—turn left again and keep walking along a hallway that was parallel to the first, or continue forward, entering a door to a stairwell. All along the two hallways that I had seen, sitting on the floor next to the walls were devices connected by strands of multicolored wires. I had seen dozens and dozens of the devices as we neared the end of the hallway, and I'm sure there were just as many along the other main corridors. Omar leaned over and clicked a button on the last device in the line. There was a beeping noise as he entered a quick code and then *05:00* showed in red on a little screen. A timer. Omar seethed, "You remember these from the helicopter, don't you, Matt?"

I nodded. "Those were in the boxes that go boom."

The helicopter had been almost completely full of large plastic crates, and each crate could probably have held a dozen or more of these explosive devices.

Omar continued, "You have five minutes to bring me Dr. Adams' research computer. Completely unlocked. I know you have the keys; everyone has said so for the past two days." Omar reached in his pocket and pulled out a long cylindrical tube with a red button at the end. "If you try anything clever, I have a dead-man's switch. You know what that is? If I let go of this button," he said as he held up his injured hand that was holding the cylindrical tube. With his thumb, he was pressing a button on the end of the tube. "It doesn't matter what the timer says.

This place goes boom, and people will be picking bits of you out of their hair and off their cars for weeks. You want to be long gone before the boom. Understand? One last mission, Matt, the ultimate mission. Get to the computer and find the research. Unlock it. Bring it to me on the roof. Save the girl. You've got five minutes, starting…"

"*Wait!*" I shouted. "Know this, Omar. Mark my words. You might not realize it and I sure haven't been walking in it, but I have authority in this situation. I've had authority since day one." Turning away from Omar, I continued the thought, praying, "Lord, forgive my ignorance."

Turning back to Omar, I finished my thought.

"I will get the information, the computer and have it unlocked when I get to you, but you *will not* shoot her. You will not shoot me. No weapon turned against us will succeed.[81] Do I make myself clear?"

Omar just laughed a maniacal laugh, hatred in his eyes, devil in his heart.

"You've got five minutes left, Bible-Boy. Starting *now!*" He pressed a button on the explosive device and the timer started clicking, counting down backwards. Then toward Jessica, Omar shouted, "To the roof! *Go!*"

They started running, and I clicked the stopwatch feature on my wristwatch.

---

81 Isaiah 54:17 (NLT)

Chapter Twenty-Six

04:59 (4 minutes, 59 seconds left)

The clock was ticking. Omar and Jessica opened the door to the stairwell, and I watched them go up two stairs before the door shut. I leaned down and looked at the explosive devices to see if there was a way that I could turn it off. Maybe there was, maybe there wasn't. I didn't know anything about bombs, and I wasn't about to take a chance. I started running and prayed as I went.

"Father, Your Word tells me that Jesus said that He gave me authority over all the power of the enemy, and nothing shall by any means hurt me.[82] That means this man, his gun, his bullets, his explosives cannot hurt me and therefore if he pulls the trigger, You must do something with the bullets. You must do something with the shrapnel if he detonates his explosives. I *expect* You to do something with the bullets, with the shrapnel. For Your Word's sake. Not for my sake."

04:42 (4 minutes, 42 seconds left)

I had a lot to do and less than five minutes to get it done. The next thing I did was turn and start running back to the bank of elevators to hit the call button and see if the same elevator would return with my gun. If it didn't, I was going back to the lobby to get it. I had one key, but if I couldn't figure out the second, I wasn't going up to the roof

---

82 Luke 10:19

empty-handed. I had only taken about three or four steps when I heard Jessica scream in a way that I had never heard before. A scream of absolute horror, absolute terror. I knew the only way to help her was to get my gun, get the research and get to the roof.

I made it to the elevator bank and slapped the call button. I had a one in six chance that the same elevator would return. It was the only one I had seen moving tonight. Possibly, at this time in the evening, some of the elevators might be disabled and my chances would be closer to one in three.

From the elevator bank, I sprinted. And when I say sprinted, I mean I ran as fast as I could in the condition I was in. I sprinted to Jessica's office, pulled her phone out of my pocket and plugged it into a charger she had sitting on her desk. I said to myself, "I don't know if this will work, but it's worth a try." Jess had told me that she left me a clue about the software key. She said the clue was in the voicemail she had left. I had listened to that voicemail twice, but I still wasn't sure what the clue was. Maybe I could get enough juice into the phone while I retrieved the gun and unlocked the computer in its cage on the desk to check the voicemail again.

I heard the elevator *ding* and sprinted back toward it. It was the same elevator I had taken, and I was just able to slip my hand between the doors before they closed. The gun was still sitting on the floor. I picked it up, stuck it in my waistband, and breathlessly ran back to Jessica's office, pulling the lipstick key out of my pocket along the way. I could see the screen on Jessica's phone had lit up, turned on by being plugged in. Possibly there was enough power to play the voicemail. I looked down at my watch.

03:29 (3 minutes, 29 seconds left)

"Less than four minutes left. Hurry up, Matt!" I shouted to myself. I hurried around Jessica's desk and fell into her chair. The momentum rolled the chair away from the laptop, and I scrambled to get back to it.

With the lipstick tube in hand, I pulled the cap off and twisted. The key appeared and I moved to unlock the computer.

Where is the lock? Where is the lock?

I was scrambling, but I couldn't find the place to put the key in.

Breathe, Matt, just breathe.

Desperate and looking to divert my attention to something attainable, I turned to Jessica's cell phone. It had powered back up and I put her code in to unlock it, 6-2-8-8. Fumbling for a moment, I was able to find and play the voicemail. "Speakerphone, where's the speakerphone icon?" I shouted! I missed the opening lines of the voicemail while I found how to turn the speakerphone on.

I hit the icon and Jessica's whispered voice came to life mid-message.

"...Uh, I've got your number stored in my phone and I don't remember it. Uh, if you get this, uh, if you're listening to this, please *be careful. Don't trust anybody,* and please hold on to my stuff. That is my *favorite* tube of lipstick. I would be lost without it. I'm a virtuous woman, Matt, I really am. *Don't lose my lipstick.* Oh, here they come." The voicemail was over.

I understood the lipstick reference. Now, I knew that was the physical key to unlock the cage, if I could ever find the lock. But what was the clue for the other key? Was it in the first part of the voicemail that I had missed?

"I'll get back to that in a minute," I said to myself.

I went back to trying to unlock the computer from the desk. I shook it, trying to get it free, trying to shake a hidden lock out into the open. Nothing worked. Really, nothing moved. I was concerned that I was going to break the laptop screen or something. There was no way to get the computer free if I couldn't unlock it. Finally, on the back side of the computer, behind the laptop's screen, I found the lock. Had I not been so distracted by Jessica's phone turning on as I entered the room, I would have seen it easily. It was out in the open, just on the wrong side of the screen for me to quickly see sitting at the desk. The key fit in on the first try and the lock popped open. Within seconds, I had the computer released from its cage.

I pressed the power button and waited while the computer booted up. I looked down at my watch.

"Lord, this is hell! *Help me!*" I shouted.

In an instant, I was reminded of a verse out of the Biblical book of Jonah which said, "I cried by reason of mine affliction unto the Lord, and He heard me; *out of the belly of hell cried I, and Thou heardest my voice.*"[83] I immediately knew that God had heard me and He was helping me. It was God confirming, acknowledging to me that He was listening to my prayer and that He was in this with me. I again looked at the time...

02:45 (2 minutes, 45 seconds left)

The computer booted up very quickly, surprisingly quickly. A box appeared with a pre-filled username, but it was asking for a ten-digit password. The prefilled username was *Virtuous Woman*.

I played Jessica's voicemail one last time.

"Oh, Matt," the voice once again quietly whispered. I was reminded of the first time I listened to this voicemail, in the bathroom of the airplane, and I couldn't hear Jessica's voice over the quiet roar of the engines. This time, I had trouble even hearing it over the pounding of my heart in my chest and in my ears. "I hope that you're okay and you've still got my phone. I hope you're listening to this. Uh, I've got your number stored in my phone and I don't actually remember it."

"That's the end of the part I didn't hear, and I don't think there were any clues in that part," I said to myself.

Jessica's message rolled on. "Uh, if you get this, uh, if you're listening to this, please *be careful. Don't trust anybody,* and please hold on to my stuff. That is my *favorite* tube of lipstick. I would be lost without it."

---

83 Jonah 2:2

"There's the first key," I said out loud. "What comes next? What's the clue?"

"I'm a virtuous woman, Matt, I really am. *Don't lose my lipstick*," she said adamantly. "Oh, here they come," and then the message was over. She had obviously hung up.

What was she trying to tell me?

She referenced her lipstick a couple times but right in the middle, between the two lipstick references, she said she was a "virtuous woman." *That* was the clue!

I should have spotted it sooner, recognized that was the clue. The prefilled username to unlock the computer was *Virtuous Woman* and she had said, "I'm a virtuous woman," in her voicemail. I should have connected the dots. But at that second, everything clicked. I knew what the clue was, what all the clues had been. I opened the sliding panel on Jessica's desk, the one where her handwritten letter had been taped. Again, I saw the "virtuous woman" scriptures. Nuria had been surprised when she saw me snapping a picture of the letter when I was here earlier. She said, "You found it." Then later, she told me that I "had the keys *now*," and that *now* part had been confusing to me. At the moment, things were making sense. I had snapped a picture of the letter when I was here yesterday and when I looked at that picture on the phone, later, I noticed some of the letters looked darker. I didn't have time to think too much about it, because the phone had died, but now I knew, those letters were the clues.

A good woman is hard to find,
   and worth far more than diamonds.
Her husband trusts her without reserve,
   and never has reason to regret it.
Never spiteful, she treats him generously
   all her life long.

She shops around for the best yarns and cottons,
    and enjoys knitting and sewing.
She's like a trading ship that sails to faraway places
    and brings back exotic surprises.
She's up before dawn, preparing breakfast
    for her family and organizing her day.
She looks over a field and buys it,
    then, with money she's put aside, plants a garden.
First thing in the morning, she dresses for work,
    rolls up her sleeves, eager to get started.
She senses the worth of her work,
    is in no hurry to call it quits for the day.
She's skilled in the crafts of home and hearth,
    diligent in homemaking.
She's quick to assist anyone in need,
    reaches out to help the poor.
She doesn't worry about her family when it snows;
    their winter clothes are all mended and ready to wear.
She makes her own clothing,
    and dresses in colorful linens and silks.
Her husband is greatly respected
    when he deliberates with the city fathers.
She designs gowns and sells them,
    brings the sweaters she knits to the dress shops.
Her clothes are well-made and elegant,
    and she always faces tomorrow with a smile.
When she speaks she has something worthwhile to say,
    and she always says it kindly.
She keeps an eye on everyone in her household,
    and keeps them all busy and productive.
Her children respect and bless her;
    her husband joins in with words of praise:

"Many women have done wonderful things,
    but you've outclassed them all!"
Charm can mislead and beauty soon fades.
The woman to be admired and praised
    is the woman who lives in the Fear-of-God.
Give her everything she deserves![84]

I grabbed a pen from Jessica's desk and scribbled the darker letters on my hand. The first letter was an "**S**" from the word "diamond**S**." The second letter was an "**E**" from the word "h**E**r." The third letter was an "**E**" from the word "r**E**ason" and then "**K**" from the word "**K**nitting." I had the first word, "Seek." Time was running out! I needed to hurry and get through the whole thing.

The next letter was an "**A**" from the word "tr**A**ding" followed by an "**N**" from the word "bri**N**gs." The next two letters were "**D**" from the word "**D**awn" and "**Y**" from the word "famil**Y**." The first two words were "Seek Andy."

Seek Andy? What does that mean? Oh, no. I'm not going to be able to figure this code out.

"Father, in the Name of Jesus, give me wisdom!" I shouted. And then I knew, just knew it, down on the inside.

Keep going. The key will be opened.

"The *key* will be opened? The *key* will? What a weird phrase, Lord."

I kept working on the code, and the next two letters cleared things up significantly. "**E**" from the word "ov**E**r" and "**S**" from the word "**S**he's."

I began to understand. The first two words were "Seek and" not "Seek Andy." The "**Y**" was actually the first letter of the third word. "Seek and yes?" That didn't make much sense either, but I knew the *key* would be opened. So I continued, working quickly.

---

84 Proverbs 31:10-31 (The Message Translation)

The next four letters spelled "**H-A-L-L**" and were taken from "s**H**e," "e**A**ger," and the two "**L**'s" from "ca**LL**." Now my clue spelled "Seek and yes hall."

Inspiration hit. Instead of trying to interpret each word from limited letters, I should just write down all the letters in one big word, in order, and see what it spelled.

I went through her entire letter and wrote down all the darker characters. The code spelled out "seekandyeshallfindknockanditisopened."

Written like that, I recognized it was a scripture verse from the book of Matthew, the first book of the New Testament in the Bible. It was a scripture that Jessica and I had talked about just two days before.

"Ask, and it shall be given you; *seek, and ye shall find; knock, and it shall be opened* unto you."[85] I had used that verse to get back in the hotel room to seek and find my wallet!

Jessica was brilliant. "Seek and you'll find *the password*, knock and *the computer* will be opened!" The key was opened!

I typed in the scripture reference, ten-digits with no spaces: "Matthew7:7" and with a melodic chime, the computer unlocked.

Without thinking about it, both of my arms shot into the air like I had scored a touchdown. It was painful, but I shouted in triumph, "Thank You, Lord!"

I grabbed the laptop and blasted my way out of the office. Following the exit signs, I sprinted to the end of the first hallway and then the end of the second hallway. Coming to the stairwell door, I looked down at the timer and saw that I only had just a few seconds longer than one minute to get to the roof.

01:07 (1 minute, 07 seconds left)

I never slowed down, passing the timer. I hit the stairwell door and it opened with a boom banging on the wall, sending echoes down close to fifty floors. I knew I had to go up at least seven flights of stairs to

---

85 Matthew 7:7

reach the top of the building. I was on the forty-seventh floor and there were fifty-three floors in the building. One minute to run seven flights of stairs. If I could do it, Omar would stop the timer and Jessica and I could be safe, hopefully together. Hopefully that was still in her vision of our future.

I started up the first flight of stairs, skipping two steps for every stride I took. I was making surprisingly good progress, and then I came to the landing between the first flight and second flight of stairs. I ran into the security guard, *New York Hulk*, from yesterday. Now I know why Jessica had screamed. He was riddled with bullet holes. He was a gruesome sight lying on the floor in a puddle of his own blood. That may have been the first dead body Jessica had ever seen outside of a funeral home. He must have been doing his rounds or something, or maybe an alarm was triggered that alerted the guard when Omar came down the stairs from the roof. Maybe Omar was on his way down the stairs with one of his boxes of explosives when *New York Hulk* tried to stop him. I'm sure it didn't take but just an instant for Omar to pull his gun and shoot him. *New York Hulk* was unarmed and never stood a chance.

I didn't have time to stop, and there was nothing I could do for the guard anyway. As I rounded the landing and made my way to the next flight of stairs, I saw there were several bloody footprints making their way up the stairs. There were two different types of footprints, one small and one large. I kept hustling, following the footprints up the stairs. The time on my watch kept running down toward zero and the numbers on the doors were running up toward fifty-three. My legs were burning. My lungs were burning. My head was pounding. My ears were ringing. Everything hurt, but I knew if I didn't make it up the stairs before the timer went off, Jessica and I would need a miracle to survive. Even though I hadn't seen anyone else, it seemed feasible that if an explosion went off, probably a lot of other innocent people would die or be injured as well.

Keep running! Keep running! I was willing myself up the stairs. *Don't slow down! Keep going. Jessica is depending on you! Keep running!*

00:09 (0 minutes, 09 seconds left)

I reached the top of the stairs and opened the door to the exterior. Being that high up, the wind was howling. It caught the door and swung it hard, banging it against the exterior of the building. It was very loud on the roof, but over the sound of the wind and the running helicopter, the banging noise caught Omar's attention.

I shouted, "Turn the timer off! Turn the timer off! I have the computer!" I started moving in his direction.

Omar was standing there, outside of the waiting helicopter, holding a slumping Jessica up by the arm. She looked like she had been in a mixed martial arts match with Conor McGregor and lost, convincingly. Her lip was bleeding, her face bruised and puffy. The helicopter's top propeller blade was spinning, but not yet at full speed. The engine was on, but it wasn't quite ready for takeoff. When he saw me, Omar pointed his gun at Jessica's head, resting it on her temple. Obviously, they had fought, or he just decided to beat her without reason, and he wasn't taking any chances with her now.

"Turn off the timer! Turn off the *timer!*" I screamed, now sprinting toward him. "The computer's unlocked! Turn off the timer!"

Omar just smiled and shouted, "There's no way to turn off the timer."

He had obviously lost track of time during his fight with Jessica, or he would have been waiting for me in the helicopter. The scuffle may have just ended mere moments before I opened the door. It was a miracle that the dead man's switch hadn't been activated.

00:00 (0 minutes, 00 seconds left)

Suddenly, there was a quiet rumble, a tremor below our feet that felt like an earthquake. Then the whole building, both towers, seemed to sway. Screams of breaking glass filled the night air.

The explosive charges had detonated.

Had we been standing on the ground below, we would have seen the concussive force that blew out all of the windows on the forty-fifth through forty-ninth floors of both towers. We would have seen the fire raging in the building. We would have seen the flashing lights. Would have seen the sprinkler system engage to try and fight the flames that were threatening to swallow the rest of the building. We were on the roof, and the only thing we knew was that we were in trouble. An alarm began blaring, a deafening sound even on the noisy roof.

I looked at Omar and saw panic in his eyes. In that instant, using the explosive detonation as a distraction, Jessica swiveled and leaned forward, bringing her right fist down, hard, into Omar's groin. He howled, crumpling toward the ground, and fired the gun. The shot went over Jessica's head. She gave him a hard right-cross, sending his face violently toward the right, and took off at a sprint toward the edge of the building.

I had been running toward Omar when Jessica hammered his groin. Instead of stopping when Jessica punched him, I continued to run toward them, to help Jessica get away from Omar. She broke free, but my momentum brought me directly to Omar's feet. I wasn't nearly fast enough to help Jessica or to get to Omar in time to effectively use her distraction, and I found myself standing face-to-face with Omar and his loaded gun. I still had the research computer in my hand. It was unlocked for him.

The tower was rocking relentlessly. I had stopped running no more than three feet from where Omar stood. We were eyeball to eyeball, close enough to have a conversation, like two friends would in a coffee shop. When I realized my mistake, I started to back away.

Omar shouted, "Give me the computer or I'll kill you."

I shouted back at him, "There is no weapon formed against me that can prosper!"

I took another step away from him and Omar pulled the trigger.

Point blank range.

I heard the shots.

I heard each one ring out a deafening blast.

I saw five mini-explosions mere feet from me.

I watched five empty shell casings ejected from the gun.

It wasn't in the realm of possibility that he could miss.

But at that moment, we weren't in the natural realm. The *super*natural realm imposed its will.

Five bullets stopped in mid-air and dropped to the ground at my feet.

I knew the Lord had saved me, sent an angel to deflect those bullets. I wasn't going to give Omar time to reload, so I began running away from the helicopter and toward the edge of the building. Jessica altered her angle, and we ran toward an invisible apex at the edge of the world.

Still running, I looked over at Omar. He was standing with eyes wide open. He was confused, scared and obviously torn. He wanted the research, but he realized he needed to get off that building and his time was short. He started to chase me, but after only a few steps gave up and jumped in the helicopter. The propeller blade sped up and turned quicker and quicker.

It genuinely felt like we were in an earthquake, the world's worst, most violent earthquake ever. The building was swaying, and it was incredibly hard to run. Jessica fell and got back to her feet. I fell and struggled to get up. Something was tearing at my leg.

Get up! You have to keep running.

Finally, Jessica and I came together, in one final embrace. I said, "Do you trust me?"

"Yes!" she said.

But before she had even said it, I was already diving off of the building, clutching her and her laptop in my arms. We were alone in the world.

"Pull the cord on my chest!" I screamed. "My hands are full, and I can't get to the cord."

I felt Jessica struggling to get her arm free and to my chest. A moment later, there was a gentle tug as the parachute opened and we began our glide toward the ground. I looked up at the rectangular-shaped parachute and realized it must have been stolen. In the center was the logo for the United States Airborne Division, a black shield that was overlaid with the head of a bald eagle and the word 'AIRBORNE' written across the top in capital letters.

"You can stop screaming now," I said, holding her in my arms. "Open your eyes. We're going to make it. We're going to be fine. Look and see!"

Looking into her eyes, I added, softer now, "Jess, look up. 'But they that wait upon the Lord shall renew their strength; they shall mount up with *wings as eagles*; they shall run, and not be weary; and they shall walk, and not faint.'[86] The Lord has truly delivered us! We're on eagles' wings!"

It was just a matter of moments, a splattering of seconds and then we were on the ground, but those few moments, with Jessica in my arms, the grace of God's deliverance in our hearts and on our lips, were the best few moments of my life to that point.

We landed with a crunch, a block away from the Azrieli Sarona Tower. The crunch was a thousand glass shards, a mass of destruction beneath our feet.

For the second time that night, the city was alive. Alarms blared and sirens screamed. The cavalry was on the way. Everything after that was a blur.

---

86 Isaiah 40:31

Chapter Twenty-Seven

My eyes sleepily cracked opened, and drowsily shut again. I slowly awakened to the gentle electronic beeping sounds of monitors and machines. My head felt… blurry and unsure, but it was pressed into a cloud-like pillow that was beckoning me back to sleep. I lay there, peaceful. The sheets and blankets were a colorless, clinical white. Through the window, I saw the sun, high in the cloudless sky. It was truly a beautiful morning.

"This is the day that the Lord has made. I will rejoice and be glad in it,"[87] I whispered with difficulty.

Shifting my weight attempting to roll over, the pain took my breath away. I was connected to hoses, tubes and wires running to breathing machines, pulse monitors and bags of fluid. I didn't know how I got here, but I seemed to be in a hospital bed.

On either side of my bed were chairs, empty now, but with evidence of recent use. Coffee cups sitting at their feet and on side tables, let me know that my room might be empty now, right at this second, but people had definitely been here with me.

"Hello?" I coarsely asked. The sound of my voice surprised me. "Hello? Is anybody here?"

The door opened and a nurse dressed in scrubs walked in. She hadn't heard me and didn't notice I was awake. Her timing was perfect, even if she didn't know it. Never looking directly at me, she checked

---

87 Psalm 118:24

my chart at the foot of the bed and went to look at the readouts on the machines.

I watched her work and as she was finishing, I said, "Hello. How are you doing today?" Startled, the nurse started stammering.

"Can you tell me where I am and how I got here?" I asked.

The nurse, with wide eyes, said in a foreign accent, "Thanks God. They will be so glad you are awake. Wait a moment," and rushed out of the room.

With the way I feel and the position I'm in, I think the "wait a moment" part of her instruction was a little unnecessary.

My body *ached*. I glanced down at my right hand and it was swollen, purple and bruised. My left arm was in a cast. Before I had a chance to survey any more of the damage to my body, the door to the hospital room swung open, and Jessica and a tangle of people rushed in.

"Hey, gorgeous," I said as Jessica neared the bed. I saw her beautiful smile and compassionate eyes. She blushed and raised a hand to try and cover the bruising on her face, bruising inflicted by Omar.

"I missed you," she softly responded. "You remember the first three words I said to you?" I nodded, trying to smile. She continued, "You're not alone. I'm here, and I'll always be here. I didn't have a chance to tell you that the other night. I'm *so* sorry. For everything I said, I'm *so* sorry."

"It's okay, Jess. I knew you were hurting, and I just happened to be the one you were taking it out on. I know you didn't mean any of it." I tried to smile and then looking around said, "Where am I and how did I get here? Who are all of these people?"

"What's the last thing you remember?" Jessica asked me.

"Why do all of you science people answer a question with a question?"

We both laughed a little because she knew I was right. Nuria had done it to me, the "good" Omar had done it to me and now Jess was doing it to me. It must be the way their brain was wired or something.

"Just answer the question, Mr. Bond. What's the last thing you remember?"

"The parachute and being on eagle's wings. The crunch of glass and handing you your laptop. I remember sitting down… and then… everything else is sort of… I don't know… everything fades after that."

"That's right, Matt," Jessica said, "You saved my life, and you saved my research, but that was three nights ago. You've been in the hospital, here, in Jerusalem since that night. You're going to be just fine. This is Dr. Padan," she said, motioning to a man in a white lab coat and a friendly face. "He's the one who performed your surgery. He was just telling us what to expect in the coming days and weeks when you woke up."

Jess stepped back and let Dr. Padan move closer to me. He started checking my vitals, pulse, eye dilation and the like.

"Hi, Doc," I said and then suddenly fighting panic added, "Why did I need surgery? What happened? What did you do to me, and do I still have all my body parts?"

Understanding, the doctor paused what he was doing and replied in accented English, "Matt, you've got all your parts and you're going to be fine. You had some cracked ribs and have a lot of bruising, but the reason you had the surgery was to set your broken femur. We had to put a metal rod in your leg. From what I was told, you jumped from a helicopter while it was in the air, landed on a rooftop and fell to the ground. Then, later in the evening, you were on the roof when the Azrieli Sarona Tower was blown up. I'm not sure exactly when you broke your leg, your thigh bone, but I know it was broken when you managed to save Dr. Adams' life. With a little work and rehab, you'll be back to fighting bad guys in no time."

Dr. Padan smiled as he backed away from the bed, giving Jessica room to move back to me. He continued to work, scribbling in my chart, checking my machines and dosage levels.

Finally, he said, "I'll be back tonight to do a final evening check. Right now, everything looks just fine. You're doing great, Matt. It's pretty miraculous the way you're recovering. Rest now and I'll see you in a few hours."

Turning toward the group of people in the room, he said, "Not too much activity in here. Give him time to rest. He'll be here a while and will be able to answer any and all questions over the next few days. He doesn't have to do it all today."

He made his way out of the room and presumably on to his next patient.

Jessica took my hand and said, "Okay, now, these two people are from the American Embassy."

I noticed she didn't move to let them closer, so the short, stocky man with a thin beard and a slightly taller woman with tight curly hair stayed at the foot of my bed. The man wore a blue suit and matching striped tie and the woman wore all black with a bright pink jacket to accessorize.

The man spoke first. "Hello, Mr. Davenport. I'm Jimmy Gibbs and this is Nancy Rogers." He had a Southern accent, Texas maybe, but was friendly and jovial. "Like Dr. Adams said, we're from the American Embassy." He said American but pronounced it like Mercan. The 'Mercan Embassy.' Texas all the way. "When you're up to it, we need to get a statement from ya and ask ya some questions." He must have seen the concerned look on my face because he then added, "Oh no! You're kinda a he-ro right now. We just wanna know what happened, get ya to fill in some of the blanks."

Nancy continued the thought. "Israel and the United States have always had a good relationship, especially now, since we've moved our Embassy to Jerusalem. But having an American *citizen* fighting against Hamas terrorists and ruining their plans to steal state secrets is kind of a big deal." She sounded like she was from New Jersey, northern and nasally.

Confused, I looked over at Jessica. She was beaming.

"In the next few weeks, we will also need to get you back to the United States. Since you made your way to Israel without a passport, there will be some paperwork and different things to sort out. We'll help with all of that," Nancy Rogers said. She added, "We've taken the liberty of ordering you some new clothes and have made arrangements for a residence. You'll be able to stay there, it's here in the city, once you're released from the hospital and until the doctors clear you for travel. You will have plenty of security too."

The man, Jimmy, spoke again and said, "We're real proud of ya, Matt. Incredible work out there. Thank ya for your service to your country and her allies. I think you'll end up meeting the President at some point real soon." He placed a card on the table beside my bed and said, "If ya need anything, anything at all, please don't hesitate to contact me. My cell phone number is listed there. You can get me twenty-four hours a day, seven days a week."

With that, Jimmy Gibbs and Nancy Rogers said their goodbyes and made their way out of the hospital room. I thought it was curious that neither of them had asked me any questions, but at that point they probably knew more than I did. With their departure, that left Jessica and me together and a small wiry man who had been standing in the corner of the room, quietly listening. I recognized him from somewhere but couldn't remember where I had seen him.

I turned to Jessica and said, "Why do I need plenty of security?"

She said, "We'll get there. Let me introduce one more person to you, an especially important person. I know it's a lot, and you've only been awake a few minutes so forgive me, but this is Dr. Eli Kaplan. I don't think you guys have formally met until now. I'm going to let him fill you in on some of the missing pieces."

Jessica sat down in one of the bedside chairs. Dr. Kaplan went to see if anyone was outside of the room, anyone who may be trying to listen. Convinced we were alone, he closed the door, pulled a chair over and sat down beside Jessica.

I said, "I recognize you from the picture."

Dr. Kaplan asked, "Which picture?"

"There is a framed—oh, I'm sorry. There *was* a framed picture of you and Jess that was sitting on her bookcase. I asked Nuria about it while I was there. She told me that you had given Jessica an award or a raise or a new position or something, and you guys had taken a picture together. I saw you in that picture. It's nice to meet you, Dr. Kaplan. I've heard really wonderful things about you over the years."

"And I've heard fantastic things about you, too, Matthew," Dr. Kaplan replied. I noticed that Dr. Kaplan had said Matthew, not Matt, like almost everyone else did.

Jessica added, "Dr. Kaplan has been right here beside me for the past three days. He never left my side and never left you alone."

Smiling, but in an unusual, pensive way, Dr. Kaplan said to me, "Jessica reminds me so much of my daughter, I couldn't leave her alone as she was waiting for you to wake up. It's been a long three days, Matthew."

Surprised, Jessica said, "I didn't know you had a daughter! You've never mentioned her before!"

"That's because she died before you were born. I like to think that if she had been given the chance, the opportunity, to grow up, she would be as sweet, compassionate, intelligent and strong-willed as you are," Kaplan said to Jessica.

"Oh, my gosh! I'm so sorry! I had no idea," Jessica gushed.

"It's okay, Jessica. That was a long time ago, over forty years now, but I think it is time you heard the story because it will fill in some holes for *you*, as well as for Matthew," Dr. Kaplan said.

Chapter Twenty-Eight

"My daughter was born in January 1972. By the time she was six years old, she was a delightful little girl. She was so sweet and funny and had developed this wonderful personality. Every day, when I would return home from work, she would be waiting to have tea with me. I was the king and she was the princess. Every day, like clockwork, I would come home, change into some comfortable clothes, she called it 'king's clothes' and we would have royal tea, with different visiting dignitaries like Mr. Tomato, Fred the Bear and the Monkey Prince; her stuffed animals. She was so thoughtful and sweet and innocent," Kaplan said, eyes misting at the memory.

"In early March 1978, on a Saturday, a Sabbath, my wife and I decided that we would take Liat to the beach to play in the sand. Have, what you would call, a field trip. My wife knew that it wouldn't be as crowded on the holy day, the day of rest. We were secular, so it being a Sabbath didn't really affect us much at all." Kaplan paused to maintain his composure.

"My wife and I had a little argument that morning. I had been called in to work, and so I had canceled the beach trip. Rebecca said that she was going to take our daughter, Liat, to the beach without me. I say argument, but it was little more than a disagreement and a little disappointment. Liat was sad that I wasn't going, but I told her we would have a tea party after she went to the beach, and that there might even be a surprise visitor. To her, it was turning into the best day

208

ever—the beach, a tea party with the king and a new toy. That little talk, the promise of having a tea party with my princess, is the last memory I have with my daughter. That was on a Saturday morning."

"Two days earlier, on a Thursday, thirteen terrorists boarded a ship leaving from Lebanon and headed toward Tel Aviv. The terrorists' intent was to stop the peace talks being held between the Israeli leadership and the Egyptian leadership. Think about that. These creatures were planning to use terror to stop *peace* talks. It wasn't like this was a summit of generals planning an invasion, strategizing over how to invade. They were planning, strategizing on how to bring peace to the two nations, and this region of the world. Thirteen terrorists left Lebanon; only eleven arrived on the Israeli shore. After having transferred to Zodiac crafts—smaller, lightweight landing boats—they hit some particularly rough seas and one of the boats capsized, killing two terrorists. I can't help but wish that they had all drowned. Forgive me." Kaplan looked at Jess. She nodded.

"Because I needed our only car to drive to work, my family left home aboard a bus, midmorning, headed to the beach. At just about the exact same time, those eleven members of the Palestinian Fedayeen from Fatah landed on the shores of an Israeli beach, forty miles north of Tel Aviv. They were forty miles off target because of the rough seas they had encountered. After asking an American photographer for directions and then killing her, murdering her on that beach, the terrorists flagged down a taxi and killed everyone in the car."

I sat there in stunned amazement, mouth open, jaw dropped. I had heard this story before, but the *truth* sounded so different. My stomach sank as I began to see that this was *Operation of the Martyr Kamal Adwan,* the mission Omar's father had led so many years before.

Kaplan continued, "Once they had a mode of transportation, the eleven terrorists squeezed into the taxi and headed south, toward their target. From there, they were able to stop a bus, a bus full of families and tourists who were headed to the beach, on the Coastal Highway."

When I heard the words, "Coastal Highway," I immediately knew the rest of this story, Omar's story. He had told me about how brave his father had been. How he and his fellow soldiers had stormed the beach, killing the enemy, how they had fought and captured two enemy buses.

Kaplan was still talking as I was trying to remember the rest of what Omar had said. Kaplan continued, "These were families, not enemy combatants, not armed soldiers. No, these were women and children going to the beach. The terrorists hijacked the northbound bus and forced the driver to turn and drive back south. The terrorists were still trying to reach their objective, the peace talks, but wanted to hurt as many *innocent* civilians as possible along the way. I guess the terrorists saw those innocent civilians as enemy combatants, so they began throwing grenades out of the windows and shooting at passing cars on their way to Tel Aviv. Town after town they did this, relentlessly and needlessly killing innocent people. Somewhere along the thirty-mile drive to the city, the terrorists were able to stop a second bus and force all of its passengers onto their bus. Now, they had over seventy hostages, mostly women and children, trapped on one bus."

Kaplan again paused to regain his composure. I wasn't sure how often he talked about this, but now, even forty plus years later, it affected him.

"The police did their job as best as they could, but they hadn't been trained for a terrorist attack like this. Everything happened so quickly, it was hard for them to react. Several small roadblocks attempted to stop the terror-bus, but nothing managed to bring the vehicle and the incident to a close. The weight of the bus and the fear of hurting any of the hostages prevented a full-scale assault. Finally, the police were able to set up a much larger roadblock, spread nails in the road and bring the hijacked vehicle to a halt. A firefight broke out between the police and the terrorists. The result was that the bus caught on fire. We don't know if the terrorists set it intentionally, but what we do know is that the fuel tank erupted." Kaplan paused. Each of the next sentences were labored, each being harder to finish than the one before.

"Thirty-seven Israelis, including thirteen children, died that day.[88] My wife, Rebecca, and my daughter, Liat, were counted among the dead. It came to be known as 'The Coastal Road Massacre.' *Time Magazine* called it, at the time, 'the worst terrorist attack in Israel's history.'[89]

"A thing like that will change you. It changed my life forever, in more ways than one."

Jessica and I sat there, quietly, reverently, not knowing what to say. I could see tears streaming down Jessica's face. The seconds seemed like hours before Kapan continued.

"I think about the terrorists, those men and women to this day. Just like me, they also said goodbye to their families, but the terrorists were able to do it on their own terms. I wonder if, on the day before they left their families for good, on that Wednesday if they spent the day with their children. Did they shave their beards so as to blend in with the Israeli population? Did they take their sons or their daughters to the park to play? Did they give their children the gift of memories before they went off to die for their beliefs? Would their children follow in their footsteps, grow up to be just like abee or umee, their dads or moms?"

Jessica and I just sat there crying. Jessica for the pain that her friend and mentor had experienced and kept experiencing each day. I was crying because I was with the son of the man who had carried out these attacks against Dr. Kaplan, his family and all of Israel. I didn't know how to explain to the man what I knew, so I sat there silently, crying tears of pain. It struck me at that moment, how radically different the

---

88 Michael Omer-Man, "This Week in History: Israel's deadliest terror attack," *Jerusalem Post,* March 11, 2011, https://www.jpost.com/Features/In-Thespotlight/This-Week-in-History-Israels-deadliest-terror-attack
89 "Middle East: A Sabbath of Terror," *Time,* March 20, 1978, http://content.time.com/time/magazine/article/0,9171,919454,00.html

two men were. One man, Omar Khalid, took his pain and channeled it into creating more pain, so that millions would feel that same pain of loss. The other man, Dr. Eli Kaplan, took his pain and used it as fuel to help people, to try and keep others from ever feeling the same sadness of loss that he had experienced.

Again, we sat for long moments until Dr. Kaplan again spoke. Slightly changing thoughts, Kaplan looked at Jessica with a different, puzzled look on his face.

"I don't think I ever told you about the first time that I met the Israeli Prime Minister, Menachem Begin, did I, Jessica?" he asked.

Jessica shook her head and through tears and a runny nose answered, "No, you never mentioned it. I can't believe you've never mentioned it. Believe me, if I ever meet the Prime Minister or the President of the United States, people will definitely hear about it."

She pulled out the same kind of travel Kleenex kit I saw her with the first day we met. She handed me a Kleenex, took one for herself and wiped her tears.

"I think the both of you will most likely have the opportunity to meet the Prime Minister, the President, and any other leader of the two nations you'd like to meet. You have a wonderful reason to meet them. As for me, I guess I wouldn't have a reason to reference our introduction in normal conversation because I try my best to not bring up this part of my life.

"The Prime Minister called me to his office one day shortly after Rebecca and Liat's death and expressed his deepest sympathy for my horrible loss. He had some very eloquent words to say that I don't have the strength to repeat at this moment. They are seared into my heart forever."

Kaplan said, "I made a decision then, one that would direct the course of my life over the coming decades. I decided that I would no longer stand on the sidelines and wait for the enemy to attack me again. No Israeli ever deserved to go through what I had endured. I told

Prime Minister Begin that I wanted to donate to Israel and her people, my most valuable possession, my best weapon, my mind. By that time, he had been briefed about my background and he saw potential in me. The two of you can tell by looking at me, I'm no soldier, not even back then in my prime, but I threw everything into my scientific research, working hours on end. It was all I had left to live for."

"After years of exemplary service behind the scenes, working with all the government agencies in this country, the military recognized another opportunity. Because of my potential, my research, my gifts, I was set up as an independent business owner, contractor, scientist, philanthropist, in the civilian world. I was in the civilian world, but not really 'in' the civilian world. The change was made with the thought in mind that I would have access to even more information if I was able to communicate through scientific research with the civilian world. I still have connections to the military and to the Mossad. Actually, the lines kind of blur with the different agencies and institutes. I am connected to them all and I funnel information and research to them. It's one of the many reasons why Israel, along with her ally, the United States of America, continues to lead the world in technology and discovery."

Dr. Kaplan stood up to stretch his legs and again checked to see if anyone was listening at the door.

When he returned, Jessica said, "Well, that explains how we got connected to the Mossad and my rescue. Or, really, how you got connected with Mossad and we worked with them to rescue Matt. All this time I've known you, all these years I have worked for you, I had no idea who you really worked for. I didn't even have a clue. It's amazing that we have spent all those hours together and you never once even hinted at it. You never even let anything accidentally slip."

"I'm sorry, dear Jessica. I was under the strictest of orders, from people who I would not want to cross, to never speak of my relationship with the Mossad to anyone. Only now, because of the incidents over the last week have I been given permission to tell you *some* of the back story. Never, in a million years, did I think anything we were working on would have had terrorists at our door."

"*Some* of the back story? That's not all of it?" I interrupted.

Kaplan ignored me and continued his thought. "I also need to ask you two for your forgiveness. I told you both a lie, and that is not in my nature."

Jessica and I looked at each other, confused. I said, "Dr. Kaplan, I just met you. There's no way you could have lied to me. I don't know what you told Jessica, but you saved our lives, and I think I speak for both of us when I say you're forgiven."

Kaplan said, "Thank you, Matthew. Let me explain. I told you that I was too sick to attend your presentation last week, Jessica, where you were going to reveal our findings...your findings. I wasn't too sick in the conventional sense. I didn't have a cold or come down with cancer. It was the thought of losing another daughter that nearly killed me. I was orchestrating things behind the scenes, trying to keep you safe. Omar Khalid was one step ahead of us. But that explains why I was in the Humvee that rescued you. I had to be there. I wasn't going to lose you too."

"Oh, Eli. You're such a wonderful man." Jessica took his hand in hers and placed her head on his shoulder. "And I understand why you never said anything about your family, your loss, any of it. Who would want to relive all that pain? Thank you for sharing with us." Kaplan put his arm around Jessica, and we all sat in silence for a few moments until Jessica finally said, "But I still don't know why the terrorists even wanted my work. I don't really know who the terrorists are."

I added, "And Omar, the bad one, kept talking about geothermal energy. Jess said she doesn't know anything about that. Do you?"

Dr. Kaplan nodded. "Jessica mentioned that you had been told that. The geothermal energy story was just a cover, a believable way, to deceive you, Matthew. Let's start at the beginning, shall we?"

I half shrugged, half nodded. Both hurt.

Dr. Kaplan smiled, realizing my painful dilemma. He continued, "Since the beginning, since Israel became a nation, the government has been aware that different Arab governments, neighboring countries, but enemies of Israel, have been funding terrorist factions, supplying them with money, weapons, soldiers, ideas and training. Really, since day one as a nation, we have been under attack. Israel has worked diligently to protect her people and the land in a peaceful way whenever possible. The military has done well to close the borders, making it harder to smuggle weapons into our nation. It will never be perfect. Terrorists will work hard to get into our country, just like they did when they killed my family. However, with satellites we can, in many cases, prevent air attacks. Our Iron Dome has been a Godsend to prevent inbound rocket attacks. Are you familiar with our Iron Dome?"

Jessica nodded, having lived in the country for years. I shook my head, again another painful movement and said, "No, I have no idea what you're talking about."

Kaplan, the scientist, was back in his element. He said, "Terrorists continue to try and kill innocent civilians. Again, women and children are the targets of these murderers. A relatively new tactic is to stand just outside of Israel's borders and shoot missiles or lob rockets into the country, into our cities. The Iron Dome is a mobile, all-weather, air defense system. The system is designed to intercept and destroy short-range rockets and artillery shells fired from distances of four kilometers to seventy kilometers away and whose trajectory would take them to a populated area.[90] So, when terrorists, unfriendly countries or even lone crazies try to shoot a rocket into Israel, a warning sounds and everyone takes cover, and the Iron Dome hopefully shoots them out of the sky."

I was pretty amazed at the technology this country had and equally as amazed at the necessity of it. It was all so sad.

Kaplan continued, "Our biggest problem now, the gap we have noted, is that we cannot see the terrorists as they tunnel under our borders.

---

90 "Iron Dome," *Wikipedia*, https://en.wikipedia.org/wiki/Iron_Dome

There are vast networks of tunnels under our feet where military weapons and explosives, even enemy combatants are being brought into our country, daily. It's how they got the explosives that ripped the Azrieli Sonoma Tower apart. Our current defense for these tunnels is to fly large surveillance aircraft miles above ground and look for people crawling into or out of holes. Once they are spotted, using limited means, mostly by the naked eye or infrared imaging or heat signatures, we bomb them, killing whoever might be smuggling the weapons or digging the tunnels. This is a temporary remedy. All the terrorists have to do is dig a new, more well-concealed entrance and they are back in business. Understand, we can't see them when they're *in* the tunnels, only when they're entering or exiting those tunnels."

"Okay. I'm following you, so far," I said.

"Good, Matthew," Dr. Kaplan responded and turned toward Jess to continue. "Once you had developed your ideas, Jessica, and tested them, I began to see another use for your Genesis Machine. Yes, it would have an impact on subterranean mapping and yes, it would have an impact on science and anthropology. It still will. I realized that your device, with very few modifications, could be used to easily search the Earth for these terror tunnels. We could fly those same airplanes and simply use your Genesis Machine. Instead of looking for people crawling in holes, hoping we get lucky, we could find the actual tunnels and close them completely, for good. Or we could find the tunnels and use them to our advantage, to capture the people trying to inflict harm on us. The Iron Dome has been a Godsend for airborne explosives. *Your* Genesis Machine will be equally as important for smuggled explosives and tools of terror. This truly is a game-changing technology for the future safety of our nation."

Jessica just sat there with a stunned look on her face. Trying to speak, she said, "I… I… wish…"

Kaplan said, "I was under strict orders not to tell you my connection to the Mossad. I wanted to tell you about the implications I was seeing but couldn't. You understand, don't you? Does it make sense, then, why I installed the titanium desk and cage for your computer? Do you understand why I implemented all the safety protocols? You don't know how many times I was tempted to break my standing orders not to speak. I'm so sorry. I hope you'll find a way to forgive me."

We sat in silence for what felt like an eternity.

Finally, Jessica leaned over to Dr. Kaplan, kissed him on his cheek and said, "Of course, I forgive you. I only wish I would have known so that I wouldn't have been so cavalier about revealing my discoveries. I could have revealed my findings in a peer-reviewed scientific journal. Not only that, I could have been working on modifications to help you and help the Mossad, modifications that would help the sweet people of this beautiful country. It makes the Genesis Machine that much more special, knowing it will have lasting effects on the people of Israel and will help prevent more attacks."

When Jessica and Dr. Kaplan had finished with their moment, I said, "I'm still confused. There's something, one part that I still don't understand. Why did the terrorists want the research, or why did they want the machine? What good would it have done for them?"

"It was twofold, Matthew," Dr. Kaplan said. "The first and most obvious reason they wanted the research, the machines, was to keep it out of our hands. If they had the technology and we didn't, we couldn't use it against them. We couldn't disrupt their operations. That's the easy one."

"Makes sense," I said, again trying to painfully nod.

"When we raided the airport, when you and Omar Khalid were able to get away in the helicopter, we took several dozen prisoners and scores of valuable intel. I say 'we' like I was in the fight. I wasn't. I was back at command central. But anyway, that's how we learned about the second, more sinister reason they wanted the technology. I need to give a little background for context. You may or may not know that Israel actually sits on a major fault line, the Syrian-African fault line to be exact."

"You're not going to believe this," I interrupted, "but when I was at Moho Magnetic Machines, I read a newspaper article about Israel experiencing tremors because it sits on a fault line. It seems like I remember reading that Israel has an earthquake once every eighty to one hundred years. Is that right?"

"That's right," Kaplan said. "The intel that we recovered from the terrorists at the airport suggests that they intended to use the Genesis Machine to locate weak points in the Earth's crust along that fault line. The weak points would have been quite easy to find, given the nature of the machine. The terrorists planned to plant explosives, the same ones used to blow up our lab, in and around valuable military and civilian targets. They would plant explosives in those weak spots and once they detonated them, it would result in catastrophic earthquakes that would literally erase Israel from the map. Cities would be destroyed in a matter of minutes. Armies would be rendered useless. The death toll would be unfathomable. Anyone left alive would then face an invasion force similar to the one Israel faced in the Six-Day War. Every enemy state would attack at once, but we wouldn't be able to defend ourselves. They would be free to rebuild a Palestinian or Arab or Muslim state on the rubble of the Israeli nation. That's what your actions prevented, Matthew. The nation of Israel is in your debt, will forever be in your debt."

I sat there speechless, frozen. Tears filled my eyes and streamed down my face for the second time in a matter of minutes. It took moments for me to regain my composure this time.

Through tears, I said, "Just like Esther, God brought me here for such a time as this."[91] Jessica immediately knew the reference and smiled, tears welling in her eyes. Kaplan looked confused.

"What are you talking about, you get to be like Esther? I don't understand."

Thinking of how to explain this to Dr. Kaplan helped me get my emotions in check. Now I got to be the teacher.

---

91 Esther 4:14b

"In your time of study, you must have learned the story about the origin of Purim, the Jewish holiday, right?" I asked Dr. Kaplan.

"I know the holiday. I really enjoy the holiday, but I don't know how or where it started," he replied. "I learned the word 'Purim' means 'Lots' in Persian, which is like a type of dice. We wear costumes and get really, really drunk."

"Right," I said. "Let me explain it to you. Purim is a holiday that is celebrated by the Jewish people because God was able to deliver the people of Israel out of the hands of their enemy. They were on the brink of extermination due to…you know what? Let me back-up a little in my story. Is that okay? Give a little history first?"

Dr. Kaplan nodded. "Please."

"The people of the nation of Israel have been displaced a number of times through history, from the land we know today as Israel. One of those times, we now call it the Jewish Diaspora, might be better known to you as the 'Babylonian Exile' or just as the 'time of Exile' from the land of Israel."

Kaplan kind of shrugged, one of those, *I've heard the term but don't remember anything about it,* kind of shrugs.

"Well, the nation of Israel was captured by a Babylonian king named Nebuchadnezzar and almost all of her people were relocated to Babylonia. So, imagine all, or almost all, of the people in the country marching from here to Iran. That was basically what took place, a great displacement. So, they spent years as captives of the Babylonians. Eventually, years and years later, the Babylonian Empire fell to the Persian Empire. The Persian king, Cyrus the Great, came into power. During Cyrus' reign, the Jewish population found favor and grace in the foreign land. They grew in number and in wealth. Eventually, a petition was made of Cyrus for the Jewish people to return to their homeland and rebuild their temple. Cyrus agreed. This was a miracle for sure. He let any Jewish person return to their homeland who wanted to go, and large numbers went. He even sponsored the trip! That virtually guaranteed their safety. However, a large number of the Jewish people were really happy where they were and decided that they had a great life, a great future, safety and a just leader, so those Jewish people decided to stay in Persia. You with me?"

"Yes, Matthew. I'm following you. Please continue," Kaplan said. Jessica smiled and nodded enthusiastically, one of those, *keep going, keep going!* nods.

"Now, let's fast forward a few hundred years. There's a large number of Jewish people living in Persia, but there's a different king, one who doesn't necessarily have the best, or really *any,* relationship with the Jewish people. Being Jewish isn't as readily acceptable as it once was. Jewish people continue to thrive, but they aren't as open about their heritage as they once were; that ancestry is hidden.

"Anyway, the Persian King at the time, a man named Ahasuerus, had a beauty contest of sorts to find the woman he was going to marry. A woman named Esther caught his eye and stole his heart. King Ahasuerus married the beautiful woman, but Esther had a secret, something she hadn't told the ministers—the ones who performed the beauty contest—and she definitely hadn't told the king. Esther was a Jew."

I looked at Dr. Kaplan and noticed I had his undivided attention.

"King Ahasuerus had a man named Haman as his Prime Minister, and Haman was doing everything in his power to keep the king's confidence, grow his lands and his wealth. He was doing the things a good Prime Minister should do. But Haman had a fatal flaw; he wanted to be the center of the King's attention and wanted to be honored and revered by the common people. One man, a Jewish man named Mordecai, refused to bow to the Prime Minister and it made Haman so mad he wanted to kill Mordecai. When he saw that it wasn't feasible, Haman hatched a plan to kill all of Mordecai's people. Haman hated the Jewish people because of Mordecai. Here is what he did: Haman told King Ahasuerus that there was a rebel group that was causing a problem in a part of the lands that the King controlled. Haman told the king that these people were wealthy beyond measure and should be exterminated. Then, their lands and possessions would go into the royal coffers. The king was deceived into thinking that these people were causing a problem in his kingdom and their extermination was the best solution to solve that problem. King Ahasuerus trusted his advisor and agreed to set forth a royal decree to have those people killed. He just didn't realize Haman was plotting the destruction of an innocent group of people, the children of Israel." I paused while I gathered my thoughts.

Dr. Kaplan was completely engaged and said, "Please continue."

"The decree was given that all Jewish people would be killed, and Haman rolled dice, or lots, called 'Purim,' to determine which day it would be carried out. Queen Esther, living in the safety of the palace, had no idea any of this was going on. Her uncle and legal guardian, that same Jewish man named Mordecai, came to see her, told her of the imminent danger and begged her to speak to the king on behalf of her people. Mordecai told Esther, 'Don't think that just because you live in the king's house, you're the one Jew who will get out of this alive. If you persist in staying silent at a time like this, help and deliverance will arrive for the Jews from someplace else; but you and your family will be wiped out. Who knows? *Maybe you were made queen for just such a time as this.*'[92] Esther decided to put her life on the line to reveal to the king that she was a Jew, and in doing so, she was able to save all of the Jews in the kingdom. God looks after His people. He did it then and He's done it again, now."

I smiled, concluding my story.

"Oh, wait! I forgot to say, that's why the holiday, Purim, is celebrated in Israel, to celebrate God's deliverance of his people from the hands of Haman."

Dr. Kaplan was a little stunned and asked, "How do you know about this? Do you celebrate Purim in America?"

---

92 Esther 4:14 (The Message Translation)

I said, "No, the story is one that is found in my Bible, in the book of Esther. I believe in God and His delivering power. I believed it when I read about Esther and I believe it now, that God has used me in this manner, *for such a time as this.*"

Dr. Kaplan turned to Jessica and said, "You're right. He is an incredible man of God. A prophet or a sage. I'm glad the two of you have found each other. I'm glad you're happy. That's all I ever wanted for my daughter."

"Dr. Kaplan," I said, "there's one more part to Esther's story. You see, Haman, the evil Prime Minister was hanged for his wickedness, for his role in trying to kill the Queen's people. He was hanged on the same gallows he had built to kill Mordecai. In *my* story, the wicked one is Omar Khalid. What happened to him?"

Dr. Kaplan paused and said, "I'm sorry, Matthew. He slipped through our fingers again. He managed to escape in the helicopter that was taken from the airport. He'll turn up, somewhere, sometime and we'll get him. Until then, we want to keep your whereabouts private and security with you at all times. Before the week is over, you will be a nationally recognized hero, and we can't have terrorists hurting our national heroes."

Chapter Twenty-Nine

T hroughout the following hours, different people stopped into the hospital room. I saw people from the United States government, the CIA, the US Ambassador and the like. I saw people from the Israeli government, the Mossad and even a few historians. There were photographers and official state inquirers. Dr. Kaplan stayed with Jessica the entire time, helping to keep the crowds down and helping to direct, to steer all of our conversations.

After everyone had left for the evening, after all the goodbyes were given, Jessica walked Dr. Kaplan to his car. A little while later, she came back into the room and lay down on the bed next to me.

Jessica gently took my hand and said, "I'm so proud of you. I've worked for Dr. Kaplan for years and tried to share my faith on numerous occasions. He was so uninterested; it was always like talking to a brick wall. I never understood why there was so much resistance whenever I tried to talk about God's goodness. I guess when someone deals with a devastating event, if they don't know any better, it's easy to blame God. Today was the first time I ever saw him speak of God in a good light. You did that for him. You helped him begin to see who God *really* is and what God's nature is really like."

I squeezed her hand and said, "God is so good, gentle, kind, loving. I'm sure, at some point, God's goodness will lead him,[93] will draw him

---

93 Romans 2:4

closer. I think you and I will have a part to play in it," and smiled a sleepy smile. It had been a long day.

Jessica said, "I know you're very tired, Matt, but I want to ask you something. There's something I don't understand. I've gone through this story over and over with different groups, agencies, teams, and I haven't told them about this one thing. I saw something on that roof. I saw something that defies explanation. The explosives detonated and I punched Omar. I threw my best right-cross and popped him in the cheek. Before he knew what had hit him, I took off at top speed. You, watching what was unfolding, ran right up to Omar and I watched him point the gun at you. I saw the two of you talk and then I watched him shoot you. I *watched* it. I watched him pull the trigger five times from point-blank range. If he had been any closer, the gun would have been touching you. What I don't understand is what in the world happened? How did he miss?"

I smiled and asked Jessica, "Do you remember when I came up the elevator at your building?"

Jessica laughed and said, "Now, *you're* answering a question with a question! Yes, I remember. Omar had me on my knees and was pulling my hair. It's kind of hard to forget."

"When I was riding up the elevator, the Lord spoke a couple of things to me. He told me two things: to 'use my authority,' and he said the name, 'Terry Mize.'"

"Oh yeah. I remember you saying 'Terry Mize' when you first saw us. I remember thinking, who is Terry Mize?"

"Well, let me tell you," I said. "Terry Mize is a missionary I saw one time. Now, he's been a missionary in several countries, but the story I'm most familiar with has to do with his time in Mexico. He was driving through a particularly barren and sparse region of the country when he saw a man hitchhiking. Reverend Mize decided it would be a great opportunity to share the Gospel of Jesus Christ with the man as they were driving through the country. What he didn't know was that the man had just escaped from prison. Before he really knew what was going on, the hitchhiker pulled a gun on Reverend Mize and forced him out of the car."

Jessica gasped, "What happened?"

"Reverend Mize said this with a gun in his face: 'Father, your Word tells me that Jesus said that He gave me authority over all the power of the enemy and nothing shall by any means hurt me.[94] That means this man, his gun, his bullets, cannot hurt me and therefore if he pulls the trigger, You must do something with the bullets. I *expect* You to do something with the bullets. For Your Word's sake. Not for my sake.' Then he turned to the man and said, 'You cannot kill me. I have authority in this situation, and you cannot kill me.' The hitchhiker and Reverend Mize were standing nose to nose when the hitchhiker pulled the trigger. He emptied the gun into Reverend Mize's gut, except that none of the bullets made it to Reverend Mize. The bullets dropped at his feet. It was a miracle of epic proportions. As I was coming up the elevator, God reminded me of my authority, and He reminded me of Terry Mize[95]. I expressed my authority and I knew that God isn't a respecter of persons.[96] That means if He'll do something for Terry Mize, He'll do it for me too."

"I wish that I had asked you about this earlier, when Dr. Kaplan was still here. I wish he had heard about how God rescued you. I think you'll really have a chance to minister to him, to show him how good God is, how much God loves everyone. God isn't out to get people. He's not looking to squash them like a bug. He is a loving, compassionate God. In fact, He loved us so much, and He hated that sin had separated Him from us, so much, that He sent His Son to fix the connection. I wish that Dr. Kaplan had gotten to hear your story."

---

94 Luke 10:19
95 Terry Mize. "I Was Shot Repeatedly but a Force Stopped the Bullets." *Sid Roth's It's Supernatural*. April 19, 2017. Available on YouTube at https://youtu.be/_NS9a_ie4Co
96 Acts 10:34

"Jessica," I said. "I'll tell him tomorrow, if you want."

"Oh… yeah! Duh!" We both gave a tired chuckle. It had been a long day for the both of us.

I asked Jessica to turn on the television and find something I could drift off to sleep watching. We flipped the channels for a few minutes and Jess found a movie, *7 Days in Entebbe*, that was just starting. The opening scene showed a group of professional Israeli dancers sitting in a semicircle, beginning the rehearsal of their performance. As they began their dance, block letters appeared in the empty spaces on the screen. It read:

In 1947, the State of Israel was recognized by the United Nations.

Immediately, the Palestinians began fighting for the return of their land.

They were joined by left wing revolutionary groups from around the world.

They carried out attacks on Israeli civilians.

*They called themselves **Freedom Fighters**.*

*The Israelis called them **Terrorists**.*

I turned to Jess and said, "It's been over seventy years, and nothing seems to have changed. Israel just wants to live in peace, for her citizens to be safe and to be left alone. I think I've had enough of this conflict for a while. Do you mind if we find something else to watch?"

Jessica smiled and said, "Oh, thank goodness!" She picked up the remote and began flipping channels again.

I thought to myself, *It's such a shame that the Israeli people haven't been able to 'change the channel' on this conflict and live a peaceful life with their neighboring countries. It's amazing; hate breeds hate in other countries, but these Israelis don't hate their enemies. They just want to be left alone. They just want peace.*

There were so many things going through my mind, so many things I was thinking about, that I wasn't sure that I would be able to fall asleep. Again, I was reminded of a Bible verse from the book of

Matthew. It says, *Give your entire attention to what God is doing right now, and don't get worked up about what may or may not happen tomorrow. God will help you deal with whatever hard things come up when the time comes.*[97] I began to focus on God's goodness, on the things that He had done for me and Jessica, on His mercy and grace in our lives.

Jessica continued to flip channels, but I fell asleep before she found what she wanted to watch.

"For the Lord is good and His mercy endures forever." — I Chronicles 16:34, II Chronicles 5:13, II Chronicles 7:3, Ezra 3:11, Psalm 100:5, Psalm 106:1, Psalm 107:1, Psalm 109:21, Psalm 118:1, Psalm 118:29, Psalm 136:1, Jeremiah 33:11.

The end.

---

97 Matthew 6:34 (MSG Translation)

Final Word

Dear Reader,

Thank you for finishing this book! I hope you enjoyed the thrill and adventure of it, but more importantly, I hope you understood something that I genuinely believe. God loves YOU, and He genuinely wants the best for you. He's not mad, upset, or disappointed with you. It doesn't matter what you may have done in your past. Just as with Matthew Davenport and Jessica Adams, God *wants* a relationship with YOU and in order to have that relationship with YOU, He was willing to sacrifice everything, even His Son, Jesus. You don't have to do anything to earn that relationship or even prove you're worthy of it. All you have to do is accept it.

A relationship takes two, and God is ready and willing, if you are. Starting that relationship is as easy as saying something like this: "God, I want a relationship with You. And I believe we can have that relationship. I believe Jesus made a way, even if I don't understand it. Through His death, burial, and resurrection, He made a way for us to communicate! I want to be saved from a life without You in it." It really is that simple.

You might not feel any different, physically, after saying that prayer, but if you truly believe that you have a relationship with God, I promise,

God is moving to make Himself known to you, just like He did with ME and with our book's hero, Matt Davenport. It doesn't matter what you feel like; God is making a new life with you and in you. Now you are connected with God, and in His eyes, you are completely new. One translation of the Bible says it this way: *"This means that anyone who belongs to Christ (Jesus) has become a new person. The old life is gone; a new life has begun!"* You are starting a brand-new journey as a brand-new person, connected to God and brand-new in His eyes! *That's* the good news of the Gospel.

Finally, if you prayed that, especially if you prayed it for the first time, let someone know or let me know. I have a 'Contact Me' page on my website, DavidPorterBooks.com, and I would love to hear from you!

David

Supporting scriptures:

God is Love. (I John 4:8) For God so loved the world (that's YOU) that He gave His only Son (Jesus) that whosoever believes in Him would not perish, but have everlasting life. For God sent His Son (Jesus) into the world not to judge the world, but to save the world through Him. (John 3:16-17)

This means that anyone who belongs to Christ has become a new person. The old life is gone; a new life has begun! (2 Corinthians 5:17)

For whosoever shall call upon the name of the Lord shall be saved. (Romans 10:13)

About the Author

Author David M. Porter has been in church since nine months before he was born. In addition to a college degree, David has three Bible school degrees, including a Master of Theology that his wife, Lauren, is elated he has finally put to good use. David writes thrilling stories with characters of integrity, who find themselves sucked into the cloak and dagger world of mystery, lies and deceit—the total opposite of his everyday life as a boring, small business owner.

Bush Publishing & Associates, LLC books may be ordered at bookstores everywhere and at Amazon.com.

CPSIA information can be obtained
at www.ICGtesting.com
Printed in the USA
BVHW031519060221
598963BV00013B/9

9 781637 520505